Praise for Nikki Turner

Forever a Hustler's Wife

An *Essence* #1 Bestseller!

"Few writers working in the field today bring the drama quite as dramatically as Nikki Turner. . . . [She's] a master at weaving juicy, 'hood-rich sagas of revenge, regret, and redemption." —Vibe.com

"A fast-paced tale of just how far a woman will go for her man . . . Turner's characterizations are true to life, and the ease with which she switches from the hardness of the streets to the love between the characters is to be applauded. . . . An open and honest portrayal of the possible consequences of the gangsta lifestyle."
—*Romantic Times Book Review*

"Nikki Turner has once again taken street literature to the next level, proving that she is indeed the 'Queen of Hip Hop Fiction.'" —UrbanPublicity.com

Riding Dirty on I-95

"*Riding Dirty on I-95* is USDA hood certified."
—TERI WOODS, author of *The Dutch Trilogy*
and *True to the Game*

"[A] gritty, fast-paced street tale with heart."
—*Publishers Weekly*

Street Chronicles: Tales from da Hood

The Glamorous Life

Black Widow

Also by Nikki Turner

NOVELS

Forever a Hustler's Wife
Death Before Dishonor
(with 50 Cent)
Riding Dirty on I-95
The Glamorous Life
A Project Chick
A Hustler's Wife

EDITOR

Street Chronicles: Girls in the Game
Street Chronicles: Tales from da Hood
(contributing author)

CONTRIBUTING AUTHOR

Girls from da Hood
Girls from da Hood 2
The Game: Short Stories About the Life

Black Widow

a novel

A Nikki Turner Original

One World ⬛ Ballantine Books | New York

A One World Books Trade
Paperback Original

Copyright © 2008 by Nikki Turner

Published in the United States by One
World Books, an imprint of The Random
House Publishing Group, a division of
Random House, Inc., New York.

ONE WORLD is a registered trademark
and the One World colophon is a
trademark of Random House, Inc.
READER'S CIRCLE and colophon are
trademarks of Random House, Inc.

ISBN: 978-0-7394-9492-9

Printed in the United States of America

A Special Message from Nikki Turner to Her Readers

Dear beloved reader,

If you are a loyal Nikki Turner reader then you know that the novel *The Black Widow* has been in my heart for a long time—before I ever sat down to pen *Forever a Hustler's Wife*. Although the story lingered in my spirit, when I tried to write *The Black Widow*, it wouldn't flow. It's no secret that I consider my projects my babies and compare the creative process to giving birth. That being said, this was one of the hardest second and third trimesters I've EVER experienced.

The Black Widow had to walk in the shadow of such a hugely successful book: *Forever a Hustler's Wife*. The overwhelming support for that book also came with an enormous workload—promotions, touring, radio, interviews, appearances, signings, and so forth. (Thank you for making it a three-time #1 *Essence* bestseller!) And all this had to be done while selecting and editing the debut novels for my Nikki Turner Presents line. In the process, *The Black Widow* was put on hold so that I could care for and nurture the first Nikki Turner Presents novel, *Gorilla Black* by Seven (You are going to love this one!), and get *Forever* out of diapers and walking. I hope it doesn't sound like I am complaining because believe me, I am not—I feel blessed to do what I do. However, I think that once I was actually ready to sit down and write *The Black Widow*, I was totally burned out. But the clock was ticking and the deadline to turn it in to my publisher was a month away—and as you know time waits for no one.

With so much going on, I never had enough time to sit down and fully get into my zone the way I'm accustomed to doing with my novels. I found my mind and my writing were all over the place. Two weeks before the official deadline, my editor called and asked to read some of the story. I sent it over, knowing that it was rough, but I wasn't prepared for the way she responded. To make a long story short—SHE HATED IT! And don't you know she had the NERVE to tell me that my baby was on life support with a faint pulse. How dare she? It was like a dagger going through my heart. How could she have been so brutal toward something that I had longed to bring to life? But after taking a long hard look at what I had sent to her, I realized that she was just being honest and that's exactly what I needed her to be. I took her comments in stride because as my friend Robert Greene, author of the *48 Laws of Power*, would say, setbacks can lead to greater comebacks.

For the next few days I didn't even think about my love child—and when I finally did, I made a tough decision without my editor's blessings. With no regrets, I basically terminated the pregnancy and went back to the drawing board. Taking it from the top, I started banging out an amazing, heart-wrenching story. The applied pressure created another precious jewel. About a week later I sent over the first ten chapters. My editor was astounded at how quickly I had turned the entire situation around; she instantly realized that I had conceived yet another rare diamond.

Now without further ado, I want to formally introduce you to the newest member of the Nikki Turner family. Drum roll, please. . . .

Loyal and new fans alike, meet my Golden Child: *The Black Widow*.

Forever Yours,
Nikki Turner

I was once a young girl with
an open and vulnerable heart
who gave her love so freely.
But time after time, the men in
my life deserted me. Most were
taken from me, some chose to
leave, but they all let me down.
And little by little, my heart
started to close. With each
murder, each betrayal, each
death sentence, I found all my
relationships unraveling in front
of my very eyes.

    I stopped being that sweet
young girl, and I became someone else.

    I became the Black Widow.

    My name is Isis Tatum, and
this is my story.

Some men don't understand
the great influence that they
have on their daughter's lives,
because the reality is, most
of the time girls love men
just like their daddies. And
that's where this all started—
with my father.

Ronald "Ice" Tatum

Baby, you gotta love
the one that loves you,
you hear me?

Betrayal

Worn down from the day's activities, Sandy Tatum arrived home from her job at the prestigious private school where she worked as a fourth-grade teacher. She was as beautiful as she was smart, with mocha skin, coal-black hair that grew past her shoulders, and round walnut-brown eyes ringed by long eyelashes. She couldn't wait to get inside the home she shared with her husband of fifteen years, Ronald "Ice" Tatum, a hardworking truck driver who hauled whatever to wherever to make sure that he could take care of his wife and their thirteen-year-old daughter, Isis.

It had been a long day. The parent of one of her students had come to the school to cuss her out, and then her car had refused to start, so Sandy had had to have it towed. A coworker was kind enough to drop her off. All she wanted was a hot bath and glass of wine, but when she reached her front door, she found an envelope taped to it.

"What now?" Sandy sighed, throwing her arms up in the air and then dropping them to her side. *Surely all of the bills have been paid*, Sandy thought before ripping the envelope off the door. *And nothing is delinquent, not even that raggedy-ass car that I shouldn't be paying for.*

Sandy pulled the contents out of the envelope. She couldn't believe her eyes as she read the papers. Her lips moved as she read the words: *Ronald Tatum has been summoned to appear in juvenile court for a child support hearing.*

Child support? she thought to herself. *This has got to be a mistake.* It just had to be. She had been married to the man for over fifteen years. Certainly she would've known if he had fathered other children besides their own daughter. Wouldn't she?

Confused and upset, Sandy went in the house and called the number on the summons.

"Juvenile and Domestic," the clerk answered. "Mrs. Joplin speaking. How can I help you?"

"Yes. My name is Mrs. Sandy Tatum, and I'm calling in regard to a summons I found taped to my front door," Sandy explained. "There must be some kind of mistake. It's for child support and is addressed to my husband, who only has one child. Mine. And I sure haven't taken him to court for child support. He takes care of home just fine." Sandy went on and on, trying to convince the clerk that there was indeed an error. But then again, maybe she was really trying to convince herself.

"Well, let's see, Mrs. . . . aah . . . Tatum?"

"Yes, that's right. T-A-T-U-M." Sandy enunciated each letter as she heard the clerk beating away at her keyboard.

"I see. Well, let me pull it up so that we can try to solve this problem, or at least get some clarity on the issue," the clerk offered before a slight pause, as she pulled the file up on her computer screen.

"Thank you very much." Sandy waited impatiently for only a few seconds, but they seemed like hours.

"Okay. Here we go. Ronald I. Tatum," the clerk said as she read her computer screen. "The petitioner is a Ms. Brenda B. Cross, and the child in question is named Phoebe Cross."

Sandy couldn't breathe. The air had been sucked right out of her lungs and spit into the atmosphere. The phone went silent.

"Mrs. Tatum, are you there?" Mrs. Joplin asked in a sympathetic tone. She had recently divorced a cheating bastard masquerading as a devoted husband, so she knew how Sandy felt. Thankfully, in her case, there were no children involved.

"Yes." Sandy tried to regain what was left of her composure. "I'm here. Thank you very much. You've been a great help."

"No problem," Mrs. Joplin said. "I understand. I've been there, done that. If—"

Click!

Sandy hung up the phone before the nice lady could finish her sentence.

"Somebody got some explaining to do around this here bitch, and it ain't going to be me," she fumed to herself.

As Sandy looked at photos of Isis, she thought about how she wasn't going to let their beautiful daughter be cheated out of the plans they had made for her future. Her daughter wasn't going to have to go to some community college instead of an Ivy League university so that some illegitimate child could get a higher education too. Isis wasn't going to have to get a Hyundai for her sweet-sixteen gift instead of a BMW because her husband had to get a car for some bastard of a child. "Oh, hell no!" Sandy raged. She needed some answers, and she needed them now!

She paged her husband about ten times over the next thirty minutes to no avail. She knew that Ice was nearby because his big rig was outside, parked alongside the house, which was a sign that he hadn't left for work yet.

Sandy waited a few more minutes to see if her husband was going to return her page, but her patience was wearing thin. She was desperate, so she called Mrs. Joplin back.

"Juvenile and Domestic. Mrs. Joplin speaking. How can I help you?"

"Hi. This is Mrs. Tatum again. We just spoke about half an hour ago?" Sandy said into the phone receiver.

"How can I help you?" Mrs. Joplin asked.

"If you don't mind, I would like to ask you a question or two."

"Sure, if I can answer them," she said. "Go ahead."

Sandy thought about how she could best articulate the question without offending the woman. " Mrs. Joplin, when we last spoke, what did you mean by 'been there, done that'?"

"Well, honey, I was married to a cheater myself," Mrs. Joplin admitted. "After I found out what I was dealing with, I divorced that jerk."

"Well, I know you don't know me, but we do have something in common. And I don't know who to turn to because all of my friends think that my husband and I have the picture-perfect life. They would probably just love for me to call and confide in them about this, and I can't give them that kind of satisfaction."

"I do understand."

"So I guess what I want to know from you is: How did you handle your situation? I mean in the beginning. I'm over here going crazy. And you know the saying: Crazy people do crazy things. I need answers. I've paged my husband, and he isn't calling me back fast enough, and I don't know what to do."

"Well, I cut out the middleman, which was my husband, and went straight to the source. I knew all he would do was tell me lies. I hightailed it right over to the woman's house. You might not know about her, but if she knows your address, then surely she knows about you."

"I don't know anything about this woman." Sandy sounded defeated.

Mrs. Joplin lowered her voice. "Well," she said, "she lives at 1713 Lady Smith Road. And if anyone asks, you didn't get that information from me. I'll deny it on my mama's grave." This time it was Mrs. Joplin who hung up.

Sandy wrote the address down and headed out the door. When she got to her driveway, she remembered she didn't have her car. As far as Sandy was concerned, it was a do-or-die situation. She had to do something she had never done before: drive Ice's rig. She had ridden as a passenger in it plenty of times before Isis had been born, when Ice made his legitimate (and illegitimate) runs across the country. She had watched him operate it. It had to be just like riding a bike.

Sandy went back in the house and grabbed the spare key from the kitchen drawer. She then went back outside, got in that baby, and started it up. *Lord, help me.* She said a silent prayer before backing the rig out of the driveway. It wasn't exactly like riding a bike, but it was like driving a car. A big one. A very big one.

As Sandy headed to the corner, she saw Isis getting off the school bus for kids who were involved in after-school activities. Isis flagged down the rig. She was shocked when she approached it to see her mother in the driver's seat and not her father.

"Where's Dad?" Isis asked. "Why are you driving the truck?"

"I'm going to find him, so go ahead in the house and do your homework," Sandy answered.

"I want to go with you, Mom." Isis quickly ran to the passenger side and opened the door before her mother could deny her.

"I don't think it's a good idea."

"Please, Mom. Please." Isis climbed in and closed the door. She couldn't wait for people to see her rollin' in the rig with her mother. "Come on, Mom, let's put girl power in effect. Two ladies at large playing with the big-boy toys." Isis's big beautiful eyes gleamed at her mother.

Sandy knew that there was no point in fussing with her daughter about anything concerning her father. She did practically everything for Isis while her father was on the road. But when Ice was around, there was no denying that Isis's loyalty was to her father. It was Isis and Ice against the world. Isis loved her father, and no one could take that away from her. She was her father's little princess, and in her eyes, he was the king not only of their castle but of the road and the world too.

Time was wasting. Sandy placed her foot on the gas and proceeded to her destiny.

Sandy pulled the rig up to the house, which was only about a ten-minute drive away from where they lived. It sat between two streets at a fork in the road.

She took off her jewelry and placed it on the console in the front of the rig. "Stay here," Sandy instructed her daughter.

"'Kay." Isis nodded as she pulled out her Walkman and began to listen to it and try on her mother's jewelry. Isis had always loved her mother's jewelry. Ice always made sure that both his wife and daughter had nice jewelry, but of course Sandy's was way more elaborate and expensive.

Sandy got out and walked up to the shabby house. *What the hell could my man want with someone who lives in a piece of shit like this? What could she possibly have to offer?* Sandy took a deep breath and knocked on the door. A cocoa-skinned woman with a bright-colored flowered scarf and red lipstick came to the window and spoke through the screen.

"What, bitch?" the woman said in a tone that indicated she knew exactly who Sandy was and that she was even expecting her.

"Is Brenda here? Brenda Cross?" Sandy asked. She wanted to return the obscenity, but decided she could probably get more information with honey than she could with vinegar.

"What the fuck you want?"

"I don't . . . I don't want any trouble. But there must be some kind of mistake. These child-support papers . . ." Sandy held up the summons after pulling it out of her pocket. ". . . were on me and my husband's front door when I got home from work today. It's a summons for child support, and it has your name on it as the petitioner."

"And?" Brenda snapped her neck and sucked her teeth.

"*And* there must be some kind of mistake," she said to the woman.

"No, there ain't no mistake. The motherfucker been falling short of making sure me and my child gets our money."

"Huh? You and your child?" Sandy swallowed the knot in her throat.

"Yes. Why the fuck you think that motherfucker is over here eating my pussy right now? So that I might change my fucking mind about the child support."

"Ice is here?" Sandy asked, dumbfounded.

"Yup, as he always is," Brenda informed Sandy. "And unless you got some motherfucking money for me, you need to get the fuck off of my goddamn property, bitch."

"Listen, there is no need for you to get mad at me. This is the first time I heard anything of any of this."

"Didn't I say leave, bitch? And once I am done with yo husss-band," she said, moving her head from side to side, "then I will send him on home to you."

"Shut the window, Brenda!" Sandy heard Ice's voice in the background. She stood there stunned. She couldn't believe her ears. Hearing her husband's voice come from what was probably another woman's bedroom sent Sandy into a trance.

So she isn't lying at all. This motherfucker is over here with her and allowing her to disrespect me. And to top it off, he isn't coming out here to face me. I've given this nigga almost twenty years of my life, and this is what I get?

"Fuck this bitch," Brenda responded to Ice while glaring at Sandy. "It took her long enough to find out about us and our thirteen-year-old daughter. If she wanna—"

That was when Ice snatched Brenda out of the way and reached over and shut the shed right in Sandy's face.

Thirteen years old. That's the same age as Isis, Sandy realized. *This motherfucker has been living a double life for thirteen fucking years. Oh, hell no! I'm not leaving until I get to the bottom of this.*

Sandy began banging on the door, not caring if the neighbors heard. She even forgot about her own daughter, who was wait-ing back in the rig. "Ice! Ice! Come to this door right now!" Sandy yelled in between hits. "You cheating-ass nigga, you need to be man enough to face me!" She kicked the door. "Mother-fucker, open up the door and come out here!"

Sandy paused to see if she was going to get any reply. She could hear Brenda inside the house still running off at the mouth.

"Don't you know he don't want you, you proper and prim, fake wannabe-model bitch? Bitch, you ain't no model" were Brenda's muffled words.

"Ice, get out here now. You owe me that much. I'm not leaving until you come out here, so you're going to have to face me eventually, coward." Sandy kicked the door as hard as she could, hoping that somehow the lock would pop and she could get in the door.

"Obviously he don't want you, or he'd be on the other side of the door out there with you instead of in here with me. Now get away from my door, bitch. What the fuck you going to do? Come in here and get him?"

Just then, Sandy noticed the huge boulders that decorated the little flower bed next to the porch. As she struggled to pick up one of the rocks, she was distracted when she heard Isis call out to her, "Ma, what are you doing?"

"My daughter," Sandy said, realizing the last thing she wanted was for her baby girl to witness her acting like a daggone fool.

She walked quickly back to the truck. As she hopped in, she said, "Baby, I apologize. I never want you to see me act like that, and I never want you to ever act like I just did. People may envy you, but you can't let them see you act a damn fool. Even if you feel like one."

"Was Dad there?"

"Yes, baby."

"How come you ain't let me go up there to get him?"

"It's 'didn't let,' not 'ain't let,' " she said, correcting her daughter's English. "Because it's grown folks' business."

After apologizing to her daughter, Sandy drove to the strip mall up the street from Brenda's house. She gave Isis a twenty-dollar bill and told her to get something to eat.

While Isis was ordering her food, Sandy walked to the pay phone and called her brother. "Look, I need you to come and pick up Isis right now from McDonald's on Nine Mile Road. I have some urgent business that I have to take care of."

Sandy waited as Isis ate her food, and within fifteen minutes, Sandy's brother showed up. Sandy left before he could get her to explain what was going on.

Sandy climbed back into the rig, buckled her seat belt, and took a deep breath, allowing herself a moment of reason. She started up the rig and cut on the radio. Betty Wright's song "The Clean Up Woman" played. It was at that moment that Sandy headed back to Brenda's house. She decided that she wasn't leaving until she had gotten some results.

Once Brenda's house was in sight, Sandy focused in on it. *How dare this bitch tell me to come and get my husband.* A few seconds later, a wicked grin spread across Sandy's face. *Ask, bitch, and you shall receive.* Sandy gunned the engine and drove the rig smack through the middle of the house.

Bang! Crack! Rip! The house looked like a hurricane had torn through it.

Cheap furniture got hooked onto the front fender and was dragged through the bathroom to the kitchen and then to the back porch. The toilet, which was caught under the truck, made a pipe burst, sending a small stream through the house. Luckily, Ice still wasn't going down on Brenda in the queen-size bed, because half of that was on the front lawn. Everyone on the block was in an uproar, as they came out of their homes and filled the street, looking for the source of the noise. But Sandy didn't hear anything. It was as if someone had hit a mute button, silencing her world. Somehow she had blocked everything out—focusing only on one thing—getting some answers by any means necessary.

She reached under the seat of the rig and grabbed the nine-millimeter handgun that Ice kept for protection. Sandy opened up the door of the rig and hopped out. "Ice," she shouted. She was greeted by Brenda. "Betcha didn't think that I was going to come and get him, did ya?"

"Look, bitch . . ." Brenda, unfazed by Sandy or the big truck, was coming toward Sandy, but when she saw the pistol, she froze in her tracks. She changed her tune. "Look, let's work this out."

"This ain't about me and you, as I told you before. Now stay out of this." Sandy charged past Brenda, bumping her shoulder. Brenda could see the fire in Sandy's dark brown eyes.

As Sandy continued to look for Ice, Brenda came up behind her and hit her with a pot. Sandy, who had never been in a fight in her life, hit Brenda with the nose of the gun and then picked up the pan and beat the shit out of her—literally.

"Ice!" Sandy screamed, and then shot the gun up in the air, bringing down another part of the already weakened house. "Motherfucker, where the fuck are you?"

"Look, let's talk," Sandy heard Ice call from outside.

She headed outside, following the sound of his voice. "I can't believe you did this shit. Just what do you have to say for yourself?" Sandy said after laying eyes on Ice.

Ice stood there, clad only in his boxers. He was breathing hard, with his chest poked out and his shoulders square, his dark brown, six-foot three-inch frame a pose of defiance. But his eyes didn't want any part of the charade he was putting on—they were filled with sadness, hurt, and shame.

"Do you know how this looks? Do you?" Ice yelled.

"How does it look, Ice?"

"It makes me look bad. It makes me looks like I can't control my fucking wife. Yeah, so what, I had another child. So what? Shit happens. We could have handled this shit on the home front . . . not in front of every-fuckin'-body else's home."

She glared at Ice and repeated his excuse. " 'Shit happens'? 'Shit happens,' huh?"

"Yeah, shit happens. Get over it."

Something broke inside Sandy at that moment, and the life

she'd thought she had, the man she'd thought she married, the woman she'd thought she was, were no more. Sandy, the perfect wife, the perfect mother, the perfect law-abiding citizen who had never even jaywalked before in her life, felt something that neither she nor anyone else had had any idea was in her.

Sirens were approaching, but Sandy didn't hear a thing. Without blinking, she raised the gun and unloaded the rest of the clip. She missed Ice more than she hit him, but he lay bleeding, nevertheless. The sound of the gun brought Sandy back to her senses, because she now heard the sirens. That was when reality hit.

"My daughter."

Sandy took off running like a gazelle as she tried to run back toward the McDonald's where she had left Isis with her brother. With any luck, her daughter would still be there. With any luck, Sandy would get to see her one last time before the inevitable took place. But the police caught her before she could get there.

Sandy's daughter and brother heard the commotion from down the block. They followed the sound of sirens to the block where Isis had last been with her mother. When they saw the rig, their first thought was that Sandy had been in an accident. Isis was out of the car and right up in the midst of the rubble before anyone could stop her. Then she saw him. She saw her father laying on the ground.

"Daddy, what happened?" Isis asked hysterically. "Where's Ma?"

Ice looked into his daughter's eyes and smiled.

"Someone help! Someone, anybody, please!" Isis screamed after watching the blood spill from her father's wounds.

"Sweetie, we've called for an ambulance. Please, come with me," the first police officer on the scene said as he tried remove Isis from her father's side, but she remained glued there.

"Daddy, tell me something." Isis waited to hear something, anything from her father. She had watched a lot of television dramas, and it seemed like one was playing out before her very eyes.

"I love you," Ice managed to say as he looked off into space.

"I love you too, Daddy. Please, please don't die," Isis begged in between sobs. "Please, Daddy. You're gonna be okay. Just tell me what to do. Tell me what to do, Daddy. I don't know what I'm going to do if you die, Daddy. Who's ever going to love me like you, Daddy? I'm never going to love anybody as much as I love you, Daddy."

He gasped for air and tried to look at his little girl. "Baby, you gotta love the one that loves you, you hear me?"

And he closed his eyes forever.

David "Dave" Davis

Live for yourself for a
change. Let someone serve
and wait on you.

Chapter 1

Another Statistic

The woman was snapped out of her daze by a loud, irritating voice.

"Phoebe Cross!" a man's voice boomed.

Isis sat in the waiting room at the state police headquarters. She was slow to respond to the false name—her sister's, actually—that she had given to the Department of Corrections so that she could be approved to witness the execution of her man, David Davis. It had been five years since the events that caused her man to be convicted of first-degree murder. Five years of letters, phone calls, and Saturday-morning visits. Appeal after appeal had been filed to prevent his death sentence, and every single one had been denied. Today would be his final day on Earth.

Her auntie always used to say that there was more than one way to bake a cake, and not only was her auntie a master baker but also she never told a lie. In the state of Virginia, friends and relatives of an inmate weren't allowed to witness the execution of their loved one, although the victim's family can have a front-row seat and watch the convicted accuser be put to death. But if anyone thought that the state of Virginia's fucked-up laws were going to keep her from watching Dave take his last breath and sharing the last bit of air with her man, then they had shit really fucked up. Isis had told Dave that she would be there for him until the end. And by all means, she intended to do just that! Dave was her first everything: her first kiss, her first date, her first boyfriend. She had even lost her virginity to him.

It had been love at first sight for the couple. Though she had been only fifteen at the time they met, if it had been up to her, she would have married Dave the first time she laid eyes on him. Everyone said that it was only puppy love, but she was convinced it was real love from the start—that kind of real love Mary J. Blige sang about.

On their very first date, Isis and Dave made a pact. They agreed that they would stay together until death. And although such a thing was strange for a fifteen-year-old girl, Isis meant every solitary word it. She felt that kind of commitment toward him. It didn't matter that Dave was locked up on death row for most of their relationship. Isis was one of those rare chicks—rare people, for that matter—who always kept their word. If she said it, she meant it.

It was 7:15 PM, and there she sat, waiting for it all to be over. Everything that they had planned was out of the window, because of one foolish mistake.

"Phoebe Cross," the man called again.

"That's me," Isis said, quickly wiping her hands across her eyes. She rubbed her cold arms, trying to warm up a little, which made her think about how years ago, when things were good, she used to stroll through her high school hallways wearing Dave's Avirex jacket. It had been too big for her and had practically swallowed her up, but it hadn't mattered because she'd been sporting her man's jacket and had wanted the world to know it. The memory gave her a brief moment of happiness.

"I'm sorry," she told the man as she stood. "With the long wait, I must've fallen asleep." Even so, she wondered how he could not have known it was her name that he was calling out; she was the only woman in a room full of men there to be a witness.

She walked toward the officer who had been calling her alias. He handed her a green visitor's pass and instructed, "Please put this where it can be visibly seen, and get in one of the three vans outside." He gestured toward the door leading to the outside parking lot. "The vans will transport us to the prison where the execution will be performed." *Performed.* He made the ordeal sound as if it were a magic trick about to take place instead of a man being put to death.

"Thank you," she said, taking the pass from him. All eyes were on her as she placed the tag on her sweater and exited the small building to proceed to the van. There were nine people logged in to witness Dave's execution. The rest were men, seasoned vets who had witnessed many executions. They were curious about the innocent-looking young black woman whom they had never seen before.

It struck Isis as funny that none of the police officers recognized her; she had been in the courtroom every single day of Dave's two-week trial. But the new Bulgari sunglasses she sported hid the pain in her deep brown eyes. The short spiked brown wig she wore was a contrast to her normal long black hair. What she couldn't hide was her figure: Isis's five-foot seven-inch physique, with every curve well placed, was breathtaking. Good thing a lot of rednecks think that all black people look alike, because who knows what they would have done to her if they'd discovered her true identity.

The police officer who had interrupted her thoughts continued to hand out the visitor passes. "Roland Pledge. Ronald Lassiter. Dan Martin," he called out.

Each name rang a loud bell in Isis's head. They were the police officers, detectives, and the prosecutor who worked on Dave's case. Even the captain of the police department was there to serve as a witness. Because Dave had been in and out of the penal system, his execution was seen as a coup. Isis watched their demeanor. They all appeared to be ecstatic, as if their football team had just won a play-off game and life couldn't get any sweeter. Five of the men, plus Isis, were there as official witnesses. There were three others who were alternates in case anyone changed his or her mind. The state of Virginia required that there be at least six witnesses to serve at an execution, and best believe the good ol' boys were lined up to come out to see a black man fry.

After everyone was seated in the van, a couple of the detectives started to make small talk with each other. The van reminded her of one that she and Dave rode in when they had gone with her church to Kings Dominion one Saturday. She and Dave went on every single ride, including the Pirate, which had flipped them upside down and caused their spending money to fall out of their pockets. They'd had only six dollars left and had to split a hamburger. Dave had insisted that she eat the entire thing, but she wouldn't eat it unless he had half.

"So, Ms. Cross," one of the detectives asked, disrupting her good memory of Dave, "what made you want to witness the death of a monster like Dave Davis?" He asked the question that everyone wanted to.

"Are you somehow connected to the victims?" another detective probed.

"Or are you doing some kind of research?" another interjected. "You look like a college student."

Isis turned around her head, locked her eyes with Detective Lassiter, and relayed the answer she had prepared in the event she was asked that question. "I'm in therapy." Then she looked in the face of each man, one by one, as the state-issued white van started its engine and headed to Greensville Correctional Center. "And my doctor said that if I saw a life taken, maybe I would appreciate living my own a bit more."

Her answer seemed to stun the rest of the witnesses, and they all stared at her. At first, the short ride was silent, and then one officer asked another, "What kind of snacks are we going to have this time around?"

"I don't know. Hopefully we'll have the hot Krispy Kreme doughnuts."

"The last time we had those awful-tasting doughnuts that were stale."

A man is about to lose his life, and the only thing these motherfuckers can think about is some goddamn snacks, Isis thought with disgust.

As the van pulled up to the gate at the prison, the man sitting behind her, whom she recognized as the prosecutor, tapped Isis on the shoulder and asked, "Is this your first execution?"

"Yes, it is. Yours?" she asked.

Special Prosecutor Pledge answered, "No, actually this is my eleventh." To Isis, he seemed to state the number with pride as if he were a runner and it was the eleventh marathon he'd run or as if he were an obstetrician and it was the eleventh baby he'd delivered.

"Oh," Isis exclaimed. "How come you've viewed so many?"

"Actually, we've all witnessed quite a few." He motioned to indicate the others in the van. "We know this process like the back of our hands. There's no better feeling than to see what you worked so hard to make happen—take bad guys off the street for life—come to its ultimate manifestation. It's what we live for."

Isis was silent while the rest of the people in the van shared idle chatter. Then the prosecutor said to her, "You know, before the execution actually can happen, the inmate gets to appeal and has plenty of fair chances. As a matter of fact, he could still get a stay of execution."

That would be wonderful. What if he could get off? . . . Stop thinking crazy, she told herself.

"Just curious—what are the chances of that really happening?"

"Slim to none because it's a capital murder case."

"Oh."

I don't know why I am torturing myself. I know better. They got a man's head on the chopping block. It ain't no turning back now.

"Often people think that in a capital murder case, the police and prosecutor's jobs are done once they get the guilty verdict, but it's not until the scum is put to death that we know that it's a job well done." When she didn't respond, he continued. "That's the real pat on the back: when we see the bad guys go down."

And they said that Dave is a monster, she thought. *Regardless of what he did, he's still a human being—someone's son . . . someone's boyfriend. But to them he's just another statistic. Another notch on their belt to let them know they accomplished something in the world.* Inside, Isis was shaking, but she maintained a calm demeanor as the bus pulled up to the prison.

Isis and the others were led into a room where they sat for about two hours. Everybody except for Isis ate Krispy Kreme doughnuts and drank orange juice and coffee while a corrections officer gave them a brief rundown on what to expect: the basic rules and regulations of a state-sanctioned murder.

It was in this room where they found out what Dave had had for his last meal: lobster, shrimp, and crab cake, which was odd to Isis because Dave had never cared for seafood. He said it gave him gas.

"Who were his final visitors?" an officer asked.

"His grandmother and his girlfriend," the corrections officer answered.

"That broad of his was one faithful bitch, I tell you that much," another officer chimed in. "She sat in that courtroom every single day. Didn't miss a beat."

Expressionless, she sat there, wondering if they were toying with her. Did they know who she was behind the designer sunglasses and the best wig that the Korean beauty supply store had to offer? Although she was terrified on the inside—and was a nanosecond from losing it—she wasn't about to let them see her sweat and blow this opportunity to see Dave alive for the very last minutes of his life.

"Well, Phoebe. It is Phoebe, isn't it?" Detective Lassiter asked. She nodded.

"I'm not sure that seeing this slimeball die will inspire you to appreciate life," Lassiter told her.

"Why would you say that?" she asked, trying not to sound defensive.

"Did you follow the story?" Lassiter asked.

She didn't know how she should answer, because she wasn't sure if the question was a trap or not. She paused.

Are these cunning motherfuckers trying to set me up? She knew she couldn't trust these pigs any farther than she could smell them. She didn't used to feel that way about officers of the law, but seeing things from another perspective made it different.

"Umm, no. But I did read a little briefing on it," she finally answered.

"Well, since we have a few minutes before his balls will be on the commonwealth's platter, fellas, maybe we should bring the lady up to speed," Lassiter suggested.

"Let's," one of the police officers agreed, and another added, "Why not?"

"Well, Ms. Cross," one of the detectives began, "let me give you the abbreviated version of this monster's murderous caper."

As the detective droned on about his version of events, Isis let her mind drift back to what she had actually witnessed firsthand to cause her childhood boyfriend to have to lose his life to the state on this fateful day. Her memory was as clear as if it had happened yesterday, although it had been more than five years earlier.

• • •

Isis and Dave's date night was every Tuesday. This was their special night to go out and do whatever Isis wanted to do: movies, dinner, bowling—the sky was always the limit. Although they saw each other almost every day, Tuesday night was their night, and no matter what, Dave always kept the commitment. It didn't matter how much money was coming through the hood or if it was the first of the month—none of that mattered to Dave at all.

That particular Tuesday night, Isis and Dave were at the Virginia Center Commons mall enjoying steak subs in the food court after watching one of those movies that Dave liked where everything and everybody got blown up by the ending credits. That was the first time that Dave had bought Isis to that mall since he'd gotten jumped there a month earlier. Three older cats from the North Side had put a lightweight beat-down on him and in the process had taken his gold chain, which had a diamond medallion of Jesus on a cross.

The necklace had been a Christmas present from Isis. She had used all of her savings from the Social Security checks she had been receiving every month since her father had passed away two years earlier. Isis had bought it for Dave as a symbol that even after life on Earth, she would love him eternally and that they'd meet again in heaven. That even though they might not be living how Jesus had lived, they still had accepted him into their hearts, knowing that if they were saved, they could enjoy eternal life together. The gold-and-diamond medallion was beautiful and contained a diamond from her deceased father's ring. Dave reminded her of her father because of how devoted he was to her. He filled a hole in her heart.

Isis had never been to that particular restaurant before. "This sandwich is greasy, but it's delicious," Isis said to Dave, licking her fingers.

"I told you, Ice." Dave smiled. "You gotta start trusting me more." He winked at her.

"I do trust you, except for your taste in movies. Now that's another issue altogether."

"Jokes, huh?"

Then Dave saw him.

The guy was by himself. That would be his second mistake concerning Dave. The first had been when he and his friends thought it was cool to put their hands on him and take something that didn't belong to them.

"Boo, wait right here," he whispered to Isis. "That's that nigga that took my chain that you gave me." Dave stood up. "I gotta go take care of something."

"No," Isis begged. "Let it go. It's not worth it." Isis wasn't one to let people walk all over her, but she knew that some battles weren't worth fighting. She could replace the necklace when she got enough cash. But she knew Dave was nothing like her. He always brought the fire, while she kept her stuff on simmer. And she could tell by the look in her man's eyes that the flames were about to get out of control.

The dude was wearing the chain and ordering a hamburger when Dave approached him. Sometimes people were just stupid like that—go around doing dirt to people, then walking the same streets the next day as if everything was sweet. Even cats knew to cover their own piss with litter.

"That's a nice piece you got on your neck there, chief," Dave said from behind the dude. The guy turned around, and recognition slowly crept across his face. "I'm willin' to forget about the lil' scuffle," Dave said, "but I'm gonna have to get my chain up off you. By the way, where're your other two friends?"

Unfazed, the dude sized up Dave, who was five feet five inches and a buck thirty-five soaking wet. "Fuck you, lil' nigga," he spat at Dave, once he decided that he would be an easy match. "If you know what's best, you'll keep it moving before you fuck 'round and lose something else, faggot."

That was the dude's third and final mistake, and in Dave's book, three strikes and a motherfucker was out. By the time the guy saw the .22-shot Glock come out from under Dave's shirt, it was too late. In front of 129 witnesses, all hell broke out in the food court. When the ringing from the pistol subsided, Dave had placed thirteen holes in the thief's body and politely taken his chain from around the dead man's neck.

Just after Dave slipped the chain around his neck, an off-duty police officer shot him, and he fell to the ground.

Isis ran over to Dave, who was on the floor in a puddle of blood. "Help! Help! Somebody help me, please!" Isis begged as Dave lay in her arms bleeding. "Please don't die, baby. Please don't die," she cried as she saw images of her father flash in front of her.

"Promise me you won't leave my side," was Dave's reply. "I love you."

Seeing flashes of her dad and remembering his last words, she told Dave, "I won't. I promise."

In addition to killing the guy, one of Dave's bullets hit a police officer's wife. She didn't die, but still her shooting added fuel to the fire: White folk were tired of young, black, dangerous hoodlums—as the media liked to portray them—terrorizing their city.

· · ·

"We have about twenty more minutes before we move over to the death chamber," the corrections officer said, interrupting Isis's thoughts. "So at this point feel free to use the restroom if you need to, because this will be your last chance until the execution is over."

Isis was glad to be brought back to the present. She used that as her cue to go to the restroom and pull herself together. What had she done? What was she doing there? *I can't believe that I am even doing this shit,* Isis thought as she looked at herself in the mirror. Her emotions were all over the place. The love of her life was about to take his last breath. She had loved him strong and hard for five years. But another part of her was angry at Dave. *If Dave wouldn't have been so damn hotheaded about a chain, then he would still be with me. He would still be right here with me.* Just then Isis realized it was Tuesday. Date night. She began to cry but then heard a knock on the door.

"You okay in there?" one of the detectives asked.

Startled, she responded that she was fine. She took a deep breath and wiped her eyes with a cool paper towel.

After coming out of the restroom, Isis entered another van, which took the witnesses over to Greensville Correctional Center, where the death-row inmates were brought a week before the actual execution and placed into solitary confinement so that a corrections officer could watch them around the clock to make sure they didn't check out before the state-mandated checkout time.

The viewing room was set up theater style. All of the witnesses sat on one side of a glass wall and the condemned prisoner on the other. There were about thirty chairs set up in six rows, five chairs on each row. The officers started play-jostling with one another, trying to be one of the first five to sit on the front. One would think that because they were all seasoned vets, the customary thing to do would be to let the virgin, or the lady, get a front-row seat. This didn't seem to cross their minds.

Maybe it was because Isis hadn't filled herself up on doughnuts and orange juice, or maybe it was because she was just naturally quicker on her feet than the middle-aged men. Whatever it was, before anyone knew what had happened, Isis had swiftly slid around to the other side of the room and was seated on the left corner of the front row.

Isis faced the table onto which they would strap Dave and administer the lethal injection.

The walls were a depressing pale yellow. There was a stainless-steel gurney with a one-inch-thick white pad laying on it. A blue curtain hung around the gurney, hiding the medical technician and doctor who would be administering the injections. The prison guards wore blank expressions on their faces. There were three other prison officials in the death chamber who were dressed in blue dress suits. A corrections officer informed her that they were the "execution team."

The director of corrections, deputy of corrections, the warden, and two assistant wardens stood while the execution team did all the work. One of the members of the team was holding the phone that was supposed to be a direct line to the governor's office in case he changed his mind at the last minute, but someone must've forgotten to pay the phone bill, because 8:50 PM came and left and that phone never rang.

• • •

The seconds seemed like hours; the minutes seemed like days. Isis watched the clock over the door, the same clock that the doctor would use to record Dave's death. She watched it as if she were the time keeper.

Then finally, with the help of twenty guards, Dave was brought into the execution chamber. There were so many guards at first that everyone in the viewing room could barely see the prisoner, but she did. His skin was pale from a lack of sunlight, and he had lost a few pounds. Isis's heart skipped and she felt short of breath. Just when she thought she going to pass out, she took a deep breath, filling her lungs with much-needed oxygen. She watched the guards move with the well-rehearsed choreography of a Janet Jackson video. In no time at all, they had David up on the gurney, strapped in. Once he was bound, another checked the straps to make sure they were all tight.

"It doesn't matter what you muthafuckas do," Dave screamed. "Y'all can't kill me!"

Isis's heart was pounding. She could feel a big lump in her throat. She thought she was going to lose all control when tears began to form in her eyes. But with all her might, she kept her cool. She kept silent. She kept still. No way could she get found out and be forced to break her promise to Dave. She had promised to be there with him to the end. Although it was torture, she would die first before breaking that promise.

"Well, the governor hasn't given you a stay," the warden said, "so it looks like you're leaving this world tonight. May God have mercy on your soul, young man."

"Suck my dick, faggot!" Dave hissed.

A black corrections officer told Dave, "Don't go out like that, young blood."

Isis looked at the clock. It read 8:59. One of the detectives looked at the time also. Just then Dave looked right at Isis.

Why is he staring in this direction? She was freaked out. A one-way mirror separated them, so she could see Dave but he couldn't see her. Isis couldn't help thinking that maybe, just maybe, Dave could feel her presence. At that point she knew: Even if David couldn't see through the glass, he knew somehow that she was there. He knew that she hadn't broken her promise.

"David Shawn Davis." The warden stood and spoke clearly and firmly as he read the death warrant. "The state of Virginia has sentenced you to the death, and this order shall hereby be carried out on this day. Do you have any last words?"

The black corrections officer positioned the microphone close to Dave's mouth so that he could be heard.

"You muthafuckers can't kill me. You will never fucking kill me. I will never die." Dave began to spit more expletives, but someone cut the speaker off. Isis couldn't hear, but she could tell that he wasn't going down to just give up. *Even as he faces death he's a soldier*, Isis thought.

The blank expressions that were on the faces of a couple of

correction officers earlier were now replaced with smirks. And most of the detectives were laughing outright.

"Give it to him." The warden gave the order and sealed it with a nod.

The three drugs that made up the death serum were administered. The first injection was supposed to send Dave into an unconsciousness state. Then they would give him another syringe filled with a saline solution to clear his veins so that the second drug would stop his muscle reflexes.

"I am like a fucking phoenix," David continued to scream. "I'm immortal. I rise from my ashes."

Dave's head began to nod, and he appeared to be physically weakening. Isis knew he was leaving her. She wanted nothing more than to run up to the glass and cry out to Dave, "I'm here, baby, I'm here," but she couldn't. She had to sit there and hold in her hurt, her pain, her anger, and her disgust. She wanted to lose control and cry out, but she couldn't. She didn't. She had to stay strong. She could break down later.

One detective remarked to another, "It seems like the doctor is moving quicker than normal to get that poison in that boy's veins. You don't think he's a little shook up, do you?"

The third drug was administered. Its job was to stop the beating of Dave's heart. A doctor monitored Dave's heart rate on the ECG machine.

"Nah. Doc probably just got some pussy waiting on 'im after this is over," the detective joked.

"You can't kill me, muthafuckers!" Dave threatened again, his voice getting weaker, but he still had enough strength to continue ranting. He even made a last-ditch effort to struggle loose.

After three minutes and forty-two seconds, David was still hurling obscenities at everyone in the room. The warden then ordered the doctor to give him a second dosage of the lethal drug combination.

It looked as if Dave was trying to keep his promise that he couldn't be killed. It had been five minutes since the second set of injections, and he still wasn't dead. It was like watching one of those horror movies. Everybody on both sides of the glass was frantic. No one knew what to do; nothing like this had ever happened before. It was unprecedented. It was like double jeopardy. They couldn't kill him twice for the same murder.

"What do we do?" the warden asked his deputy.

Just at that moment, Dave's words started to slur to the point where they couldn't be understood. He stopped kicking, and his eyes looked like white marbles as they rolled to the back of his head. Then there was no more movement at all. There were no more sounds.

The doctor checked his vitals. "He's dead."

"Look at his face," somebody said. When everyone turned to look, each was caught off guard by what they witnessed: Dave had a smile on his face. An eerie smile like the one Jack Nicholson sported when he played the Joker in that Batman movie.

That night Isis lay in bed, unable to get the scene she had witnessed earlier out of her mind. She had experienced something that would change her forever. She had sat and watched the man whom she would have traded places with in a heartbeat die before her eyes. She hadn't so much as shed a tear. She knew she couldn't cry while at the prison, but she thought for sure she'd break down once alone. But she didn't. By pretending to be someone other than herself, she had been so far removed from the person she really was that she had no idea if she could ever find her way back again.

Chapter 2

Necessary Arrangements

The next morning the weatherman had predicted the three H's for the day: hot, humid, and hazy.

It was 10 AM and Isis was still enveloped in her leopard-print comforter. The air-conditioning was set on sixty degrees, but she hadn't slept well. She tossed and turned all night; her body and mind subconsciously fighting the sandman tooth and nail. During those rare rounds when the sandman did land a lucky punch to the chin and put Isis to sleep, the images of what the state had done to David—and the look on his face— would cause her to reawaken. Just when she thought she was about to get a few winks just before midmorning to compensate for last night, the phone rang.

Who the heck is this? she thought to herself, reaching for the phone. The caller ID read "Department of Corrections." After last night, she had thought that all of her business with them was over: no more trials, no more visits, no more collect phone calls. No more Dave.

"Hello?" she answered.

"Yes, I'm trying to get in touch with Isis Tatum," a high-pitched, cheerful voice said. "Is this she?"

"It depends on who wants to know and why," Isis snapped.

"Well, my name is Janet Smith, and I am calling from the Department of Corrections. Miss Tatum, we have in our possession the corpse of David Davis, and as you probably know, he had you listed as next of kin. We need to confirm whether you will pick it up."

Isis was shocked. "Pick *it* up?" She finally got herself somewhat together. "The body?" She was now sitting straight up in the bed—confused.

"Yes, the corpse," Janet Smith explained. "We have Mr. David Davis's corpse. Most families usually like to pick it up and make their own funeral arrangements." She paused. "Although there are those who simply like to let us deal with it. DOC policy isn't usually to call the families; we just assume you know. Some families make arrangements beforehand. But when I didn't hear from you . . ." Ms. Smith's voice trailed off and lowered. "Look, I like to give a basic courtesy call because I know if it were a loved one of mine, I wouldn't want the state to bury them in a box and just throw some dirt on them."

Isis thought for a minute and let out a long sigh before she spoke again. "Yes," she said, "I would like to claim . . . take possession of . . ."—Isis was having a hard time wording it—". . . receive the body. Where do I go, and what do I need to do?"

"We generally like to have the paperwork done before the execution," Ms. Smith said. "That's why I'm calling you this morning. The body is at the Medical College of Virginia morgue, and if you can make arrangements to come or have it picked up within twenty-four hours, that will be fine. If not, then I'm sorry, but the state will have to dispose of it. I can let them know that you will be in contact with them."

"Thank you, Janet. I mean for calling and all. I know you didn't have to do that."

"No problem," Ms. Smith said, "but there is one other thing."

"And what might that be, Janet?"

"You have to pay a fee before they will give you the body."

"A *fee?*"

"I'm afraid so. There's a two-hundred-dollar fee to have the body released to you, and they won't take checks—only postal money orders."

"That's a crying shame. The state kills him, and I gotta pay *them* to get the body?"

"I know," Janet admitted, "but they're not my rules."

That's crazy. Isis looked at the clock. "It's getting late, and I'm going to have to get out of here if I'm going to make it on time. I need to start making some phone calls, I suppose. Again, thank you very much."

"No problem." Ms. Smith shared a few more details with Isis and then said, "Let me give you my extension just in case you have any problems."

As soon as she had hung up the phone, it rang again. *What is it this time?* She peeped at the caller ID. It was her half sister, Phoebe.

Isis and Phoebe had an odd but strong relationship. Even though they shared the same father, they didn't meet each other until they both were thirteen years old, at their father's funeral. They were born four days apart; Isis was the elder. Those were tough times, especially for Isis, but despite their mothers' hatred of each other, the two girls hit it off right off the bat. There was no jealousy between them. They were each just pleased to have an extension of their father in each other.

Phoebe's mother, Brenda, didn't want her daughter to have anything to do with Isis, the daughter of the woman who had murdered her lover, but the girls paid her no mind. They became thick as thieves—better than Siamese twins, because they were joined at the heart.

"Hey, sister," Isis answered.

"Hey, sister, tell me what's wrong." Phoebe knew her sister had been through the fire, but she sensed an additional stress in her voice.

"How do you know something is wrong?" Isis tried to put a little pep in her voice.

"Because I'm your sister and you can't hide anything from me, that's why."

"I just got a call from a lady from the DOC. She told me that I could come get Dave's body."

"Well, Ice, that's good—isn't it?"

"Yeah, but it's just too much. It costs two hundred dollars just to get him from MCV. Then there's the funeral. I mean, in all honesty, I never even thought about a funeral."

"Well, sis, what did you think they were going to do with the body? I mean, after somebody dies, there's always, always a funeral. I mean, you got people out there that have funerals for their dogs."

"Yeah, I know, but . . ."

"Okay, sis, just relax. Let's think about one thing at a time. First, we have to get him. I got my half," Phoebe offered. "You got a hundred on you?"

"Yeah, but there's more," Isis said. "They said that his body was in a wooden box, and that we needed a truck or something or immediate arrangements with a funeral home, and I don't get paid until next Wednesday."

"Now that's some shit right there," Phoebe said.

"Which part: Having to pick the body up or me not getting paid until next Wednesday?"

"Both. Damn." Phoebe sighed. "Wait, doesn't Dave's mother have a truck?"

Isis thought for a minute. "Yeah, you're right. Good lookin' out, sis. I'm going to call her now. Stay on the line. I'm going to call on the three-way." Isis clicked over and dialed Ms. Davis's number and then clicked back over to Phoebe, who sat silently listening in.

The phone rang three times. *Nothing beats a failure but a try*, she thought, knowing full and well that getting a favor from the woman was going to be like pulling teeth because Dave's mother had never been a member of Isis's fan club. After the phone rang three more times, Isis was about to hang up, but then someone picked up on the other end.

"Hello?" Ms. Davis answered.

"Hi, Ms. Davis, this is Isis."

"Hey, Isis, how're you doing?"

"I'm doing fine." Isis took a deep breath and proceeded. "The reason I was calling you is because the people from the prison called me because Dave had me down as a next of kin along with you. But I don't think they got an answer when they tried calling you." Isis was lying about Dave's mother being next of kin because she didn't want to hurt her feelings. Dave would have never put his mother's name on a list. Not after the way she acted once he was convicted of the crime. She never went to see him, not one time, and refused to take the collect-call block off of her phone.

"Damn, they did kill that boy last night, didn't they?"

"Yeah, they did." Isis was silent for a second or two, and then she took another deep breath before continuing. "They called because they need someone to pick up the body, so he can have a decent buri—"

Ms. Davis cut her off. "Look, I ain't using not one iron motherfucking dime of my insurance money to bury that goddamn boy. Why can't the state bury him? Shit, they da ones that kilt him."

Most people would have been shocked to hear a mother speak like that about her child who had just passed, but not Isis. She had hoped the conversation would go differently, but when it didn't, she wasn't surprised. And even though she wanted to snap off on Ms. Davis, the woman was still the mother of the man she had loved for what seemed like forever. Besides, Dave wouldn't have wanted her to; he would have done it his goddamn self if he could've!

"No. I mean they can, but it wouldn't be much of a funeral," Isis told Dave's mother. "And he deserves way better than what they are going to give him if we don't pick up the body. I think we need to get together and handle this."

"Well, shit, I honestly don't see why."

Once again, Isis bit her tongue. "With all due respect, when he was out here, he was good to all of us. I just think that we should put him away nicely."

"When he was out here? Phuh! That was years ago. Hell, he ain't did shit for me in the past five years," Ms. Davis barked. "And I know he was hustling in that prison too, and he ain't send me not one red cent. Furthermore, that motherfucker knew he was dying; do you think he signed life insurance papers for me to be the beneficiary? Hell, no!" She raised her voice. "I'ma tell you something right now: They can bury his ass in a cardboard box and set his ass on fire for all I care. Like I said before—and I will say it again—I ain't taking one dime of my hard-earned money to do shit for that nigga." Dave's mother finally took a breather.

Isis was about to get a word in, but Ms. Davis started back up again. "Shit! The nigga is dead; he ain't gonna know nothing about no funeral or what was done with his body for that matter."

What Isis wanted to say was: "That's really messed up that you feel like that about your only son. I don't remember you feeling that way when he was out here throwing bricks from the time he was twelve years old to pay your miserable ass's bills." She wanted so bad to set the record straight, but instead she told Ms. Davis, "I wasn't calling you for any of your 'hard-earned' money anyway; I knew better. It's sad. I only wanted to borrow your truck to pick up your son's body. But forget it—you might charge me to drive it. It's okay. I will find another way." Isis hung up in Ms. Davis's ear. She had wanted to tell Ms. Davis off for a long time and still hadn't given it to her like she'd really wanted to.

Isis hit the flash button on the phone and clicked back over to Phoebe. "Phoebe, are you still there?" she asked.

"I'm here," Phoebe said. "I can't believe her."

"I can," Isis replied, and just then her other line beeped. She looked down at the caller ID screen on her phone. "Hold on; this is her calling back." Isis clicked over to answer the incoming call. "Hello?"

"Did you hang up on me?" Ms. Davis snapped.

"Well, honestly, the conversation was over."

I can't believe this lady. I swear I wish she was his sister and not his momma. I would pull a Freddy Krueger and go through this phone receiver and get that ass!

"Look, you little bitch, I didn't say 'bye yet. And was it something that you needed to say to me, because you sound like you was rushing off the phone and biting your tongue."

"Ms. Davis, trust me," Isis cackled. "You don't even want to know."

"Look, bitch, you ain't Jack Nicholson; I can handle the truth. Spit it out."

"Well, since you want to know what I think—"

"Ain't shit your little young ass can tell me, because I done been through hell and back."

"Look, Ms. Davis, I'm trying not to go there with you because sad to say, I know you are his mother."

"No, let's go there," Ms. Davis said.

"Like I said—trust me, Ms. Davis, you don't want me to take you there in the emotional state I'm in right now."

"Oh, take me there, suga. Take me there." Isis could feel Ms. Davis rolling her neck around through the phone. "But I'll warn you, you might not be able to find your way back by the time I get done with you."

Isis chuckled at Ms. Davis's threat. "All I'm going to say is that one day when all the money, cars, and diamonds are long gone and you are old and sick with no one around to love or take care of your shitty butt, and the nursing assistant is being mean to your hateful self and not changing your Depend undergarments and she is the only familiar face you ever see, then maybe you'll think about your son and all of the good things he *did* do and all the things he did risk for you. And when that time comes . . . and you're at your worst hour . . . this is what I want you to do: *kill yourself!*"

Isis hit the flash button on the phone and began to laugh. For that brief moment, she felt good.

Isis returned to the line when her laughing fit was done. "Phoebe, are you still there?"

"I'm here," Phoebe said.

"Hold on," Isis said. "Give me another minute with that no-good so-called mother—she needs to know one more thing." Isis clicked over and dialed Ms. Davis's number again. When Ms. Davis picked up the phone, Isis clicked back over so Phoebe could get an earful.

"I thought you'd call back and apologize," Ms. Davis said.

"You'd better think again. I called to tell you that there will be a funeral—and don't bother showing your face." This time when she hung up, she heard someone putting a key in the front door. Isis at first wondered if Ms. Davis had made her way over quick, in a hurry to make good on her threat, but shook off the thought. "Phoebe, is that you?"

"Yeah, I had got in the car and started on my way over here a little after I called you and you told me about the body and all. Somebody has to get you around. You are in no shape to be driving."

As she entered the house, Phoebe bent down to pick up the mail that had been dropped through the mail slot. She thumbed through it, being nosey, before she stopped at one of the envelopes. "I know you probably don't want to hear this, but you got a letter here from Dave. He must have written it the day before he died." Phoebe handed the letter to her older sister.

Isis stared at the letter, shaking her head. This was all too much.

Phoebe took the letter back from her and put it down. "Look, sis, you don't have to read it now." There was a brief moment of silence before Phoebe spoke again. "You know what I was thinking? We don't need that bitch's truck anyway. We can just call a funeral home and get them to do it."

"But they gonna want to get paid, and I don't have no money to pay for a funeral right now."

"We'll figure out something. Remember, one thing at a time." Phoebe thought for a moment. "Maybe we should call Scott's Funeral Home; they are the ones that my momma called for Daddy."

"That's a thought," Isis said, feeling even more melancholy than before.

Phoebe made the call for her sister, asked for the owner, and pleaded their case. A meeting was set up with the funeral home for 1 PM the next day to discuss payment. For now, Scott's Funeral Home was on the way to the Medical College of Virginia to pick up the body.

Later that night, exhausted after such a stressful day, Isis decided to open the letter that she had received from Dave.

My dearest Isis,

By the time you read this, the day would have come and gone, the day that we both have been dreading yet anticipating. The day that we both knew was inevitable, the day that my death will be carried out by the State of Virginia.

You've been everything to me since the first time that I laid eyes on you, when you were only 15 years old. You were the most beautiful girl I'd ever met, seen, or read about. I knew that we could never be together for long. Girls like you grow into the kind of women who don't have guys like me show up on their radar. So the day that we would grow apart was also inevitable. It had nothing to do with the execution.

I'm not writing this letter in an attempt to make you feel bad or guilty for anything; you have nothing to feel guilty about. You've been great to me. Better than any of my so-called friends, better than my family, better than my own mother. You've given me everything and asked for nothing in return. For that, I just want to say thank you and I love you for it. But now I must say, "No more."

During our last visit together, when I looked into your eyes, I saw the future. I saw your future and I wasn't in it; and that's the way it should be. You've wasted enough time on me. You were my wifey, girlfriend, sister, and best friend when everyone else got ghost (including my mother), before the ink even dried on the death warrant. Now it's time for you to move on. From this point on, I want you to forget that I ever existed.

I want you to give the same love and dedication that you have given me for all these years and put it toward your future and career. Live for yourself for a change. Let someone serve and wait on you. You deserve it. But always remember this one thing: No one's going to give you anything in this life without a price. It may cost a little, it may cost a lot—but it will cost you.

Dave

BKA The Phoenix

P.S. Just so that you know, those crackers are going to have to bring the noise, because I'm not going to just roll over and die for them. Mu'fuckas best pack a lunch.

See ya in the next life!

Isis was standing with a blank look on her face, staring at the letter she held in her hand, when Phoebe walked into the living room carrying the house phone with the mute button activated. "It's Bam," she said. But after looking at her sister's bloodshot eyes and vacant stare, she asked, "Do you want me to tell the nigga you busy and to get at you another time?"

Bam was an old acquaintance of Dave's. They had gone to school together, and he always called Isis to check on Dave or just to see if she needed anything.

Isis wiped her eyes. "Nah, he might need information on Dave or something," she said, reaching for the phone. "Give me the damn thing." Isis shut off the mute function. "This is Isis," she said, slowly wiping her eyes, chasing the tears that were trickling down her face.

"Hey, gorgeous, how're you feelin'?" Bam said cheerfully, trying to lift her spirits.

"Not so good, but I've been done worse by better." She tried to sound confident. "What about you?"

"You know me—fine as wine, all the time. But I didn't call to bore you with shit that you should already know," Bam boasted. "Fill me in on what's been going on in your world today, and let me know how I can help to make it better." Bam had a pretty good idea as to what was going on. A moment passed, and Isis hadn't responded. "You know our boy wouldn't want you teary-eyed. That nigga was a soldier; probably went out like Scarface. He would want you to be a soldier too, not sad with watery eyes."

"What makes you think that you know what's in my eyes?"

"I can hear it in your voice. Plus, your mute button must be broke, and Phoebe can't whisper worth shit."

"No, you got ears the size of an elephant, that's all."

"That's not all I got that's like an elephant, but that's another story. Now who do I need to fuck up for my good friend?"

"Nobody," she answered. "I just had a really horrible day."

"Now we're gettin' somewhere."

"I don't want to get more worked up than I already am. Shit has just been fucked up ever since they executed Dave last night. It was awful."

"I know. I heard them talking about it on the news," Bam said.

"I was there."

"You were what?" he said, not believing what he had heard.

"I was there," she repeated. "I watched it all go down, and I haven't been able to sleep since," she confessed. "But that wasn't the half of it. This morning the people from the prison called to tell me that since I was listed as Dave's next of kin, I would have to come and get his body if I wanted to give him a proper burial."

"You gotta go get the body?" Bam questioned, surprised.

"Yes. And I don't have any money for a funeral. Then to top it off," she continued, "that mother of his . . . I don't even want to talk about it."

Bam let out a small chuckle. "What she do now?"

"Why you laughing?"

"Because Ms. Davis is a fool, and I don't even want to imagine what her latest stunt might be."

Her sister handed her some juice, and Isis took a sip before continuing. "Don't you know that she had a fat-ass insurance policy on Dave, and she could give a flying fuck how he gets buried?"

"Is that all?" Bam said consolingly. "Fuck her. Don't let her miserable ass get to you. She ain't never gave a fuck about nobody but herself."

"I know, but how could a mother literally leave her son for dead?"

"I'm telling you, it's not even worth the stress trying to figure the old bitch out. Just tell me: How much do you need to send my man off in style?"

"Me and my sister are supposed to meet with the man at the funeral home tomorrow. I won't know until then."

"Well, let me know as soon as you know. Whatever it is, I got it. It's gonna be okay," Bam assured her. "Now how about I carry you out to dinner tonight?"

"I'm going to have to pass on dinner," she said. "But I know Dave would've been pleased to know that one of his old friends came through for him."

Bam brushed off her comment. "Well, call me tomorrow and let me know how much it is."

"Okay," she said. "Thanks a bunch. I'll call you then."

As soon as Isis put the phone down, Phoebe looked at her sister and said, "He gonna pay for it, ain't he?"

A look of relief appeared over Isis's face. "Yes," she said, nodding her head. "How did you know?"

"Because that nigga has been in love with you from day one. He's always wanted to find a way to get next to you, even before Dave." Phoebe paused for a moment and then mumbled under her breath, "I guess he's finally figured out a way how."

Chapter 3

R.I.P.

Bam came through with the money needed for the funeral just as he promised, and it could never be said that Isis did not put Dave away in style. Although Isis had never planned a funeral before, she made do with the information learned from her Aunt Samantha, who'd practically raised her after her mother was sent to prison for killing her father.

Always dripping in fabulousity and ultraglamorous, Samantha stood five feet nine inches and was model thin. She wore only the best push-up bras that money could buy to make the small breasts God probably considered a blessing look like a B cup. Dressed, as always, as if going to a *Vogue* photo spread, she was at the funeral in a fierce black dress that complemented her small waist. Her long black hair was always kept up to par, and she was never caught without her makeup. Samantha was blessed with the beautiful eyes that Isis and Sandy shared, but the difference was that Samantha was never without long false eyelashes to enhance them.

After the funeral, Isis was walking out of the funeral home toward the limo when, out of nowhere, she was greeted by an unwelcome guest whom she saw walking from a red limo.

"Let me ask you one question." Ms. Davis approached, wearing candy-apple red from head to toe. The two-piece skirt set was matched by stockings and pumps that were both the same shade of red. She was wearing a big-brimmed red hat with a lace veil, with red-and-white drop earrings, a red pearl necklace, and a wristful of gaudy red bracelets.

Before Isis could regain her composure, or her vision, from the shock of Ms. Davis having taken things too far both by showing up for the funeral and by sporting such a hideous *coordinated* ensemble, Dave's mother was in her face, nose to nose, as if they were professional boxers posing for a pay-per-view fight advertisement.

"How da fuck you gonna have a motherfucking funeral for *my* son," Ms. Davis said to Isis, "and not invite his momma, bitch?" She was moving her shoulders and neck from side to side like she was doing a stiff version of that dance, the snake.

It took everything in Isis's power not to dropkick the woman. She answered with all the decorum she could muster. "Ms. Davis, you don't send invites to a funeral." Isis flashed a fake smile. "And besides, I thought you didn't care if he was left in a cardboard box. Why should I go out of my way to make sure you were here to see that he wasn't?" Isis had no intention of punking out to Ms. Davis ever again.

"It don't make no motherfucking difference what I said, you little bitch. I am still his mother!"

Isis's face twisted ever so slightly. She wasn't going to be called a bitch too many more times by this hag. "Surely a real mother would have *never* collected the insurance money from her son's death and not taken care of the burial of her son, would she?" Isis took a step back so she wouldn't be in arm's reach of Ms. Davis before continuing. "Not any mother that was worth a damn anyway."

"Listen, you little bitch! I will beat yo' young ass."

"Whatever, lady." Isis brushed off the threat. "Don't come at me sideways just because you feel guilty that you've always been a piss-poor mother to your offspring."

Aunt Samantha wasn't far away and had overheard the conversation. Samantha, who was a little taller than Isis and about the same height as Ms. Davis—but much prettier—got right into Ms. Davis's face. "My niece ain't gon' be called nan nother bitch from yo' stank ass." Samantha, like always, wanted to protect Isis from the unnecessary madness around her. "You want to put your hands on someone, honey, take it up with me."

Ms. Davis looked Samantha up and down, observing every inch and detail, right down to her bone structure. "You must be crazy if you think I am going to stand here and fight a *man*."

That statement got Isis worked up. "Oh, no you didn't," Isis said to Ms. Davis before hauling off and spitting at her. The spit landed right on her red pointed toe pumps. "Don't you ever call my Aunt Samantha a man."

Ms. Davis put her hands on her hips. "Shit, why not? Sa *man* tha. *Man*tha. *Man*! Take away the 'Sa' and the 'tha' and what you got? *Man*. The only somebody who might not be able to tell that your *aunt* Samantha is a man is Eddie Murphy."

Aunt Samantha was actually Isis's mother's only *brother*—

Sam Jones. He was living proof that God sometimes makes mistakes, just like the rest of us, because God had definitely given Sam the wrong body at birth. Sam had been getting shots to make her butt bigger and rounder and was taking the necessary steps to get a full sex change. For over twenty years, Sam had been dressing in drag, living the life of a woman.

When Isis's mother had gone to prison, Sam had been forced to take on the responsibility of caring for his niece. His crazy, reckless lifestyle, the unprotected sex with various men, the casual drugging and drinking—all were reduced to a minimum when Isis had come to live with him. Isis was probably the best thing that had ever happened to Sam, because the AIDS epidemic swept through the gay community during that time. Most of Sam's friends didn't have a lifesaver like Isis to pull them away from the unhealthy lifestyle that they were living. Unfortunately, many of them battled the deadly disease to a losing end.

Missing her original target, Isis spat at Ms. Davis again, this time making her mark. Ms. Davis was caught off guard but still managed to swing and hit Isis with an open-handed smack to the face. That was the beginning of the end.

Aunt Samantha balled up her manicured fist and commenced to whip up on Ms. Davis as if the woman was a bitch who had just tried to steal her man. A few people were watching from inside the funeral home, but no one dared to break it up.

After a couple of well-placed blows by Samantha, Ms. Davis hit the ground. She should've stayed on her feet, because Samantha used her fall as an opportunity to stomp a young mudhole in her ungrateful butt. The only thing that made Samantha stop was looking down and noticing that she'd run her panty hose to the point that they were starting to look like large-holed fishnet stockings.

After leaving the imprint of her pointed-toe pump on Ms.

Davis's behind, Samantha warned, "Think about that the next time you want to call my child a bitch," and followed that with another kick. "Bitch!"

Ms. Davis was balled up in a fetal position, afraid to move, afraid that another blow was on its way, when Samantha stepped over her to get to Isis and give her a hug. "I'm sorry, honey," Aunt Samantha said, "but don't let this affect today any more than it already has."

"I won't," Isis assured Samantha. "You always told me that sometimes a girl's gotta do what a girl's gotta do." They pulled themselves together and made their way to the burial ground to finish what they had intended to do from the start: put David in the ground in style.

Chapter 4

Sick as a Dog

Isis was eating breakfast at her favorite diner when her phone vibrated. Normally she turned the phone off when she was in a restaurant so that she could enjoy her food in peace and not distract other patrons from their dining with a one-sided phone conversation. She thought about just letting it go to voicemail, but when she looked down at the caller ID, she was glad that she hadn't; it was Phoebe calling.

Phoebe was in Texas trying out for the Dallas Cowboys Cheerleaders, which had been a dream of hers since she was a little girl. The Cowboys had been her father's favorite football team, and once he passed away, she had become even more determined to make the squad.

"Hey, sister," Isis answered. "How is everything?"

"I'm sorry I couldn't be there for you at the funeral," Phoebe told her sister, sadness dripping from her voice. "I feel like I let you down. I really wanted to stay and help with everything going on with you right now."

"I know, sis, but I really want you to do great at your tryouts. You know this has been your dream since we were young."

"I know. But there are so many girls here to try out. I don't know if I'll make it anyway," Phoebe said.

"Sure, you are going to make it. You were the head cheerleader in high school and led your squad to three straight championships. You're a natural." Isis tried to increase her sister's confidence. "How many black chicks are there?"

"Probably." She hesitated, "about ten."

"Okay—they gotta have at least two black girls on the team, so you should be a lock. Plus, you got the looks and the talent. Besides, they gotta add some flavor, in my opinion."

"I know, but—"

"But nothing. You're incredibly beautiful, you have a cute figure, you're model thin, and in shape, plus you can dance your ass off."

"That's sweet of you to say, but you're my sister," Phoebe said. "Will they see that?"

"Sister, please. You are cuter than any cheerleader I ever seen, and you know that I've seen some cheerleaders in my day with all those football games that Daddy took me to. Gurl, I need to be down there in Texas judging y'all."

"You right," Phoebe said with a slight chuckle. "I guess you would know." But Isis could hear a little hurt in her voice. "Sister, I've always been jealous of the relationship that you and Dad shared. He was your full-time dad and only a when-I-see-you dad for me, which was only when he had to stop by to drop off money or get a quickie with Brenda. That's all Brenda cared about. She didn't give a damn about Dad having a father–daughter relationship with me. Sure, sometimes he would stay a little while, but I never got to go out to eat with him or to the movies or go to the park or football games."

Isis had never known that her sister felt that way. Though they'd formed a bond as strong as any blood sisters could, Phoebe had never talked much about her feelings toward their father.

Phoebe continued, "Then when Sandy killed him, my chances of us ever having a deeper relationship were killed right along with him."

"Sister, I'm sorry that you didn't have a closer relationship with our father, but we both suffered great losses when he died," Isis said. "I lost both of my parents on that day."

Sandy had received a thirty-year prison sentence for the killing. Isis had never understood how her mother could have done something so horrific, and so she had never forgiven Sandy or ever visited her in prison. As far as Isis was concerned, her mother had died on that day as well.

"I'm sorry for peeling the scab off old wounds," Phoebe said. "Let's change the subject."

"Sister, you have nothing to apologize for. You should always feel free to share how you feel with me. If you can't be honest with me, then who can you be honest with? Your mother?"

"Yeah, right." Phoebe chuckled. She was closer to Isis than she was her mother, a fact that wasn't lost on Brenda. "Did you call in to work today?"

"Yes, but I have to bring a doctor's note. I know they are sick of me. Last week it was the funeral, and now this shit."

"You'll be okay. You just gotta take care of yourself, and pneumonia ain't nothing to be taken lightly," Phoebe cautioned.

"I know; it's just hard to lie around all day," Isis said, knowing that she should have her butt at home in bed. But she was finally regaining her full appetite, and she couldn't stand any more of the soup Aunt Samantha had been bringing her. Cooking had never been Aunt Samantha's strong suit, but Lord knows she tried.

Just then a loud voice in the background warned Phoebe and the other participants: "Warm-up in five minutes, ladies."

"Sister, I gotta go. I need to make one more call before warm-up," Phoebe said.

Isis started coughing. "Okay. Good luck, sister," she said between sniffs and coughs before hanging up the phone. She knew that she should have kept her tail at home.

Isis left the restaurant and went home. For the next hour or so, she lay in bed, blowing her nose and flipping through TV channels, until her phone rang.

"Hey, Boo, I heard you were sick." It was Bam.

"Yes, I'm sick as a dog," Isis said, coughing.

"Well, if you need a nurse, then you are in luck, because I know a good one."

"I do too, but you do know that I am not only a member of the Broke-Ass Friends Club but also the president?"

Bam chuckled on Isis's play on the words of one of Biggie's old joints. "Shit, the emergency room don't refuse no one."

"I've already been there."

"What did they do?"

She hit the mute button to blow her nose and then returned to the phone. "Nothing much. I got pneumonia. Hold on." She sneezed and wiped her nose. "But I'll be okay."

"I know you will, because I am on my way over there with tea, juice, crackers, soup, and some other goodies."

"No, I'm good." Although she tried to control the next round of coughing, it blasted out anyway. "You've done enough already."

"No you're not. That cough right there is why I am on the way. I'll be there in ten minutes."

She tried to stop him. "No. I look a mess."

"I know you're beautiful, but you can't be glamorous and sick at the same time. Not even Naomi Campbell can do that. And for real, Shorty, I done seen you dolled up; I know how you do yours," he told her. "I'll be there in eight minutes. Gotta go."

Although she was weak, Isis managed to wash her face and brush her teeth and hair so she could be a little more presentable. She didn't want to be seen in a vulnerable state by Bam, but once he arrived, she liked the idea of having him there to take care of her. She dozed off a few times, and each time she woke up, he was right there. He would make quick runs to handle his business, but he was so fast about it that she would never even have known that he'd been gone if he hadn't told her.

"I know your being here is cutting into the other things you need to be doing. You've been great. You can go take care of the streets now," Isis suggested to him as he sat on the side of the bed feeding her chicken noodle soup. She felt bad that Dave's boy was taking care of her the way he would have.

"It's not an inconvenience at all. Actually, it's kind of convenient in its own way."

"Really? You aren't just saying that, are you?"

"Nope, it's real talk. See, I've been staying out in the country with my aunt, but I'm about to get my own place."

"For real?" she asked. "Out here? In the city?"

"Naw, in the country. See, I don't be trying to fuck with these niggas for real. You know, they see a nigga getting money and they want to run up in they spot. They feel like they should reap the benefits of another man's labor."

"I feel ya," she said after a big sneeze.

Bam handed her a tissue. "So to protect myself from that shit, I can keep that place good and booby-trapped just in case a nigga wanna try his hand. Usually when I get calls, I have to drive up here and meet dudes, but now that I am here with you, it's been more convenient. I like the company. Plus, you got a nice little place—no kids, nothing."

She smiled but thought about how much longer she would have her place. Her rent was already one month behind before the funeral, and then she got sick, and now with her missing over two weeks of work, she had no idea how she was going to play catch-up. "So you don't like kids, huh?"

"Naw, I am not going to say that I don't like the li'l monsters, but I don't want any right now."

Isis seconded his opinion. "Me either. I need to get my shit in order first." She opened up a new box of tissues.

"That makes two of us."

"You seem like you got your shit together: nice car, you making money. What more could you want?"

"There's always more to be had. I want more out of life than drug money and trick bitches."

"That sounds like a plan." She blew her nose.

"Yeah, so bringing kids into this world isn't a good look for the lifestyle I'm living right now."

"I agree, but are you protecting yourself?" Isis had no idea why she was asking such personal questions, but she kept firing. "If it happens, then what?"

He smacked his lips at her as if she was asking him a crazy

question. "That cold must really got you delirious. Damn right I'm wearing armor. I've got to look out for me."

"That's good. I was just checking."

* * *

Over the next few days, Bam slowly nursed Isis back to health. But as she grew stronger, Bam got weaker—she'd passed the virus on to him. So the next thing she knew, their roles had reversed, and now she was being his nurse.

Finally, after about a week, Isis felt well enough to return to the jewelry store where she worked. She worked the entire day with her boss, Bob. She was still busy even after she had finished her official eight-hour shift.

"Isis, what time had you planned on leaving today?" Bob asked.

"Well, I have so much to do to try to get things back on track."

"Like what?"

"I really need to follow through on all of the special orders to see when they will be in and call my clients to let them know the status so they won't be left in the dark."

He nodded, and Isis continued. "Then I have to find a company that we can order an eight-carat trillion tanzanite ring from for another customer, but because it may be hard to get, I am going to get the price of the same ring in sapphire because it may be another option as far as the look. Plus, I'm sure it would be a lot cheaper."

He nodded again and smiled. "That's awful nice of you."

"I do what I have to do to make sure that we keep them coming back. With all the competition out there, they can go anywhere they want to purchase their gems, but it's important that we treat them as valued customers so that they'll choose us."

A huge smile covered Bob's face. Isis had learned well. "That's right. So how long you think before you'll be finished up?" Bob asked.

"Well, I'm going to do as much as I can here, then I will do some research from home."

Bob looked at his watch. It was after six. He left and went to dinner. When he returned, Isis was putting the clearance items out.

"After I get all of these clearance items tagged and ready to be put out tomorrow, I'm going to go ahead and head out, Bob." Isis felt good about her day. It had been very productive. She had caught up to the point where it was almost as if she had never been gone.

"Make sure you come and see me after you have everything done," Bob instructed her.

Isis finished up a couple more things and then went to see him.

"Hey, Bob, you wanted to see me before I left for the day?" Isis said as she entered his office.

"Listen, you are one of the best workers that I've ever had. I've never seen any one of my employees work the customers as you do. Even if they come in with no money, you treat them so well that they come back when they do have money."

She smiled. She knew what all of this was about, why Bob wanted to see her. *One day back on the job, and already they giving me a raise*, Isis thought. *They must have really missed me. Sales must have been at an all-time low, which they always are when I am out or on vacation.* Isis was pumping herself up big time. If she'd had a dick, she could have sucked it herself.

"Working with jewelry is a gift that you possess, and I am sure your next employer will appreciate it as well. I'm sorry, Isis, but I'm going to have to let you go."

Isis snapped out of her thoughts. "What? Excuse me? Did I hear you correctly? You're letting me go? But you just said—"

"And I meant it," Bob assured her. "The problem is that I need someone that I can rely on to come to work consistently. Sorry, but I'm going to have to let you go."

"You *can* rely on me, Bob, I swear. It's just that things have been crazy lately." Isis pleaded her case. "But you can trust me, Bob."

"Not anymore. I have no idea what has happened to you in the past few weeks."

"I had a death in my family and then I was sick." None of this seemed to matter to Bob. "What about the four years that I've been working where I hardly ever missed a day? Sometimes I even came in on my days off."

"That was then; this is now. As I said, your services are no longer needed, and I'm going to have security escort you to your car after we check your bags." Employees getting their bags checked was standard procedure.

Isis was pissed off and hurt and cried the entire way home, only to be greeted by an eviction notice at her front door because she had missed her housing court date. Funny how things worked. She had never missed one of Dave's court dates, and now she had missed her very own. *When it rains, it pours*, she thought.

Bam, who was still sick and laying up at Isis's spot, heard her in the kitchen as she was putting water in the teakettle.

"You finally off?" he called out from her bedroom. She had been sleeping on the couch so that he could rest and try to get better.

"They fired me," she said, keeping her back to him because she didn't want him to see her tears.

"How they gonna fire their best employee? I saw your employee-of-the-month plaques in the other room."

"They don't care about that. I guess they didn't like it that I'd been out three weeks, and I was going to be working only two more weeks before my scheduled vacation."

"Where are you going?"

"Where *was* I going, you mean?" She started to wash the glasses that sat in the sink. She really just needed an excuse to keep her back to Bam. Slowly she pulled herself together. "I was going away to a weeklong jewelry seminar to learn about becoming a professional jewelry designer. I've been sketching different designs for years, and I thought now was the time to finally make my dream a reality."

"That's what's up!" Bam said, impressed that Isis was a chick who wanted to do something and wasn't depending on a man to come in and take care of her.

"I know, but it seems like one thing after another keeps pulling me away from my true love. I gave so much time to Dave that I put my dreams on hold, and now . . . ." She finally turned to face him.

"You shouldn't let anyone get in the way of following your dream," he said. "I wish I could do something other than sling dope."

"You do have other options, Bam. Stop selling yourself short. You're smart and are a natural leader."

"Maybe you are right, but this convo isn't about me; it's about you. Why can't you go to the class now?"

"Because like I said, something always comes up. Like . . . ," she began, but she couldn't quite get the words out, ashamed of her reality.

"Like . . . ?" Bam egged her on.

"Like Dave and having to plan funerals. Getting sick and losing my job. I was already late on my rent and other bills before I lost my job, but I've always managed to hold it together," she confessed. "I don't know what I'm going to do now."

"I understand more than you may think. I do have a mother and two sisters." He paused before saying, "It's hard out here for a woman trying to hold her own. Taking care of everyone else and putting herself last. I feel you, baby. I know times are hard."

Isis didn't respond, so Bam broke the silence. "Shit, the world is in a damn recession: gas high, milk high, everything. Shit, times is real fucked up for all of us—even the damn dope man."

Isis laughed. She was grateful for Bam's humor. Somehow he made things seem doable.

"Hard times are definitely in our city, baby. You better believe that." He sat down at Isis's breakfast bar.

"I know that's right," she agreed, joining him.

"Well, look, I know what I am about to throw at you may seem like it's coming kinda quick, but I'm goin' to put it out there anyway."

She looked at him. "I'm listening."

"I have a confession of my own to make. You know I've been feeling you since the first time I laid these pupils on you."

"That's what someone told me," she said, "but it's the first time that I ever heard it from you."

"Well, it's absolutely true. Now you've heard it straight from the horse's mouth. I've always been in love with you."

It hadn't even been a month since she had put Dave in the ground, but she couldn't deny that she had developed feelings for Bam. Isis really didn't know how to respond, so she simply said, "Damn."

But Bam wasn't finished. "And being around you these past two weeks has made me want you even more." He paused for a minute, hoping she would say something, but she didn't. "What I'm about to say may sound fucked up, but I got to say it."

"Just don't say anything that you don't mean," she warned.

"My momma always says shit happens for a reason. Even when the shit is fucked up, it happens for a reason." Bam looked at her. "There is always something good that comes along with the bad."

"Bam?" she asked. "What are you getting at?"

"My aunt is always on my ass for money, acting like I'm her personal ATM, which is driving me to get a place. You getting fired is going to allow you more time to chase your dream; it's destined that way."

Bam saw that after all these years he finally had her ear, so he didn't let up. Next, he wanted her heart. "I mean, let's face it: There was a reason for Dave being in both of our lives."

"Why you say that?" she asked, not really liking Dave's name coming up in the conversation this way.

"Because Dave was the bridge that connected us. He was the reason we met. Him dying was the reason I've been able to grow on you."

"Who said you've grown on me?"

"I can see it in your eyes," Bam said, "and if I hadn't, I wouldn't be here."

"Well, I was just trying to help a person that had my back when I was down and out."

He laughed and then took her hand. "I feel like the timing is perfect. You and Dave never had a real man-and-woman relationship."

"That's not true." Isis pulled her hand away. "Don't try to diminish what Dave and I had."

"Hold your ponies; let me finish. Don't cut off my head just yet." Bam cleared his throat and continued. "No one can deny that you two had a strong bond and that you were a hell of a friend to him—probably the best friend he ever had—but you never had a real relationship because you had only known him a few months when he caught his case, and you both were so young."

Isis had been thinking over the past few weeks about her relationship with Dave and knew that what Bam was saying was correct, but she wasn't ready to admit it to him. "Yes, we were friends, and I loved Dave very much."

"Yes, but he could never fully be your man from behind bars. He was distracted by his case, knowing that he was going to die, knowing that he could never truly be with you."

"But—" She tried to defend their love, but he cut her off again.

"I just feel that you deserve a man that could give you the world and everything in it. I feel like I could be that man."

Isis put her head down, but Bam put his hand under her chin and lifted it back up.

All she could say to that was "Really?" She was confused. She had loved Dave, but it had been a young girl's love. She was a woman now and felt guilty about moving on.

"Really. And like I said before, there is a reason you lost your job, a reason why we connected, and a reason why they decided— today—to put that eviction notice on your door."

"Please share that reason with me, then, because I can't see a good reason for getting thrown out on the streets."

"I thought you'd never ask." A big smile took over Bam's entire face as he began to run down his theory for her. "The reason is because I am going to get my own double-wide trailer in the country, and it would be the perfect place for you to concentrate on designing your jewelry. And we can take care of each other. We could have the best of both worlds with each other."

The teakettle started to sing. Isis got up to cut off the burner and make them both a cup of tea. Heading over to the stove, she glanced at the eviction notice and reality hit her. Where was she really going to go? No money. No job. Where? She wouldn't be able to get another apartment. Who would rent to her? She had no job, no money, and a bad rental history. She didn't want to go back to Aunt Samantha's house, because her aunt would rub it in that she had told Isis that she wasn't ready to move out on her own when she had. Then there was her sister, who was in Texas, and when she wasn't, Phoebe lived with her crazy mother. Brenda hated Isis with a passion.

Bam came up from behind and wrapped his arms around Isis. She wanted to resist, but it had been five years since she last had a man's arms around her.

He pressed her. "So, is it a deal?"

"I don't know. That's a lot to think about."

"Is there any way that I can persuade you?"

"No, I just need to clear my mind and think this through," she told him.

Bam started to kiss her neck and run his fingers down her shirt. Because it had been a while since she had had sex—five years, in fact—his first touch had her soaking wet.

"Stop," she moaned.

Instead Bam stuck his hand in her pants and began caressing her clit. He didn't stop until she reached that point of ecstasy. He then led her over to the sofa. Isis didn't want it to go down like this—sex this soon after Dave's death. She had to stop Bam, regardless of how good it felt, regardless of how much she wanted it to go on forever. She thought about what Samantha had taught her: *When someone knows that you need them, they are already in control, and this puts them in the position to take your neediness as a weakness.*

But Isis's thoughts were clouded by lust, so she decided to dismiss her aunt's advice. Bam laid her down on her back and removed her underwear, using his tongue to make her come over and over again. Dave had never pleased her like that. He never put his mouth down there. Once she had come, Bam got on top of her, putting his skinny, short dick where his tongue had been just seconds before. After four and a half strokes, he exploded.

From that day forward, Isis knew there was no turning back.

Ronald "Bam" Michaels

What you have in your
possession is blood money.
A lot of blood was shed in
order to obtain it. I sold my
soul to the game when I
started hustling, and a contract comes with that. . . .
There are consequences
and repercussions that
come with it.

Chapter 5

April Showers

April showers cascaded from the overcast sky, giving the newly birthed leaves of the century-old trees their first baptism of the season. Caroline County was only a hop, skip, and a jump away from Richmond, but for Isis, a person who had spent her entire life in the city, it was a world away.

Just a few days earlier, she had lost her job and had been facing eviction. Now she was starting a new life in the country with Bam. Isis still couldn't believe how quickly things had transpired between the two of them. She was staring out the window, watching a family of squirrels hide from the spring rainfall, when her cell phone rang. "Damn," she said to herself, upset about the interruption, before glancing around the small place she now called home, in search of her phone.

She followed the ringing down the tiny hallway and into the bedroom. The bed was a mess. Actually, the entire room was a disaster; she and Bam hadn't unpacked completely yet. The ringing was definitely coming from underneath the comforter. She felt around the tangled bedding but came up with nothing.

Whoever it is on the other end of the phone must really want to talk, Isis thought. The phone had been screaming with at least four or five back-to-back phone calls now.

She picked up a handful of bedspread and shook it—nothing. She shook the spreads a second time—still no luck.

Trying to find the phone was beginning to feel like trying to locate a lost ship in the Bermuda Triangle. Enough was enough; she snatched all the top covers and linen from the bed, and the cell phone fell to the floor. The caller ID read: "Sister."

Isis was elated that it was Phoebe calling, although she was a little upset with her as well. She had left messages on Phoebe's machine for two days but had gotten no return call. They always kept each other up on what was going on in their lives, regardless of how big or small, usually talking four or five—and sometimes ten—times a day depending on how much drama was in the air.

"Hey, sister," Isis answered the phone. "Where have you been?" She didn't give Phoebe a chance to answer before continuing. "I've been tryin' to reach you for more than two days."

"I'm sorry," Phoebe apologized. "Things have just been so hectic for the past few days, and I just got a chance to check my messages a couple of minutes ago," she said. "So first, please explain this to me, sister: You living where, and with who?"

"You heard it right, sister, I'm living with Bam in a real nice trailer in Caroline County."

"A trailer?" Phoebe exclaimed. "Sister, *you* have never been any trailer-park type of chick. What happened while I've been gone? Did you fall and bump your head, or has Bam drugged you?" she joked.

"None of the above," Isis assured her sibling. "It's a double-wide trailer and it's really nice. It looks just like a house, only smaller. You just have to see it." Just as Phoebe was about to respond, Isis jumped back in. "You know when we drive down I-95 and we see those houses on eighteen-wheelers that say 'wide load'?"

"Yeah."

"Well, something like that."

"Oh, okay."

"But you'll have to see it for yourself."

"I know," Phoebe agreed. "I can't wait." There was a small pause, and then Phoebe asked, "But are you happy?"

"Yes, very happy," Isis declared. "I don't have to worry about anything but creating my jewelry designs. Bam takes care of everything else. If I may say so myself, this is the life, sister."

"Well, as long as *you're* happy."

"As happy as I've ever been . . . in a long time anyway," she confessed. "But enough about me. How are things going with you in Dallas?"

"So far, so good. I made the first cut."

"That's great!" Isis yelled into the phone.

"I met someone too."

"Who?" Isis wanted to know who was courting her sister.

"All I can say is that he plays for the Cowboys."

"Really? But what do you mean all you 'can say is that he plays for the Cowboys'? What's up with him?"

"I'll have to tell you later, because we're not supposed to talk to the players like that."

"So you're going to leave me in suspense?" Isis asked.

Phoebe and Isis had never kept secrets from each other, so she thought long and hard before answering her sister's question.

"Not right now," Phoebe said.

"Okay, sister, tell me in your own time, but don't keep me in suspense for too long." Then she added, "Remember, I'm the one that has your back no matter what."

"I know." Phoebe said, and laughed.

· · ·

Although the rain showered the capital city, the streets were dry. Richmond's cocaine trade had been suffering from a drought for more than two months. There were many theories floating around the streets as to why the drug, from the high-priced, high-quality stuff to the inferior, was so hard to find, but no one really knew the answer. New York used to be the place to go at such times, but things had changed. Cats up top were asking for ridiculous prices, just like the local jokers. Some of the younger, less-experienced hustlers liked the current market. They could sell cut-up coke—that they normally couldn't give away—for a jacked-up price. Supply and demand is a mutha.

While the fiends were in the streets trying to figure out how they were going to come up with the extra money being charged to get them lifted, Bam was at a friend's house on the west end bagging up a fresh shipment of work. He'd recently met a guy from North Carolina with more grade-A coke than Bam had ever thought about selling, and the new connect was playing more than fair with the prices. The south was taking over more than just the music business.

"Tameka?" Bam called. "Bring me a glass of water." Weighing, cutting, and bagging the two and a half kilos of soft white had made him thirsty.

"Okay, give me a second." A beat later, Tameka walked into the room wearing a powder-blue Baby Phat miniskirt and matching wife beater. She was giving Kimora Lee Simmons a run for her money, body-wise. She set a bottle of Dasani on the table where Bam was breaking the coke down. "Here you go."

"What the fuck is this?" Bam asked. "Girl, you know I don't drink that bourgeois-ass shit. Water is the most abundant natural resource in the world, and them crackers done tricked you mu'fuckaz into spending two-fiddy a bottle for it. I'll take mines right out the tap." Before he could go any further into his lecture on marketing and resources, his cell phone rang.

A familiar voice on the other end said, "What up, my nig? I'm trying to do sixty-two. You gon' help me?"

The voice belonged to his best friend, Drop-Top. "Why wouldn't I? It's just like I told ya it would be," Bam boasted. "I'm almost done with the washing and folding now; just drop by the laundry. Meet me in about ten minutes."

Drop-Top knew that he was referring to Tameka's house. "I got some other important business to talk to you about when I get there," he announced. "Gone."

Ten minutes later, the doorbell rang. Drop-Top was always prompt. It was almost annoying how meticulous he was about time. Tameka opened the door. "You're late," she teased.

"Never that," Drop-Top said, seriously. "Where's B?"

"The same place he's always at."

Drop-Top slid into the den, or the lab, depending on the time of day and who you were. The two friends slapped hands. "What took you so long?" Bam asked.

Drop-Top smiled. "So now I know where Tameka gets the jokes from." He took a seat on a blue leather sofa across from where Bam was sitting.

Bam asked, "What is it that you need to talk to me about?"

"Smiley."

"What about him?"

"You went from copping from the man to fucking his girl and taking half of his clientele."

"Tell me something that I don't already know." Bam stroked his mustache with his thumb and forefinger. "Smiley can put his hands on twenty bitches at any given time, so I know the nigga ain't trippin' off one stray ho. Besides, just like his customers, the bitch chose me," Bam reasoned. "Smiley knows how the game goes."

Bam had looked up to Smiley when he'd first gotten in the game and Smiley had fronted him his first package. But over the past couple of years, Bam had gone from being a little shorty on the block to a certified bigwig.

"This is true," Drop-Top agreed, "but his ego won't allow him to accept the loss. He put fifty G's on your head."

Bam's pupils grew slightly larger after hearing the contract amount.

Drop-Top was glad to know that he finally had his friend's attention. "I don't have to tell you how many thirsty niggas that'll try their hand for that type of paper. You gonna have to sleep on point."

The Bundle of Joy

The radio in Isis's car was tuned to 92.1 FM, but her mind wasn't on the noon throwback mix that was being broadcasted across the airwaves. If someone offered to give her a million dollars to name just one of the songs that had been played while she was in the car, her bank account would've screamed out in disgust because she didn't have clue. Her mind was elsewhere. She and Bam had been living together for almost a year, and things couldn't have been better. Besides Bam's unpredictable temperament at times, Isis was completely satisfied with the way her life was going.

Bam was sitting at the kitchen table eating a grilled

cheese sandwich when she walked through the front door. She smiled at the sight of him. "Hello, darling."

"'Sup?" Bam responded back.

"We need to talk." Isis walked down the hall and into their bedroom, trusting he was behind her.

Bam was irritable. He'd been that way off and on for months now since finding out that Smiley had put the hit out on him. There had been at least fifteen attempts at his life—that he knew of. The stress was starting to get to him.

"What's good?" he asked, walking into the bedroom, where Isis was sitting on the bed.

Isis felt like a child going on a roller coaster for the very first time—excited, yet afraid of the unknown. Not wanting to beat around the bush, she blurted out the good news: "I'm pregnant."

Bam was at a loss for words. His throat started to feel dry and sticky. "You're what?"

"I was just as surprised when doctor told me as you are now," she said, "but don't you think it's great?"

"No, I don't," Bam said. "You have too much on your plate right now with your jewelry gig and all, and didn't you tell me the other day that you wanted to do some traveling?" He tried another angle. "Plus, these streets are insane; I never know if I'll survive to see the end of today, not to mention tomorrow. How are you going to take care of a baby when I'm gone?"

"Stop talking like that. . . . You could get hit by a car while crossing these *insane* streets also—and so could I—but I don't live in fear of it."

"It's not just that," Bam said. "I told you before we ever moved in together, that day right there in your old apartment, that I didn't want any children, and you agreed."

Her eyes searched his. "So what are you saying?"

"That I love you and the whole nine yards," he told her, "but

I ain't trying to have no baby. So you know what needs to be done."

She was quiet for a moment. "It's not that simple."

"Yes, it is, Ice. People go and have it done every day."

"No," she said. "I am three and a half months pregnant, Bam. I'm out of my first trimester."

"So you knew what I would say," he questioned, "and you kept this shit from me?"

"Stop it. I've never hidden anything from you. For some reason, I never missed my period. Today when I went for my checkup, the doctor told me . . . well, this . . ." Isis put her hand over her flat stomach.

Bam's eyes softened. Gently stroking her cheek with the back of his hand, he said, "I'm sorry."

Before Isis could process his odd response, suddenly she felt a sharp pain in her side. She had no idea where it came from. She put her hand where the pain was and doubled over. Bam had landed a well-placed sucker punch to her kidney. And then he hit her again, harder, sending her to the floor. Stunned and in excruciating pain, she curled up into a fetal position to try to protect herself from the blows. She thought that he would stop if she didn't fight back. She thought wrong.

"Bitch, don't lie to me again." This time he kicked her in the stomach.

"Please, Bam, no!" she begged. "What are you doing?" Bam had never put his hands on her before. Maybe a little play-wrestling or a shove here and there, but never anything like this.

Bam was in monster mode. She no longer knew the man who was beating the living crap out of her. When he was finished with her, she looked as if she had been walking in Central Park after dark wearing a miniskirt and high heels and carrying a suit-case filled with money.

Isis lay on the floor in pain.

"You will appreciate me when your career is booming and all is going well," he said. "When the time is right, we will have us a baby," Bam promised before leaving the house.

After he was gone, Isis drove herself to the hospital. Before the doctors even took any X-rays, they noticed blood on her underwear. "I'm pregnant," Isis said to the doctor.

"Can you tell me what happened to you?" he asked.

"I fell down the steps." The doctor knew that her two black eyes and cracked ribs had not come from falling down stairs, but his first concern was to make sure that she was all right before reporting the incident to the police.

After examining Isis thoroughly and checking all the X-rays, the doctor asked if this was her first pregnancy.

"What do you mean by *was*, doctor?" Isis knew what the doctor was going to say even before he said it. She had known when Bam was beating her, but she hadn't wanted to believe it.

The doctor regretted telling her. "I'm sorry, Ms. Tatum, but the bleeding was too severe. You've suffered a miscarriage."

At that moment, Isis hated Bam with every fiber in her body for killing her baby.

• • •

Isis called her Aunt Samantha from the hospital for a ride home after the doctor said that she shouldn't drive. Samantha saw the bruises on her niece and grilled her about them. Because Isis was mad at Bam, she confided in Samantha about everything. Samantha might have been living her life as a woman for the past umpteen-plus years, but under all the makeup, padded bras and support garments, make no mistake about it, she was a man.

Samantha took Isis home and made sure that she was resting and doing everything that the doctors had recommended. Once

Isis dozed off, Samantha went to her truck and got out a gym bag that contained her "just in case I have to fuck up a nigga" clothes. She transformed into the man she was born as, except for the false eyelashes, and waited for Bam to come home.

As soon as Bam walked into the trailer, Samantha shouted, "Bitch-ass nigga," and snuck him with a powerful punch that made Bam stumble and trip over the Air Jordans that he had left in the middle of the floor. Before Bam could catch his balance, Samantha hit him again with another blow, and then pulled out a pink-pearl-handled .22. "This asswhipping is your free pass; you don't get another chance, motherfucker. Keep your hands off of my niece."

Samantha let Bam go and looked down at her own hands. "Shit, you made me break a goddamn nail." Then she threw in one last kick.

Bam wasn't the toughest kid on the block without his gun, but it wasn't wise to try him and let him live. He got up, brushed himself off, and warned Samantha, "Muthafuckas get killed for shit like this, but I am going to spare your life this time because I know how much you mean to Isis. I'm going to leave now, and when I get back, your ass better not be here."

Samantha had made her point, so she didn't press her luck by staying much longer, but before she left she said, "I'm not afraid of you. You'd just better not put your greasy hands on her again."

Bam asked his aunt to sit with Isis for the next couple of days while he ran the streets and made things happen. He wasn't about to let her Aunt Samantha tend to her.

Isis was resting in bed when she heard Bam's key in the front door lock. She involuntarily cringed at the thought of his presence. She could hear his footsteps as he walked into the kitchen, opened the refrigerator, and poured something to drink. When he started toward the room, she closed her eyes and pretended to be asleep.

His footsteps stopped once he entered their bedroom. Isis could smell his cologne mixed with the aroma of perspiration and the outdoors.

He whispered, "Ice, you awake?"

She used to like it when he called her *Ice*. Her mother used to call her father Ice; she missed her father. For a few seconds, thoughts of her father flashed through her head. What would he do if he knew a low-down coward-ass motherfucker had put his hands on her and beaten her as if she were a man?

"Wake up, baby." This time his tone was slightly louder than a whisper, but not quite his normal talking voice. "I have something for you."

She still didn't open her eyes.

The man who had forced her to lose her baby—their baby—kissed her on the forehead. "I know this has been tough on you, but I want to make it right." He sat a box down on the bed beside her.

Besides her diaphragm pumping up and down from her shallow breaths, Isis remained motionless.

Bam wasn't used to this type of treatment from her. In his own selfish way, he really thought that he'd been looking out for their best interests by causing her to lose the baby. He asked, "You still love me, right?"

"I love you, but I hate you." Isis decided to speak, parroting the line that famous radio personality Wendy Williams had used so many times on her show.

"Well, I love you," Bam said, happy that she was speaking to him, "and I need you to get better because you gotta get ready for what's in this box."

She opened her eyes and saw the gift for the first time. "What is it?"

"You're gonna have to open it to find that out." Sitting on the bed next to her, he picked up the box. "Let me help you out . . . you're going to love it." He put a couple of extra pillows behind her head so that she would be sitting up and unwrapped the box before gesturing with a nod for her to remove the lid.

Isis couldn't believe what she was looking at. The box contained ten stacks of fifty-dollar bills. Each stack had 100 bills. And there was a plane ticket to New York. $50,000. That was just what she needed to buy the diamonds to complete some of her ring designs. *So this is what my baby's life was worth to him?* Isis thought as she gazed at Bam, who acted as if he genuinely cared about her future.

Bam took one of her hands in his. "I want you to design a ring for yourself that lets men know they gotta back the fuck up and support what you do at the same time."

"Bam, this doesn't make up for what you've done to me. You do understand that, right?"

"I know, Ice, but we just weren't ready."

From this point on, Isis thought, *I gotta really get myself together and make sure that I am okay, instead of always worrying about these niggas. I'll take his money, but nigga better sleep with one eye open, because there will be some get-back.*

* * *

It took Isis two and a half weeks to get her body and mind back in shape to make the trip, but when she returned from New York not only was she rejuvenated but she also had established a great wholesale diamond connection.

Isis was now able to turn the designs that once existed only on paper into actual creations. The six-carat yellow diamond engagement ring she made for herself was nothing less than fabulous. The attention she was getting because of it was priceless. Drop-Top wanted her to make one just like it for his girlfriend, only in a different color. All of Bam's hustling friends wanted one of her original pieces. She flipped all the rings that she had purchased on her first trip to the Big Apple, and six months later, she was making regular runs for more material. The more diamonds she bought, the better the price got. She even sold a few of her ideas to other jewelers. For the people who wanted one of her rings but didn't have a lot of money to spend, she used her same hot designs but used lesser-quality diamonds. Business was up and down because people didn't always have cash on the spot, but she made it work.

. . .

Isis was on the phone with her sister. Phoebe had made the squad and was dishing on the other cheerleaders, and Isis was telling her about how her jewelry business was flourishing. Call-waiting beeped. "Phoebe, let me call you back. This is the third time this number has come up since we've been talking; it may be important."

"Okay, sister, but don't forget what we talked about. I want one of your pieces for the guy I'm seeing. I'm headed to rehearsal."

"I won't. See ya." Isis pushed the connect button on her cell phone. "Hello?"

"Why haven't you been answering your phone?" the caller asked.

"Bam?" she replied. "Whose number are you calling from?"

"Who the fuck you thought it was—Pebbles?" he half joked.

"I'm at the mall. I was on the phone with my sister, and I didn't recognize the number you were calling from, so I didn't take the call. What's up? Where are you?"

"I'm in jail."

Chapter 7

Nextacy

It had been seven months, six days, and thirteen hours since Isis had received what she now just refered to as "the call." From that point on, she faithfully showed up for every court proceeding related to Bam. Because Bam was a convicted felon, the Commonwealth of Virginia showed him no mercy whatsoever.

Finding out that Bam had killed a man named Smiley, for reasons still unclear to her, raised mixed emotions in Isis. The prosecutor said it was a psychopathic, premeditated act. Bam's lawyers said it was the act of a man in fear for his life and the lives of his family.

. . .

Bam had broken into the house of Thomas "Smiley" Raskins through an unlocked basement window and waited for more than twenty-eight hours in a small pantry. The room was only five by five feet. It was unclear how Bam, at six feet two inches, had managed to wait for his prey for so long in those cramped conditions, but nothing can stop a man from achieving something that he's determined to obtain. It doesn't matter if that goal is to get the girl of his dreams, buy a new home, build a multimillion-dollar business, or kill a man.

It was 2:17 AM on a Monday morning when Smiley returned home. Bam heard Smiley's Mercedes 550 pull up into the driveway. The sound of two car doors being closed pierced the silence of the quiet neighborhood.

Smiley was with a dancer whom he'd met at a club, Bare Essentials, three weeks earlier. Her stage name was Nextacy, and her body was the *next* best thing to Beyoncé's, but she was prettier. She didn't need a ten-thousand-dollar glam squad to make her look that way either. She was hands down the baddest chick in the club the night he met her.

"Nothing has changed; you have to take your shoes off at the door," Smiley said as he and Nextacy entered the house.

Nextacy's perfectly manicured toes disappeared into the three-inch-thick white carpet. "This house is even more beautiful than I remembered," she cooed. "You sure you don't have a woman living with you?" Smiley had brought her to his house the previous week while he took a shower before going out. They never did make it up to his bedroom that night because she had played the not-on-the-first-date card.

Smiley had a white baby grand piano, white furniture, and a picture of a white albino panther on the wall. The panther looked like it was smiling. "Ya damn right I don't got no bitch staying up in here with me, and I like it that way," he said, flexing his independence.

Smiley's sharp tongue didn't faze Nextacy one bit. He was a man, and she knew that once she gave him some real head, not that amateur shit that he'd been used to, and a dip between her legs into some of the best pussy on the East Coast, by morning he would have her ass on speed dial, money on the table, and a freshly cut key from Wal-Mart. Nextacy rubbed the front of Smiley's pants; he was hard.

"I feel you, playboy," she teased. "Can I get a sip of something wet before I empty your tank?"

Smiley knew that the bitch was superhot in the ass when he first laid eyes on her. That's why he had to have her. "I got more than enough to quench your thirst," he said, "but what else would you like?"

Nextacy looked at his crotch and licked her lips. "Some Patrón, a can of whipped cream, and you will do just fine."

"Make yourself comfortable. I'll be right back."

Bam heard Smiley enter the kitchen, get glasses from a cabinet, and take something out the refrigerator. He was tempted to come out and slump him right then, but the time wasn't right—the girl. It had to be perfect. Patience pays the piper.

Bam's military timepiece showed that eight minutes had elapsed since he heard the two of them go upstairs. Another thirty minutes had passed when he heard the headboard of the bed banging against the wall. He smiled.

It was time to come out of the closet.

When Bam got to the top of the staircase, he followed the noise to the master bedroom. The door was slightly ajar. Looking through the opening, Bam witnessed one of the finest women he'd ever laid eyes on on her knees and handcuffed to the bedpost, and Smiley was behind her, shoving about ten inches of muscle in her ass. Unless this chick had taken acting lessons from Halle Berry, she was loving every stroke of it.

Bam walked through the door and tossed his own set of cuffs onto the bed. Smiley jerked around, staring down the barrel of an AK-47. "It ain't no fun if yo' homie can't have none," Bam sneered. "Put 'em on."

When Nextacy saw the gun, she mouthed a silent prayer.

Smiley looked at the cuffs, then at Bam, then at the assault rifle Bam was holding.

"This ain't no multiple-choice test," Bam warned. "Wrap 'em around the other post just like you got the bitch."

Smiley did as he was told, and then Bam walked over to the side of the bed where Nextacy was and uncuffed her.

"It's about time," she said. "What took you so long?"

"You stankin' bitch," Smiley hissed. "You set me up?"

Bam rubbed Nextacy on her backside. "Teach that fool how to treat a lady for me." He nodded toward a dildo that was on the night table.

She grinned.

Smiley was horrified. "What do you think you're going to do with that, bitch?" Smiley spat.

Nextacy smacked the twelve-inch phallus in her hand one time and then spit on it. "I'm going to show you how to treat a lady."

If Bam hadn't put the rag in Smiley's mouth before Nextacy violated his private space, the noise from his screaming would have woken the dead. After she finished having her fun, Bam removed an eight-inch, razor-sharp hunting knife from his small gym bag with his latex-gloved hand. He pressed the blade against Smiley's throat and said, "You shoulda just been satisfied with sharing the pussy. No ass is worth dying over."

Then he swiftly maneuvered the cold steel from one side of Smiley's neck to the other, severing everything in its path. After he watched Smiley bleed to death, he placed the knife back in the bag, and this time came out with a .22-caliber revolver with a silencer and pointed it at Nextacy's head.

"Why, Bam?" she asked. "Please don't hurt me."

"It's nothing personal." He fired the small weapon three times into her skull.

• • •

Isis sat and watched from the edge of her seat as Nextacy's friend, Revlon, took the stand and told all the sordid details about how Nextacy had planned to stop dancing because of the money she was going to be paid by Bam for helping him set up a man named Smiley who had been frequenting the club.

The prosecutor showed Revlon a picture and asked, "Is this the man you know as Smiley?"

Revlon took a long look at the photo. "Yes," she said, "that's him."

"And is the man you know as Bam in this courtroom today?" the prosecutor asked.

"Yes, he is."

Then the prosecutor asked, "Can you point to him, please?"

Revlon twisted around in the witness chair, looking more like a secretary than a stripper in her gray business suit, and pointed to Bam. "That's him right there."

• • •

It took the jury just two and a half hours to bring back a verdict of guilty for both murders. Bam's sentencing date was scheduled for two weeks later. The jury had to decide whether to give him a life sentence or the death penalty. It didn't make much difference to Bam. To Bam, life inside of prison was death. But he wasn't going to cry about it. The way he looked at it, you do what you do and you get what you get. That was all there was to it. He wouldn't go out like a sucker in order for them to spare his life.

Although Bam had mistreated Isis, she was still willing to stand by her man. He had rescued her when she was being evicted and made sure that she had all the necessary funds to chase her dream, and like her daddy had said, "You gotta love who loves you."

So at least Bam was alive and well, and that was more than she could ask for. So as long as Bam loved her, she was going to love him.

When Bam was first arrested, he sent her to his stash, which contained just over a half million dollars. After she paid for his lawyer, the investigator, money on his books, and some other expenses, there was still a pretty penny left.

It wasn't that Isis had forgotten what Bam had done to her—she could never forget—but she had forgiven him. All couples had their problems; some were just larger than others. And although Bam had abused her, she was prepared to make his prison stay as comfortable as humanly possible, even if it meant paying a guard to turn his head while they snuck into the prison restroom to have sex. Maybe they would even make that baby that he had promised her that they would have when the time was right.

Bam told her that he loved her and that he would never cross her. He said that she had been his only true love from the first time that he had met her, and that she would be his only true love until the day he died. In return, Isis vowed that she would stay faithful to him until the bitter end, much like the promise she had made to Dave when he was sentenced to death.

Chapter 8

The Motherfucking Ring

Not knowing her man's destiny caused Isis to have many sleepless nights. On the day of Bam's sentencing, she ended her fight with the bed by throwing in the towel and getting up to get dressed. After she got her gear on, she hit the road early enough to stop for breakfast. The traffic on the highway was as slow as a snail going up a San Francisco hill, but she arrived at the courthouse at 8:55.

"Ladies and gentlemen," a guard yelled, "empty out your pockets of change and any metal objects. Cell phones are not permitted in the courtroom. We are not allowed to keep them at the desk, so if you have one, take it to your car now. It'll save us the trouble of having to pat you down twice, and save you from having to stand in line wasting time." He recited his spiel as if it were a nursery rhyme.

Though long, the line moved quickly. In fact, the lady in front of Isis couldn't get everything out of her pockets fast enough with her son on her hip. The woman caught her attention for several reasons. First, she was there unescorted with a baby, so she was fairly certain that the lady was there for the same reason as she: to witness the fate of her man, who was probably her baby's father. Second, she felt sorry when she saw the lady struggling with her baby, a Gucci diaper bag, and a Gucci purse, which matched her and her child's Gucci sneakers.

Are kids even supposed to be in the courtroom? The thought ran through Isis's mind as she smiled at how the mother was holding it all down. *That's the shit we do, that superwoman shit, whatever we have to do to make shit happen for our men. Now that's the part that Maya missed in her poem "Phenomenal Woman,"* she thought.

The last reason was the jewelry that the lady sported. Isis had a habit of peeping fly jewels; it didn't matter if it was on a person walking down the street, in a magazine, or in the window of a jewelry store. All of the girl's pieces were immaculate. The watch was a Cartier, as thin as a silver dollar. She was wearing a beautiful tennis bracelet that had to have at least ten carats of diamonds running through it. The sparkle was reflecting off the Gucci shades that covered her sad eyes. From the looks of the rest of her outfit, Isis knew that the ring on the girl's finger would be nothing short of stunning, but she would have to get a little closer to see it.

The bejeweled woman could tell that Isis was peeping her, so she held her hand at an angle to better flaunt the ring.

Isis finally just came out and said something. "That's a beautiful ring you're wearing. Can I look at it?"

"Yup." The girl threw her hand out there as if she were Elizabeth Taylor before adding, "My man had it specially made for me." Before Isis could get in a compliment, the chick was quick to say, "Yes honey, they're pink dye-mons, not pink sapphires. A lot of peoples gets dem mixed up."

Isis recognized it as one of her own creations. Then the woman spoke to her son. "Stop, Bam-Bam. Don't do that. Don't make me tell your daddy." Isis felt as if a frigid dagger had been plunged into her heart.

Could it be? she thought. "What?" she said, stunned by the little boy, who had an uncanny likeness to her man. Isis had been so busy looking over his mother that she hadn't paid much attention to the little boy until now.

"I was talking to my son," she pointed at the little boy. "Are you finished admiring my ring? Because I got to get into the courtroom to find out what these crackers are gonna do to my man today."

To add insult to injury, Isis noticed a tattoo on the woman's arm that was identical to the one she had on her inner thigh that read *Bam*.

The woman said, "Come on, Bam-Bam," and the little family stormed off.

Isis didn't quite know what to think as her man's son and other woman strolled away. She couldn't find the words to call the woman back, and if she did know what to say, her tongue didn't want any part of the conversation. She just stood there as if in cement boots, trying to process what she had just seen.

This is some motherfucking, fucked-up-ass shit. This bitch is wearing the same fucking ring that I designed—for myself—as a make-up gift from Bam, after he whipped my ass and made me lose my baby, she thought.

The room started to spin when she reflected back on the brutally effective tactic Bam had used to ensure that she was no longer four months pregnant. "You have too much on your plate right now with your jewelry gig and all, and didn't you tell me . . . that you wanted to do some traveling? . . . You will appreciate me when your career is booming and all is going well. When the time is right, we will have us a baby," he had told her.

Bam had played her like a video game. His best friend had even played a part in his little game of charades. He had had Drop-Top convince her to make him the exact same ring as hers—only in pink instead of yellow—as a Valentine's Day present for his girlfriend. But in reality, it was for Bam's girlfriend. Bam was sick. Only a demented, twisted person would do something like that.

Isis started to feel light-headed. Her only thought before she fainted was *I can't let him get away with this shit.*

• • •

When Isis regained consciousness, she was at the hospital, where the doctor informed her that she had had a panic attack brought on by stress and anxiety. The doctor told her that the best way to avoid having another one was to try to stay stress free and do stress-relieving exercises.

Isis listened as the doctor gave his diagnosis and decided that she had the perfect tension-breaking exercise: it was called the Pay Bam Back theory.

Like mother, like daughter. History would indeed repeat itself. Just as Isis's mother had killed her father for being unfaithful, she would kill Bam. But she was going to slay him in another way. That $313,000 he had left with her was history. She didn't care if he didn't have enough money on his books to buy a bar of soap; she was done with him.

The way Isis saw it, because the other woman had the same ring, same tattoo, and his seed, he had probably left her double that amount of money. Let her take care of him; Isis was out. Now all she had to do was to convince herself that the $313,000 was enough severance pay for her broken heart.

• • •

After court, Bam tried to call her. He wondered why she wasn't in the courtroom when the judge followed the jury's recommendation and gave him life in prison. He tried calling her all day, but she never answered his calls.

She decided to take the advice that Dave had given her in the very last letter that he ever wrote: *"Live for yourself for a change. Let someone serve and wait on you. You deserve it."* She could hear Dave's voice in her head saying the words over and over.

"Thank you, Dave. I will," Isis said out loud.

All she needed now was a change of scenery, somewhere she could go to clear her mind, to find herself, to discover what she really wanted.

She called Samantha to get some suggestions on where should she escape to.

"Child, there's only one place," Aunt Samantha said.

"Where?" Isis was curious.

"Vegas!"

"Vegas?" she questioned. Vegas didn't seem like a place where she could find peace of mind.

"Yes, Vegas. There you could see and meet all kinds of people. The shopping is fabulous; the shows and entertainment are great. You loved it that one time I took you, back when you first came to stay with me, remember?"

"Yes, but I was hanging with a bunch of drama-filled drag queens."

"Which you loved, and besides, the weather is hot just like you like it. . . . And what happens in Vegas stays in Vegas."

Isis let out a small chuckle, but her aunt knew her mind was somewhere else, so she called her on it. "Where is that little mind of yours roaming around to?"

"Nowhere," Isis quickly answered.

"Oh, it's somewhere, Ms. Thang. Spill it out. You know I know when you tell me lies." The mother in her poured out in her tone.

Isis took a deep breath and then began to speak. "I don't know where to start."

"Pick a place, baby, and we'll work through all those weeds."

"Well, it's my mother," Isis blurted out.

Samantha was caught off guard but didn't voice her surprise. "So it's my sister that has you all flustered."

"I thought I would never understand how she could just kill my dad, but now I know. I truly understand." Tears welled in Isis's eyes. "I feel bad because I've been hating her for what she did and never thought how she must feel; how she must've felt then."

"Yes, your mother snapped because of her feelings. She loved your father so much."

"I loved Bam too, and we were together for only two years. I can only imagine how she felt; she was with Dad for over sixteen years. They had a child and a promising life together."

"They really did," Samantha agreed.

"And then to discover all the lies—the side relationship and child. After all she went through, I turned my back on her too."

Samantha sighed. "I think you need to go see her."

"She must hate me."

"She loves you!" Samantha smiled. "And you know every time she calls, she asks about you. I keep her informed about everything."

Samantha had always known that one day the time would be

right for daughter and mother to reconcile. This was definitely the right time. "Her visiting day is Saturday; we could go see her, and you could stay over here on Saturday night. Then I could take you to the airport Sunday morning." Samantha had the plan all mapped out.

"We'll see." Isis didn't give a definite answer, but she knew that she had to go.

Chapter 9

Love Is a Dirty Game

As Isis parked her seven-year-old Honda Accord outside the women's correctional facility where her mother was being housed, she made a mental note that when she returned from Vegas, she would treat herself to a new car, courtesy of Bam, of course.

It had been more than ten years since Isis had last seen her mother, and although this was far from her first trip to a maximum-security prison, because of her visits with Dave, she was surprised by the butterflies fluttering in her stomach as she and Sam entered the main building.

Sam somehow knew what Isis was feeling, so she spoke a few comforting words to her niece. "There's no

reason to be nervous, honey. Your mother loves you. She's going to be glad to see you."

Isis looked at Sam with questioning eyes. "Are you sure?"

Sam replied with a warm, reassuring smile and then approached the corrections officer at the sign-in desk to get the required paperwork. "May I have two visitation forms, please?" Sam wasn't in drag today. He had on sweatpants, a T-shirt, and a pair of tennis shoes and wore his shoulder-length hair in a ponytail.

The corrections officer working the desk looked at Sam oddly at first, probably because whether in drag or not, Sam never left home without his extra thick, extra long false eyelashes. But the officer decided to keep everything moving along instead of holding up the line trying to figure out the character before him. Pointing to a black tray, he said, "Here you go, sir. Drop the paper off right there, and someone will call you when we're ready."

Sam knew that the officer was watching him as he sashayed over to his niece. "Here you go, baby." He handed Isis a form.

Isis started to panic. She wasn't even sure if her name was o: her mother's visiting list.

Sam dropped the sheets off in the tray after they finished fi ing them out, just as the officer at the desk had instructed. L than five minutes passed before the same officer said, "Will Tatum please come to the desk?"

Damn. I guess I wasn't on the list. Isis stood up, wiped sweaty palms on her jeans, and walked to the desk as she pared herself to have to come up with a story to get the offi override the policy. "Yes?" She stared at him.

"I'm sorry, but we have a problem here," he said, hold: form Isis had just filled out.

I knew it, Isis thought before he could even finish. It v

to go to plan B, but what was plan B? "I would like to see the major, please," she stated.

"Well, all you need to do is put your license plate number right here." He pointed to the spot on the paper that she had failed to complete.

As soon as she wrote it down, the officer said, "You two can step right through those doors."

Isis was relieved. After she and Sam were searched, they proceeded through the steel bulletproof doors that led to the visiting room. Once they were inside, another prison guard directed them to sit at a table that had the number ten written on it.

Isis whispered to Sam, "I can't believe that I am still on the list."

Sam rolled his eyes. "Why would you think otherwise, little girl? You are her only baby."

"But I was so awful to her, for so long. I refused to talk to her and told her that I hated her."

"Listen, Miss Lady, we're talking about your mother. A whole lot of shit may change in your life, but the love my sister has for you won't ever change. You hear me?"

Isis tried to avoid becoming emotional by turning her attention to the visiting room. There were so many children there who were visiting with their mothers and loved ones. A few men were visiting as well. Isis imagined they were there to see women who could have been their wives once upon a time or who still might be if they were holding her down the way she did Dave and had been willing to do for Bam until he betrayed her. Two female prisoners sat at a table across from them. One of the women had a short fade haircut; she looked like a little boy. Growing up with Sam, Isis was used to women like her. The other was a young girl holding a newborn baby. Looking at the mother and child tore at Isis's heart. The young girl had a proud

look on her face as she held her child. The baby's grandmother, who was over by the vending machine, had brought her. Isis wondered how long the girl would be in prison, separated from her child. She didn't look old enough to be out of high school. What type of crime did she commit? All kinds of questions about the young girl's circumstances ran through her head.

Isis sat there, waiting and watching for the door to open through which the inmates entered. Disappointment overtook her each time the door opened and it wasn't her mother, but still she kept her eyes glued to the door.

An hour passed, which seemed like an eternity, but once her mother entered the room, time seemed to stop. Sandy glided across the room. She was still so beautiful. Her skin was smooth and her hair was still as pretty and silky as ever. It almost felt as if the Ghost of Christmas Past was walking toward her. Everything about her mother was the same as Isis had always remembered, except the prison-issued outfit that she wore. Sandra Tatum would have never worn something like that.

When Sam saw his sister, he stood up and started waving. When Sandra realized that her only daughter was with him, she covered her mouth and tears began to form in her eyes as she walked faster toward them. For ten years, Sandra had been waiting for this day. She'd had no idea if and when it would ever come. She wasted no time getting to the table, almost knocking a few people over in the process.

Without hesitation, Sandra hugged her daughter. She had the same look in her eyes that the young mother with the newborn baby had had just moments ago. "I love you," she whispered in her child's ear. Isis was speechless as the tears flowed from her eyes. Until that very moment, she had had no idea just how much she had missed hearing those words from her mother. People stared as they shared their emotional moment.

Women who knew Sandra asked her, "Is that your baby girl?"

"Yes." She proudly nodded. "This is Isis."

Some prison guards just can't stand to see people happy, and Wilma Buster was one of them. She marched across the room until she got in front of Isis and Sandra. "The two of you are going to have to be seated or I'll have to terminate your visit," she warned.

Sandra shot a look toward the guard that said, *Bitch, please!* Then she turned her attention back to her daughter. "Thank you so very much for coming. I'm so glad to see you, baby. I can't begin to tell you how good it feels to see you." Tears streaked down her checks.

Isis nodded through her tears. What she thought would be a hard task, turned out to be a piece of cake. The conversation between the two of them flowed so naturally, just as a mother and a daughter's should. Unless you knew them, you'd have had a hard time telling that it had been a decade since their last time together.

"So how are you, baby?" Sandy asked her daughter.

"Sandra, how the hell you think she is?" Sam butted in. "She needs her damn momma."

"Listen, Sammie, I know that, you know that, and she knows that—and your point is . . . ?"

"The point is—" Sam began.

Sandy talked over her brother. "The point is, some shit don't ever change. You still just like the police, in everybody's business and ain't saying shit." She turned to Isis. "Baby, don't pay that knucklehead no mind."

"Mommy, God knows that I love Uncle Sam, but I already knew he was crazy."

Sam finally got a word in, "Oh, Ms. Thang, you turning on

me now since you here wit' yo' momma, huh?" Isis could only smile. "That's my cue. I'll be right back; I'm going to the ladies' room."

"You mean the boys' room," Sandy said, correcting her brother. Isis laughed.

Sam glared at his niece. "Keep it up, and you gon' be walking. It's a long ways back to town too." Sam seemed to forget that it was Isis who had driven.

"I know damn well you ain't gon' leave my child out nowhere. You know what happened to the last person that left my baby?"

"The bus driver," both Sandy and Sam said in unison while laughing. Isis didn't understand the inside joke.

"The media like to say that Sandra snapped when that god-awful incident took place." Sam shook his head, "Negative, honey. Yo' momma been crazy long before then." Then Sam strolled off to the restroom.

Once it was just the two of them, Isis asked her mother, "Ma, what is Sam talking about?"

Sandy saw the befuddled expression on Isis's face and decided to share the joke with her. Sandra waved her hand as if it were nothing. "Chile, when you were in kindergarten, the bus driver discovered, at the end of her route, that you had missed your stop. And she didn't want to go out of her way and take you back to school or to your regular stop. So she told you to get off the bus. She just left you there, but you were so smart that you knew where one of my friends lived in that area, and you walked to her house." Isis looked at her mother as if she were making up the whole story. Sandy added, "It was a long walk, over a mile, and you were only five, but you did it."

Now Isis was convinced that she'd made it up. "I don't remember."

"Well, I remember the way I beat the hell out of that bus driver and got her ass fired," Sandra said, admonishing Isis.

"You joking, right, Ma?"

"If I ain't whip that bitch's behind, my ass ain't black," she said. "I wanted to homeschool you after that, to protect you at all times, but Ice wouldn't let me."

"Well, Ma, I learned to take care of myself pretty well. It must be in our DNA."

"Did you really?" Sandra asked, searching her daughter's face. "A mother needs to know these things."

"Yes, Momma. Aunt Samantha took great care of me too."

"I know you probably hated me for what I did, leaving you alone. But I didn't know what else to do. I loved you and your daddy so much. If I had thought things through, I never would have done it. Not because I'm behind these bars, but because of what it did to you."

"Ma, you don't have to explain. I miss Daddy, but I understand that whole thing more than you think I do. I've suffered a broken heart a few times myself, but I'm fine. Experience is the best teacher."

"That's where you're wrong at," Sandra said. "I do need to explain myself to you, and not only that, I need your forgiveness too."

Isis was happy to hear that she needed something from her, even if it was only forgiveness. "Of course I forgive you, Mother."

"Baby," her mother said, "there ain't no man, woman, or shield that can protect you from a broken heart. You just gots to learn to not wear your feelings on your sleeve."

"I thought that if I was faithful, honest, and trustworthy, I'd get the same back in return."

"Baby, don't be reading those damn romance novels; that

shit'll fuck your head up. Without a doubt, love is a dirty game. But just to keep it on the up-and-up with you: I used to think the same thing myself—until reality showed me love ain't got shit to do with it."

Just then the stud with the short hair that Isis had seen earlier walked up to their table on her way back from the trash can. "Sandy, is this Isis?"

"Yes," Sandy answered with a smile, gloating over her daughter.

"Hi, Isis, my name is Pam; I'm a friend of your mother's. I've heard so much about you."

"Nice to meet you," Isis said.

"You know you mean the world to your mother, don't you? I'm glad you came up to see her."

Sandy cut in. "Well, let us enjoy our visiting. We only got an hour to catch up on ten years."

When the youthful-looking stud walked away, her mother shamelessly said, "That used to be my lover."

Isis wasn't shocked that her mother was bisexual. After all, she had been in prison for ten years, and she had gone in with a scorned heart. But Isis was surprised that her mother admitted it to her so openly.

"There's no sense in hiding it from you," Sandy said. "I want you to learn from my mistakes. Don't do the same crazy shit I've done and end up in here. They say, 'lead by example.' Well, chile, I'm your living testimony."

Isis smiled, thinking that her mother could probably school her on quite a few things. The moment was interrupted when the stud returned to their table. "Hey, y'all want some cards? We done playing, and before I put them back, I wanted to ask."

Sandy gave the chick a cold look this time. "Nah, we straight," she said dismissively.

"Dang, Mommy, that girl really got the hots for you, huh?"

"What can I say? I look good as a motherfucker," she teased. "But I ain't thinking about her fast ass."

"Then who are you thinking about?"

"None of these penitentiary bulldaggers, that's for sure."

There was a brief silence; Isis felt that her mother had more to say.

Sandy was the first to pierce the bubble of silence that had momentarily enveloped them. "The one person I really cared about isn't here anymore. Praise the Lord for that one. She went home a couple of years ago."

"Does she keep in touch?" Isis was curious.

"Faithfully . . . but things between us are complicated."

"I'm not sure if I'm ready for this." It was Isis's turn to tease her mother now.

"Not that complicated," she said. "It's just that she sends me money and things, and I don't want her to feel like she owes me anything."

"Why would she think that she owes you?"

"Because I saved her life," Sandy said. "There's no doubt that I love her and I know that she loves me, but I don't know if she feels devoted to me because I saved her life or if it's genuine love. You know?"

Isis was about to respond, but before she could, Sam returned. "You know Ms. Thang is leaving for Vegas tomorrow," Sam informed his sister as he walked up.

"Really?" Sandy was happy that Isis was traveling and getting out of Richmond. She wished that her daughter had shared the news with her instead of her loudmouth brother, though.

"I just need to go somewhere to get my mind right," Isis admitted.

"What has my baby's mind so not together that she has to go

clean to the other side of the country, and when are you coming back?"

"Well, I'm just having boy problems, and I'll be back in a week or two."

"Let me be a living testimony to you," Sandy said. "Boys can be the worst problem a good woman can ever encounter. The best thing a woman can do is to avoid boys at all cost and sit back and let the men find us."

Chapter 10

Blood Money

Isis sat poolside looking as beautiful as ever. The whiteness of her Christian Dior bathing suit enhanced her brown skin. Her big, walnut-colored eyes and long eyelashes were hidden behind a pair of white Dior sunglasses that she had purchased from the Forum Shops at Caesars Palace just the day before. They were a perfect match for the suit. She had been at the pool for only an hour, and already four people had complimented her.

After writing a postcard to her mother, Isis enjoyed the warm weather. Earlier she had browsed through some of her bills and junk mail that she had picked up from her post office box on the way to the airport. Her intention had been to sort through the mail on the plane, giving herself something to do. But after she'd boarded the aircraft, her sleep-deprived body had other plans for her, and she slept for most of the flight. Now, she figured that while she was chilling in a pool cabana was as good a time as any to read mail. While doing so, she ran across a letter from Bam. She was about to toss it, but curiosity got the best of her. She opened it and pulled the single-page letter from the envelope.

Dear Isis,

I stood in the courtroom last week waiting on those crackers to make a decision about my life: whether I spend the rest of my life in prison or be put to death. When I looked around the room, you were nowhere in sight. I found this to be more disturbing than the outcome of the proceedings, which was life in prison, by the way.

When I first noticed that you weren't there, I thought maybe you had car trouble or something; I knew the Honda was on its last leg, and I had intentions of getting you another car. I've tried calling you several times, to no avail, and a couple of people have said that they've seen you riding around town, so I have no other choice than to assume that you have crossed me. You know I've never begged anyone for anything—man, woman, child . . . judge or jury, for that matter—but I'm begging you now: Please don't fuck me over! Isis, please don't fuck with me.

If for some reason you feel like you can take my money and do what you want with it, I need to explain something to you so that you can have a complete understanding as to what comes with spending my money.

What you have in your possession is blood money. A lot of blood was shed in order to obtain it. I sold my soul to the game when I started hustling, and a contract comes with that. You see, some niggas in the street, as well as squares, think that type of money is free money, but nothing is ever given to you for free. There are consequences and repercussions that come with it. For some people, the repercussions just come quicker than for others.

If you spend any of my 313,000 dollars without my blessing, you take on everything that comes with it.

"So what, motherfucker!" Isis laughed to herself, waving the pool waitress over. "Excuse me, but can I get another apple martini, please?" She gave the hostess a twenty-dollar tip, courtesy of Bam and his blood money.

Looking up from the drink, Isis noticed four guys in street clothes, walking toward the pool. They were searching for a spot at the pool to chill. She smiled as they pulled chairs from other places to make their own little area. One of the men from the group caught her attention. He wasn't the best-looking one, but there was something about him. He looked slightly older than the other three. His head was bald, his beard was perfectly manicured along his jaw, and his body was chiseled with the precision of a jeweler cutting a rare diamond.

As Isis watched this work of art disrobe, her cell phone rang, competing for her attention. The number had an 804 area code, but she didn't recognize it. Isis decided to answer it anyway. "Hello." Just as she spoke into the receiver, Mr. Perfect Body made eye contact with her.

"Hold on a second," a female's voice on the other end of the phone said.

"All I want is my paper from you." This time the voice on the phone belonged to Bam.

"Whose phone are you calling me on?" Isis asked.

Bam answered nonchalantly, "A friend's."

"You mean your baby momma's?"

Bam was quiet for a minute.

"Hello? Is anyone there?" Isis said. No one said anything. "Hello, Bam?"

"Yeah, man," he said slowly.

"Yeah, it's your baby momma, or yeah, you on the phone, or the both?"

"Man, look: I gotta call however I can since you put a block on the phone."

"Look, despite what you think, I was at the courthouse on the day of your sentencing. I got sick and had to be rushed to the hospital. And I became sick after meeting your goddamn baby momma!" Isis continued her rant. "You got some motherfucking nerve."

"Look, let's talk. Let's work this out." Bam had a much more accommodating demeanor now than in his jailhouse letter.

"You crazy, muthafucka," Isis said. "I don't have shit to say to you."

"I didn't call to hear you talk anyway," Bam told her, realizing that honey wasn't going to get his money back, so he might as well resort back to vinegar. "I called for my muthafuckin' money. If you think that just 'cause I'm in jail I'm going to let you or anybody else take something from me, you must've busted yo' head or something."

Isis pushed the button and ended the call, but before she could even look up, there was another voice in her ear. "Don't let dem niggas upset you, Princess." Mr. Perfect-Body took a seat next to her. The conversation with Bam had distracted her. She had almost forgotten that just moments ago she was in an eye-wrestling match with the man.

"Thank you for your concern," she said. "And I won't."

"You promise? Because you too cute to let anyone put a frown on your face."

Her frown turned upside down. "Thank you."

"What's your name, Princess?"

"Isis. My friends call me Ice," she said. "And yours?"

"That would be Logic." He smiled. "And yes"—he nodded—"that's my real name."

"That's a very interesting name. Are you going to drop some logic on me?" She teased.

"No, but I can logically give you reasons why a pretty girl such as yourself shouldn't be wasting a beautiful day in Vegas arguing with some fool on the phone when she can have dinner and a night of gambling and entertainment with someone that would appreciate her company."

After thanking Isis, Logic and his three friends all hung out at her cabana until 6:00 when it closed. Once the cabanas closed, they each headed their own separate ways to get dressed so that they could meet up again in an hour. It didn't take long for Isis and Logic to put the duck on his friends.

Neither Logic nor Isis were big gamblers, but one couldn't tell by looking at them. When they got in the casino, the two of them gambled and gambled and gambled, all night long. Isis's favorite game turned out to be the craps tables. Every time she rolled those ivory dice down that long felt table, she won. After about eight hours of hanging out together, they cashed out, and Logic walked her to her room.

When he got her there he asked, "Am I going to see you tomorrow?" Snapping his fingers, he said as if he'd forgotten something, "That's a crazy question. But of course I'm going to see you tomorrow. I have to take you shopping tomorrow so that we can spend some of our winnings."

Isis agreed and smiled. "Pick me up in time for brunch."

Logic was all teeth. "It's a date. I'll pick you up at eleven."

As soon as Logic got back to his room, he dialed Isis's room number on the phone, and she answered on the first ring. Somehow she just knew it was going to be him.

"Hello."

"I was thinking, Ice," he said. "So that I won't run off with all our winnings, perhaps it would be better if I sleep on your couch. That way, you know all the money is safe, and plus, that way I won't miss our brunch date."

She hesitated for only a second before agreeing. She reasoned, *What happens in Vegas stays in Vegas, right?*

• • •

Getting what he wanted was an effect that Logic had on 98 percent of the people he met. He had a way of getting his point across and never raising his voice to do it. Thirty-one years of age, Logic had been on his own since he was fourteen. He started out hustling on the corner, but he didn't stay in that occupation for long. He knew the value of saving and investing his money. By the time he was eighteen, he was loaning money to other drug dealers to buy work. By the time he was twenty-one, he was loaning young entrepreneurs money for DVD companies, record labels, artist-development projects . . . it didn't matter to him, as long as they paid his money back with thirty percent interest. And the majority of them always did, because there was another side to Logic that people had heard of but didn't want to deal with personally.

No one really knew how many people Logic had actually killed, not to mention those he had someone else kill for him. But overall he was fair. He always kept his word, and he demanded the same from whoever he dealt with. Disloyalty was punishable by death in his book. That was it, period and dot. So for those reasons, he almost always got paid, and he made lots of money.

That night, he did as he promised: He slept on the couch in Isis's room and woke up only when he heard her get up and try to tiptoe to the restroom.

. . .

Although nothing sexual jumped off between the two, being with Logic felt like a dream. Isis found herself imagining what it would be like to be his girl, but in the real world she knew that a man like Logic was way out of her league. Yeah, she had been with drug dealers before, but somehow they just didn't seem to measure up to Logic's stature. She was sure that he had plenty of women chasing him, not to mention a wife, mistress, and a few girlfriends on the side. But of course, he told Isis that he wasn't married.

Why wouldn't he be married? she asked herself. *All of that charisma and money, and no one has locked him down?*

After racking up in the Forum Shops, Isis and Logic went to see Elton John's show. Afterward, they decided to try their luck at the casinos again. Before they started gambling, Logic ran into his boy, Jacob, who needed some money, claiming that it had not been his lucky night.

Jacob was a compulsive gambler. From the time they arrived in Vegas, he showed no interest in any women, shows, or sightseeing. The only thing that kept his attention was the roulette table. Jacob not only looked like he had been up for days but he really had been up for days—losing. On a normal day, Jacob was a pretty handsome guy, always dipped in the latest crisp gear, but this day was a different story. The bloodshot rings around his green eyes gave them the look of Christmas ornaments. And both his hair and clothes were disheveled. Vegas had put it on him, and put it on him hard.

While Logic stepped off to the side to talk to Jacob, a lady

with long, stringy, dark hair and a colorful crocheted pocketbook with long straps crossing her chest walked up to Isis. "Excuse me. Would you like a psychic reading?"

Isis had never had one before, but she thought, *Why not?*
"How much?" Isis asked.

"Well, I charge"—the frail lady cleared her throat—"different
prices. It depends if I do a tarot or a palm reading," she said.
"Palms, fifteen dollars, and tarot cards, twenty dollars."

Shit, twenty dollars. What the hell I got to lose? I am on vacation,
she thought.

"Princess"—she heard Logic's voice call out—"come here."

"Hold on one second," she told the psychic chick as she went
to see what Logic wanted.

Logic informed Isis that before they would be able to start
gambling, he would have to run up to his room to retrieve more
money. He had given everything in his pockets to Jacob.

"While you run upstairs, I'm going to look in those two shops
we passed."

"A'ight. Just don't stray too far from them, because I am going
to be right back." He kissed her on the cheek, and then headed
through the crowded casino to the elevators.

Isis almost bumped into the palm reader when she turned
around. She had forgotten about her just that quickly, but Miss
Psychic must've *known* that she was open to the experience.

"Let's get it popping," Isis said to the hippie-looking lady.

"Let's go over here to a quieter place," the lady suggested, and
took the lead. There were really no quiet places in any Vegas casinos. They sat at two nickel slot machines and faced each other.
Isis held out her palms for the lady to read.

"What do you want to know about?" the self-proclaimed psychic asked. "Love? Money? Family? Work? Health?"

Isis answered, "All of the above."

"Okay. First, within ten days, you're going to take a trip," she said.

Yeah, I am going home, Isis thought.

"You have never experienced real love in your life."

"What?"

"The man who will really love you will address you as his princess."

Okay, step up your game, lady. We both know you just heard Logic call me Princess.

"The first man that you loved . . . didn't love you back."

Warm, but that could pertain to almost anyone. The one we love hardly ever loves us back.

"He thought of you as a sister, and he used you for his own selfish reasons. Then, the second person you thought you loved hurt you, made you do something that you couldn't really forgive him for. Now he hates that he loves you, and you don't love him."

Warmer.

"You are going to marry soon." She paused. "Within the next six months. And your husband is going to love you unconditionally."

Six months? To who? Bam and I are never going to get back together.

The psychic continued. "You just came into a lot of money. Be careful; all money isn't good money."

No shit!

"You are also going to be successful at your own business."

I hope you're right.

"You had a great childhood, but your mother had to leave you. But when she left you, it was only because she wasn't in her right state of mind."

How could she know that? That hit home. Isis was starting to get a little scared of this woman.

"You were raised in a lifestyle of homosexuality, but you never indulged in it yourself. And you were the life raft for someone who should have been dead years ago."

Isis began to look around. This wasn't funny anymore. This lady was getting too deep and way too personal. Isis searched the casino to see if anyone she knew was there to tell this woman the stuff she had revealed.

The psychic was earning her money. "Thirteen isn't a good number for you. Stay away from anything that has anything to do with the number thirteen. Everything thirteen will forever be a bad omen for you."

Tears started to well in Isis's eyes. She was thirteen when her life took a turn for the worse. This definitely wasn't funny anymore. The things the lady was saying were all too true.

"Our time is almost up, so let me say this to you: I know you think that I am a charlatan, but this is something you won't be able to deny—someone in your family will have a newborn baby within four weeks by the name of Abigail."

You done fucked it up now, because ain't nobody in my family having a baby in four weeks, and nobody damn sho ain't going to name their child no goddamn Abigail.

"How much do I owe you?" Isis asked.

"This isn't a game to me, as you seem to think it is. It's my gift, and God will provide me with my riches. He just uses people like you sometimes to give me financial blessings. So, that'll be fifteen dollars."

Isis gave the lady a twenty-dollar bill. She looked away when she noticed Logic coming toward her, and when she turned back around, the psychic was no longer there.

For the rest of the night, Isis kept scanning the casinos for the lady, but she never did see her again. Over the next two days Isis and Logic had a ball until her time in Vegas was up and she had to go back home. Although Logic lived in Miami, he asked her to stay a few more days; she declined. She needed to go back home to pick up the pieces and move on with her life.

Chapter 11

Housejacked

As soon as the big metal bird touched down in Virginia, Isis powered on her cell phone and checked her messages. Most of them were from Bam, talking smack. He went on and on about how she wasn't shit and how she was going to pay.

"Yo' stankin' ass ain't gon' live to spend that paper," he spat in one of his messages.

"Bitch, you better give me my shit if you know what's good for you," another one said.

"I got seven words for you: pay me now or pay me later—with yo' life, bitch!"

The insults didn't let up. "You think what I did to that baby was bad . . . bitch, I will suck the life out of you."

Isis dismissed the messages as idle threats and went to baggage claim, where she retrieved the original luggage she had traveled with, plus the extra suitcase she had had to purchase to lug all of the items she bought during her shopping trips with Logic.

Samantha picked up Isis from the airport; the rain began to pour as soon as they reached the car. The weather had gotten so bad so quickly that Samantha thought it would be best to take Isis to her place until the rain let up instead of trying to make the trip all the way out to Caroline County. Because of a combination of jet lag, the time difference, and the late nights she had kept in Vegas, Isis fell straight to sleep when she got to Samantha's house. It was her aunt's voice that awakened her about five hours later.

"Yeah, she's here," Samantha said into the phone.

Isis's first thought was that Bam had tracked her down, but she knew that Samantha wouldn't have given Bam so much conversation. Samantha had never really cared for any man that Isis had dated, but she especially disliked Bam after he caused Isis to lose the baby. Even though Bam warned her to never come back, Samantha had even showed up at the trailer with her pistol ready to shoot him, but he had left before she arrived.

"She would love to see you too," Samantha said into the phone. "She'll be here when y'all get here. Bye-bye."

"Who was that?" Isis said as she rolled over on Samantha's bed. She wiped her eyes to try to focus on the clock.

"Ty and Anthony. They're on their way over," she said. "They want to see you."

Ty and Anthony were like Isis's uncle and aunt. They had been friends with Samantha since forever and had even helped raise Isis. Ty didn't work, so when Isis would get sick, he would go pick her up from school and take care of her. Ty was the woman in his and Anthony's relationship. He cooked, cleaned, kept the house in order, and was one of the best-dressed men, women, or trans-sexuals Isis had ever seen. Anthony was all man: tall, dark, and handsome and highly sought after by many straight women, but he lived with and loved a cross-dressing man.

Isis was still resting when she heard her surrogate aunt and uncle walk into the house.

Samantha walked into the bedroom. "Aren't you going to come and say hello?"

Isis sat up in the bed. "I'll be down in a few."

Once Samantha left the room, she lay back down, but only for a few minutes to get herself together, and then she got up. When she finally did make it to the front room, she was surprised to see that Ty and Anthony had brought another guest with them.

"Oh my goodness, who is this little sleeping bundle of joy?" Isis asked, walking straight over to the baby that was nestled in Ty's arms.

Anthony answered first. "This is Abbey," he said with a big simple smile on his face.

"This is your little cousin Abigail," Ty added.

Hearing the name *Abigail* sent every single hair on Isis's body sticking straight up. *This can't be!*

The entire room went into a blur, and all she could hear were the psychic's words replaying in her head: *I know you think that I am a charlatan, but this is something you won't be able to deny—someone in your family will have a newborn baby within four weeks by the name of Abigail.*

Isis went right to her aunt's bar, made herself a drink, and drank it straight down. She then made herself another one.

"Did two gay men having a baby drive you to drink?" Anthony asked.

"No, I'm happy for you, Anthony, for both of you." But regardless of what came out of Isis's mouth, she couldn't control the sweat being released from her pores. "It's much, much deeper than that." She gulped down her second drink and poured a third.

"Care to share what's going on in that pretty little head of yours?" Ty asked.

"No, not right now," she said, dodging the question. "Tell me, when did y'all get Abigail?"

"We adopted her from China," Anthony said.

"And we decided to name her Abigail after the lady who approved the adoption," Ty said. "We were running into so much red tape. After that angel of a lady made it happen for us, we had to name the child after her."

Isis chitchatted with the doting new parents for a while before making her way back to that comfortable spot she found on the queen-sized bed in her old room. The alcohol she'd consumed, along with the bad weather, took hold of her. Sleep came quickly.

The next day, Isis wasn't sure how long she had been asleep, but the constant ringing of her cell phone wouldn't allow her to continue. She tried to block out the incessant noise, but it wouldn't go away. Whoever it was was determined to be heard. She reached for the source of the rest-killer, and the caller ID read: blocked caller. *It was probably Logic. I guess what happens in Vegas doesn't stay in Vegas.* She wished anyway.

She answered the phone. "Hello." The grandfather clock struck noon, and the chimes on the antique time keeper sent roaring pain through her head, reminding her that she had been drinking the night before.

The voice on the other end of the phone said, "That dumb-ass clock gave you away. I know that you're at Sam's house. Are you ready to apologize and give me my money back?"

"What?" She was still a little disoriented from the cognac she had drunk after finding out about Abigail.

He laughed. "I know you don't want to be living there, listening to that faggot-ass mu'fucka telling you how he told you so."

Enough was enough. Isis refused to sit on a phone and listen to a psychotic murderer refer to Samantha as a faggot. The next voice that Bam would hear would be the operator telling him that his call had ended. She closed her phone, got up, took a shower, gathered her things, and borrowed Samantha's spare car to get home.

She made a mental note to get Samantha's car washed before returning it, because the red mud in her neighborhood was something awful. The car may have been an early model Lincoln, but Samantha kept that baby in tip-top condition, and Isis didn't want to hear her mouth.

Once she turned onto the road where she lived, something felt out of place. The closer she got to home, the more intense the feeling got. From a distance it looked like someone had left trash bags and debris all over her yard. But as she got closer, the picture got clearer. She couldn't believe what she was seeing—or wasn't seeing: The lot that she had called home for almost two years was now just that, an empty lot.

The trailer was gone. Isis thought her eyes were deceiving her. *"Fuck!"* Tears rolled down her cheeks. Isis saw some of her clothes scattered about and sticking up out of the mud as if they were trying to save themselves from drowning or something, but it was too late. Everything was either gone or destroyed. Nothing was left. Was it a storm? No one had told her about any bad storms while she was away, and even if that was what had happened, why wasn't anyone else's trailer gone or messed up?

One of the neighborhood kids whom she occasionally watched

after school when his mother was running late from work spotted her. The young boy came running toward her—calling her name, "Ms. Isis, Ms. Isis." He was happy to see her, yet he wore a long expression on his face. "Ms. Isis, I'm not going to have anybody's house to go over since you let them take your trailer somewhere else."

At that very moment it hit her: She had been housejacked. Bam had moved the trailer. And the picture kept getting worse. Her car was vandalized. It was tireless; sitting on four bricks. The windows were broken, the doors were off the hinges, the engine was smashed, and even one of the seats was missing.

She wanted to respond to the little boy's remark, but all she could do was fight back the tears. She had seen worse. She could dare to cry over a missing house . . . right? Once again, her phone started ringing. It was probably Bam calling to gloat. She peeped at the screen. The area code read 305—Miami. Bam was real crafty; he'd been trying to reach her by using blocked and out-of-town numbers for the past two weeks.

The phone kept ringing.

The phone continued to ring and she continued to fight tears, ignoring the intrusion. Then something inside of her, something that she would never be able to explain, told her that she should—no, needed to—answer the phone. In a way she was wishing it was Bam so that she could at least cuss him out and let go of some of the frustration she was feeling inside.

She answered with an attitude. "Yes?"

"Is that the way you answer the phone for the man who just showed you the best time of your life?"

Hearing Logic's voice took her back to her trip to Vegas and away from her current madness. "No one can ever accuse you of having low self-esteem, that's for sure," she shot back. "How are you doing, Logic?"

"Why the sour voice?" he asked, sensing that something was wrong. "I did show you a good time, didn't I?"

"It's not you. I'm sorry, but I just got something going on here," she said. "I'm going to have to call you back."

"Nope. Talk to me now." He wasn't going to let her get away that easy. "I miss you and I want to see you. Why don't you take a flight down to Miami?"

With the back of her hand, she dried some of the moisture that had earlier started to form in her eyes. "I can't."

"*Can't* isn't a word; it's a device designed to hold you back."

"My shit is real fucked up right now, Logic. I'ma have to call you back." She hung up. But just when she thought that she would have a nervous breakdown, her phone rang again.

It was Logic calling back. She ignored the call, but he kept calling and calling until she picked up.

She finally did. "Hello?"

"Listen, Princess, you need to know that I'm not a big fan of chasing women that don't want to be caught, but I know something isn't right with you right now, and I'm not going to stop calling until I help you fix it. Everybody needs somebody every now and then," he said, "and I think you need me right now."

"I'm going to get it together. And when I do, I promise I'll call you back," Isis assured him.

"I got a better idea. Pack a bag and hop on the next flight smoking to Miami. My treat," he offered.

"It isn't that easy." She broke down and confessed, "I can't pack anything because I don't have anything to pack." She took a deep breath. "I don't have shit to pack."

"Is that all?" Logic said. "For a minute there, I thought that you had just been diagnosed with terminal cancer. This is what you do: Go home and book a flight, and we'll go get you everything you need when you get here."

"I don't have a home."

"What you mean?" he questioned, not fully understanding.

Isis sighed. "I'm homeless."

"You ain't never homeless," Logic sympathized with her. "You always got a place . . . with me."

"Look, Logic, I appreciate what you're trying to do here, but the last nigga that told me that just took the fucking trailer back, and that's why I am homeless now."

"I don't have anything to do with the last clown you fucked," Logic said. "Just come and see me and we'll sort this shit out. Then we'll find a way to get back at that bitch-ass nigga. I promise."

"But you don't understand everything." Isis was still rationalizing why she couldn't go. *You think I'm going to go to a place I ain't never been before, to see a dude who I don't really know anything about? You could have two wives, three girlfriends, and a number-one hooker. Or worse, you could get me down there and kill me.*

"Yes, I do. The sucker you were dealing with took a damn trailer back. I get it," he said. "That's some bitch shit right there. Bitches take shit back, not men. Real men move on."

Logic was making a lot of sense to her at the moment, so she kept listening. *Maybe he can help.*

"Princess, you're not homeless; you've just been victimized by a sucka. It ain't much to it. We gon' get you a place to stay—a much nicer place."

Isis was quiet. Listening to Logic helped her to calm down and pull it together.

Logic took the phone away from his mouth for a second as he hollered at his boy real quick. "Jacob, call the travel agent and see what time the next flight leaves Richmond, Virginia, to get here." Then he came back to the phone. "Princess? Go ahead and bounce back to the airport and I'll call you back in a few with your confirmation and flight number."

"Logic, do you understand that other than the clothes on my back and the stuff in my suitcase, I don't have shit, nothing, nada, zero?" Isis did have $20,000 left in her suitcase. Other than the money she had given to Samantha and the money she spent in Vegas, the rest of Bam's money had been hidden in the trailer.

"Baby, you ain't said nothing but a meatball. Now hang up the phone and get to the airport."

Isis looked around at her lot. What did she have to lose?

Logic Wiseman

All bitches ain't
female; they just have
female traits. A dude
can have a dick as big
as an elephant's and
still be a ho.

Chapter 12

Miami

Logic was true to his word about Isis not needing any money. When her plane landed in Miami, he took her straight to an exclusive boutique on Collins Avenue. Logic had called in advance and arranged for the owner to pull a few hot new trendy pieces in her size from the rack for her to model. The owner and Logic had been associates for quite some time, so she was more than happy to offer her assistance.

Isis and Logic entered the store, and before Logic could even introduce the store owner to Isis, she rushed over to the couple and introduced herself. "Hi. I'm Lola, and I am going to take great care of you." She placed her hand on Isis's shoulder as if they had been sistah-girlfriends forever. Lola had a warm smile and sweet spirit.

Lola's perfect tan stood out on her otherwise naturally fair skin as if she was a permanent resident on a nudist beach year round. Her bleached-blond hair dropped past her shoulders, down her back, and stopped just above her narrow butt. The lace-trimmed tank top that she wore showed off the cleavage created by her double-D implants paid for by another good client who came in monthly to shop for his wife but weekly to see Lola. Yet her most striking asset was her ocean-blue eyes; they were captivating. She could have been in a commercial. Isis found it hard to keep from staring into them.

Lola noticed Isis picking through some of the high-end garments that she had taken out for her and said, "I tried to pull a variety of things for you. I didn't really know your taste, but I sell only the best here, so I'm sure you will find plenty to your liking."

Isis continued to browse through the things. "You did a great job. Everything is so beautiful." She had to give Lola her props.

"I'm sure we are going to have to play with the sizes a little. Logic tried to describe you to me the best he could, but you know men." Lola winked at her. "If there's anything else you see that interests you, feel free to pull it from the racks or shelves. We are all here to help you find exactly what you want."

As Isis put aside outfits that she liked, Lola called one of her friends from a shop on the same block that sold shoes and accessories. She described the garments she had pulled and that Isis seemed to favor, and within minutes, another lady whirled into the boutique, pushing a cart filled with shoes, pocketbooks, belts, and hats that matched most, if not all, of the outfits. Logic watched Isis model outfit after outfit for him while he mostly talked on the phone. Once he saw that Isis was pretty comfortable with Lola and her team, he headed to one of the back offices to conduct more business in private. Before he left, he gave Lola the address to the condo. "Have everything that my Princess wants delivered to this spot."

They had been going through clothes for almost two hours and were about finished when Lola told Isis, "I hear you are going to be here in Miami for a while, which means you have an open account here. Anything you need—whether you want to come in or if you need us to pull some things for you or if you want me just to get one of the girls to bring you a few things to choose from—it's not a problem. We are here to make sure your needs are met," she said. "And the good thing is that you get to keep your money in your pocket." Once again, Lola winked. "We'll send the bill to Logic." She laughed.

Logic had just stepped into the store area and overheard the statement. "You can, and I'll bet she'll take you up on that offer, Lola."

"Well, we mean it." Lola showed her pretty white teeth.

When Isis and Logic were back in the car she asked him, "Can I ask you a personal question?"

"You can ask me anything you like."

Isis cleared her throat, then said, "Do you bring all your women here to buy clothes?"

"Actually, I don't," he said. "You are the first. Now can I ask you something?"

"You can ask me anything you like," she said, mirroring him.

He smiled. That was one of the reasons that he liked her so much: She had swagger. "Will you promise me that when you do take Lola up on her offer, you won't just wait for the sales?"

Isis laughed and gave him a kiss on his cheek. "I have another question," she said.

"Shoot."

Isis paused. She didn't want to sound jealous or anything, but she did want to know the story behind him and Lola. If he had never brought another girl into the store to shop before, then why was it that Miss Lola was so quick to oblige to his called-in favor? "Lola and her people were really happy to see you. I mean they truly rolled the red carpet out for you—well, us. Have you known her a long time?"

"I helped her to get her business started. It took her about six years to finally pay me back, and I didn't charge her one dime of interest, which is something I almost never do." He looked over to her from behind the wheel of the Bentley that he was driving. This was the first time that Isis had ever ridden in a Bentley. The closest she had ever come to one was the picture that Bam used to have on the wall in their trailer. She had gone from admiring the GT in a photo to riding shotgun in one. She smiled on the inside and thought, *Damn, shit changes.*

After they left the boutique, Logic drove Isis to his condo. From the moment she walked in, she loved every inch of it. It was located in the heart of trendy South Beach on Collins Avenue, and the back of the building faced the Atlantic Ocean. The wraparound balcony overlooked an enormous tropical-style pool, and the panoramic view of the paradise on the other side of their bedroom window was enough to make her want to make herself at home forever. The luxurious 2,000-square-foot condominium was heaven sent, and Isis loved everything about it: the big Jacuzzi tub in the master-suite bathroom, the king-sized bed—just one glance had her mind wondering about all the things that they could do in that bed. All the white appliances and white furniture made it feel so Miami and serene. This was her first time in the state of Florida, but Miami was treating her fabulously thus far.

Their first night together, Isis shared a bed with Logic. It wasn't like it was the first time: They had gotten good and wild while in the city of sin. But Logic was all over her, as if it was his first. His excitement showed in his performance. He came much too quickly. The next couple of times were better, but still nothing to write home to mother about, or in Sandy's case, Fluvanna Correctional Center for Women.

The next day was totally different. Logic was like a tiger in bed. As hard as she tried, Isis found it hard to keep up. She knew he had probably taken something, trying to make up for the night before, so she bit her lip and rolled with the punches. After the sex was over, Logic got up and rolled up a large amount of marijuana with a brown leaf. Once it was lit, he attempted to hand it to her.

"No thank you," she said. "I don't smoke."

"You've *never* smoked?" he asked. "Or you just don't smoke *anymore*?"

"Never."

"Never?"

She shook her head. "Nope."

"Well, now is as good a time as any to give it a try," he suggested. "I haven't done anything to harm you yet, have I?"

Isis wasn't really afraid of smoking weed; she just never had. All of her friends did, and even her sister. She viewed the serene look in Logic's eyes and decided, *Why not?*

Isis accepted the blunt, holding it between her thumb and index finger. She put it up to her mouth and inhaled—deeply. The smoke from the exotic weed caused her to cough uncontrollably.

Logic gently patted her on the back. "It's going to be okay," he said soothingly. "Don't pull on it so hard the next time. You have to start off small because your lungs aren't used to it yet." He waited a few seconds. "You want to try it again?"

Isis's eyes were already starting to feel a little heavy, but she gave it another try. "Like this?" This time she didn't inhale quite as hard, and then she passed the spliff back to Logic.

"Uh-huh. That's it, Princess," he said. "Now, I want you to promise me something, though."

"What?" she said.

"Promise me that you'll never smoke anything with anyone other than me."

A curious expression passed across Isis's face when he asked her to make that promise. "Why do you want me to smoke it only with you if it's not harmful to me?"

"Because niggas are the most shysty animals in the world," he said. "They may put something inside of the weed that'll fuck you up for life; they sometimes call them mickeys." He could tell that he had her attention, so he continued. "I'm not trying to scare you. I just don't want you to fall victim to another sucka pretending that he or she is your friend." He passed the weed back to her. "A jealous bitch will act like it's all about you but all the time be trying to tear you down. And all bitches ain't female; they just have female traits. A dude can have a dick as big as an elephant's and still be a ho," he explained. "Okay?"

Isis wasn't sure if it was the weed or what, but everything that Logic said sounded deep and thoughtful. The room was filled with the pungent aroma of top-shelf marijuana. The smoke wafted above her head. She took another toke, this time bigger than the last one, but not quite as large as the first time.

"I promise." The words came out along with a puff of smoke.

Three days had passed with Logic and Isis doing nothing but smoking weed, having sex, eating gourmet food that they had delivered to the house, and swimming in the pool at night—and sometimes in the ocean.

On the third day, Logic announced to Isis after he had gotten out of the shower and was getting dressed, "I've got to go to work to make us some money if we want to continue to have a place to live."

"You know I love this place," Isis said, smiling, "so by all means don't let me stand in your way."

"That's my girl," Logic told her. Most chicks would have been whining, saying, "Oh, baby, but I don't want you to leave." Isis knew the deal. She respected his hustle and understood the game. Daily she gave him reasons that could make any man fall head over heels for her.

Dressed all in black, Logic said to Isis as he grabbed his keys, "Okay, I won't be gone long. There should be plenty of things to keep you occupied until I return. You can sit by the pool and work on some of your hot-ass jewelry if you want to. Hopefully, the atmosphere will propel your thoughts into a creative frenzy," he said, encouraging her. "But if you need a break from that, there's always shopping, sightseeing, or lunch at any of the four- and five-star restaurants. Two of my credit cards and some cash are on the nightstand by the bed. Have fun, Princess."

Did this man just say cash and two credit cards? Isis had to ask herself. *Dreams do come true, huh?* "You make it all sound so wonderful. I'm not sure what I want to do, but I know one thing you can let me do, and that's to let me make you breakfast before you leave."

He looked at his watch, jingled his keys, and then thought, *what the hell.*

Isis prepared sunny-side-up eggs with toast and sausage. She was going to make some fried potatoes, but with Logic being the bachelor that he was, he didn't have any potatoes. To wash every-thing down, Isis cracked open a bottle of champagne instead of juice, because he had none. She worked with what she had.

After they were done with breakfast, Logic went into the second bedroom of the condo, which doubled as his office space. He removed his .40-caliber Glock pistol from the closet and placed it between the waistband of his pants and the small of his back. Then he fixed his shirt and walked back out to the kitchen, where Isis was putting the dishes in the dishwasher. He walked up behind her and gave her a kiss on the cheek before heading to the door.

"Thank you for cooking me breakfast. It was delicious," he said. "But next time, do dat shit butt naked." He smacked her playfully on the bottom and then headed for the door.

"Be safe, Logic," Isis said to his back with a smile on her face.

He turned around with a grin on his face, and asked, "Is there any other way?"

Chapter 13

A Gangsta in Bed

Logic paraded Isis around the city all week as if she was his prized trophy, introducing her to big wheels as one of the finest hidden secrets on the East Coast. He damn near forced them into being jewelry clients of hers, but hey, they would do anything for Logic. Once he took her to a nightspot called Club Opium, where multiplatinum rapper and entrepreneur Smooth Breeze was giving a big party. Of course Logic had platinum VIP status, walking to the front of the door and straight to VIP. He wasn't really feeling up to dealing with a loud hip-hop crowd tonight, but he thought there would be some good contacts for Isis. Besides, the rapper owed him so many favors, it was indeed his time to collect one or two.

Logic nudged Isis's arm. "That's the guy over there that I want you to meet," he said. Smooth Breeze was sitting in a giant booth with three other men and about eight women who looked like models.

"He looks occupied," Isis observed.

"He's not too busy to meet you. Besides, I'm sure he'll want to meet any friend that's a friend of mine."

When Smooth Breeze saw Logic walking toward his table, automatically he had two of the women get up to make room. "Logic, my man, what's good?" Smooth Breeze greeted him with a homeboy hug. "I didn't think you were going to make it. I know this isn't your type of crowd."

"No crowd is my type of crowd," Logic answered. Then he gestured toward Isis. "I want you to meet my lady, Ice. She makes top-notch original jewelry, and I want you to expose her to the hip-hop market." Logic got right to the point. "Nobody buys jewelry like you cats." Isis was stunned at the way he spoke to the famous rapper.

"No problem, Logic," Smooth Breeze showed his platinum teeth. "You know I'm going to need to see you tomorrow to take care of that business. If I'd known you were coming, I would have brought that with me."

"I know, but I'm going to have Doc or Jacob to meet with you to handle that tomorrow."

"That's what's up." Smooth Breeze nodded, then said to Logic and Isis, "Y'all's cups been good all night, right?"

"Yeah, we good on the cognac," Logic replied.

"Is that all you need from me right now?"

Logic answered with two quick words: "For now." Then he smiled.

"Anything you need, let us know."

"Just make sure you handle that B-I with my Princess." Logic kissed her on the forehead.

"I got dat."

"Let someone serve and wait on you." If Dave could see me now, he sure would be proud! Isis couldn't help but smile.

Sitting in VIP with a full waitstaff waiting on her hand and foot and having the full attention of one of the most respected men in the club—if not *the* most respected—made Isis truly feel like the princess that Logic had labeled her when he first laid eyes on her at the pool in Vegas. A couple of times Logic had referred to Isis as his lady while introducing her. She loved seeing the way that people flocked to her new man, damn near kissing his ass just to get a hello out of him. She watched how one of the guys in Smooth Breeze's entourage passed off a sack of pills to Logic while he sat there smoking a blunt in the middle of the club like it was a cigarette. Logic smiled at the small gift.

Isis overheard the guy that passed him the bag say, "I know you probably got this shit by the pound, but Breeze wouldn't have it in here if I didn't break bread off of his stash."

Isis was getting turned on by the power that Logic exuded. He caught her looking at him. "What did he give you?" she asked.

"Some E pills. They're not as powerful as mine, but the gesture is what counts."

"Is that right?" She smirked, totally infatuated. "I didn't know that you took those."

Before he could answer, a business client approached him. "What up, Logic? I've been working hard trying to get your money back," he said. "I'm in production right now with the film, finally. It shouldn't be long before we generate some revenue."

Logic just looked at the negligent filmmaker. His boy, Doc,

jumped into the conversation to alleviate some of the uncom-
fortable tension. "Yo, Tre, so how you loving that Ferrari you
driving?" he asked.

"It's a perfectly tuned machine. I had to pull some strings to
get the limited edition on the first shipment that they sent
through the Port of Miami, but the red tape I went through was
worth it."

"Plug me in with them motherfuckers you dealt with, 'cause
I can't get a bitch to pay me no mind," Doc told Tre.

"That's nothing. I will take care of that for you."

While Doc and Tre continued to talk, Logic redirected his attention back to Isis. "You have a problem with that?"

She wasn't sure what he was referring to. "What, you handling
your business?"

"Me and E?" he asked like her opinion really mattered to him.

Isis shook her head. "I was just asking."

"I mix the E with the V from time to time. They call it sex-
tacy."

"I know what the E stands for, but what are V's?" she asked.

"Viagra."

She recalled their sex episodes from the other night. *That's
why I couldn't keep up with that nigga.*

"Actually, the pills that Breeze sent to me are nothing close to
the ones that I get. They won't even do anything for me."

Ecstasy is Ecstasy, she thought. Then she asked, "Can you let
me try one of them, then?"

Logic studied her face. "Have you ever taken one before?"

"You know I am the original square from *Green Acres.*"

"Then why now?"

"Curiosity," she said. "And you're the only person that I can
trust to satisfy my curiosity."

He sat there feeling himself, loving the way that Isis tuned into him, and then Doc whispered something in Logic's ear. It must have been something funny because a big smirk appeared on his face. He grabbed her hand, signaling to Isis that it was time for them to leave. She grabbed her Chloe bag and started toward the door, led by Logic through the crowd. She was more than ready to go home and hit the sack. She hadn't gotten much rest the night before and had been functioning all day since 6 AM on only four hours of sleep.

Once they were outside of the club, Isis watched as Tre, the film guy, headed over to his car with two six-feet-tall white women, one attached to each arm. She watched as they stood next to the banana-yellow Ferrari making arrangements on what the next move was. Isis couldn't even imagine the freaky festivities that they had in store for the rest of the night.

Logic handed his keys to Jacob. "Take my baby to the car," Logic said, referring to Isis. The car was parked only four spots from the entrance of the club. He turned to Isis. "Princess, wait in the car. I'll be there in a minute. I gotta talk to Tre right quick."

Isis did what she was told, but Logic was only a few feet away and she could hear him talking to Tre. "Let me hold them keys to that Ferrari until the revenue from the film is proper."

Tre knew that it wasn't a request that Logic was making. He had three options: produce the money that he owed, which he didn't have; give up the car; or die. With moisture in his eyes, he gave up the keys. That car was the love of his life, but it wasn't worth his life. Logic tossed the keys to Doc. "Put some miles on her for me."

"Will do," Doc assured his boss.

Before Doc could pull off, Isis heard Logic tell Jacob, "There's too much money owed to me in these streets. I think niggas are starting to think that shit is fucking sweet. What the fuck a nigga doing in a club driving a Ferrari, dicking not one but two white bitches, while he owes me a quarter-million dollars and counting? I need you to go to the strong-arm collection tactic to let cats know that it is that serious. So for the next couple of weeks, keep your feet the fuck out of them casinos and on the pavement collecting my gwock."

Although he tried to conceal it, Isis read the angry look on Jacob's face as Logic pulled off.

Logic took another look at Isis before he turned onto the main highway. He admired every stitch of the all-white rhinestone halter dress that she wore. In fact, this was the first time that he had noticed that since she had been in Miami, she had worn only all black or all white. He found it interesting. He also liked the fact that she asked him for permission to take the Ecstasy. She never whined or complained about anything, although there wasn't much to complain about. He put his right hand on her left leg and then slowly ran it up her thigh, and he didn't stop until he reached the prize. She wasn't wearing any underwear for fear her panty lines would show through the form-fitting dress. Between her legs was hot and wet like a rain forest in South America. That night, she would break another one of her never-haves. Hot sex on Ecstasy was definitely on the menu.

When they got in the house, Logic gave her a small blue pill. She wondered if it was one of the blue dolphins that she had read about, but she didn't ask. She took the pill that he gave her, and he swallowed a different-colored one. Not really knowing what to expect from the drug, she wanted to be prepared.

"I want to go freshen up," Isis said. She turned her back to him to unzip the sexy number she was wearing and let it drop to the floor.

As she strutted off to the bathroom, Logic's voice stopped her in her tracks. "Thank you for trusting me," he said.

"I was born to trust you," she told him, "but please don't betray my trust. Okay?" she said with a look of hope in her eyes. *Now, if this motherfucker right here betrays me, it's going to be the damn straw that broke the camel's back.*

Logic didn't even get a chance to respond to Isis's query. Next thing he heard was Isis in the bathroom vomiting. He came in behind her and handed her some paper towels as she leaned over the toilet bowl. "It's one of the side effects to the E the first time you take it."

He sat there and talked to her for a few minutes before she insisted that she get into the shower. He agreed.

Logic was lying in the king-sized bed stroking his manhood when she returned. Steam emerged through the door from behind her as if it was trying to race her when she stepped on the carpet. She looked like a black angel emerging from the gates of heaven, and she was coming his way. As she got closer, she slowly turned her back toward him. Logic could make out the black sheer Claire Pettibone nightgown that she had purchased earlier that day, along with some black, strappy, come-fuck-me sandals. She was ready for attack. Logic had no idea that the E had her so high that it had taken her an extra fifteen minutes just to get the sandals laced up correctly.

She stood in front of Logic, striking a sexy pose with her back to him. She slowly turned back around.

Damn, I hope I don't fall, she thought as she made the spin. *This shit got me fucked up already. Lord, please be with me.* She could feel her body being super lightweight.

In his eyes, everything was perfect, right down to the slight bow in her legs that made a gap just the right size at her mound. He sat up and pulled her to him so that she could sit on his lap. He had to have her closer, right then and there. Forget trying to play it all out like one of those old romance movies.

Her long black hair was pinned up with a black-and-rhinestone hair clip, which provided a perfect opportunity for him to kiss her on the neck. He then reached around and cupped her breasts, massaging them gently. By the time he got around to playing with her nipples, she rolled her neck back, wishing that he would move faster and take it to the next level. And just when the thought crossed her mind, he slid his fingers into her moist vagina. His fingers moved around her clit so deftly, she was sure that at one time in his life he must have played a piano or some other instrument that took great digital dexterity. Isis breathed deeply and her body began to quiver. She moaned as his fingers rubbed in a circular motion, dipping in and out of her canal.

"Ooohhh, that feels sooo good," she moaned.

Feeling her juices made him hunger for the taste of them. Licking his lips, he turned her onto her back and kissed her inner thighs before he buried his face in that magical place. He parted her lips and lapped the sweet-tasting nectar dripping down her legs. She could feel her body shaking and knew that she was about to climax. He loved the fact that she had no control of her actions. Her body was in overdrive. She balled her fists and locked her legs around Logic's neck, using his face as her personal fuck toy.

Both of them were drunk with lust, but the Ecstasy had Isis so hot that she wanted to taste him. She wanted to share with him the exhilarating feeling that she was experiencing. He had an urgent desire to explore her insides with another part of his body. She decided that she would succumb to his desires. She would put hers on hold.

Isis discarded her sexy lingerie. It made a puddle of silk at the side of the bed. They emitted a heat from their bodies that was indescribable. Now that Logic was released from her headlock, he guided his shaft toward her shaved pussy. He entered her without a condom, and she didn't object.

The E was in his system and he was laying dick to her like a madman, stretching her vagina to its limits. She gyrated her hips and threw her pussy back at him like the destiny of the world depended on whether she made him come or not.

All five of the CDs in the disc changer had played; no music crooned from the speakers. The only music to be heard was the moans and grunts coming from the two of them. His balls smacking against her butt because of his intense thrusting created a rhythm to their duet. Ashford & Simpson, Method Man and Mary, and Peaches & Herb combined ain't had shit on the harmony of Logic and Isis. When he glanced at the sweat rolling down her beautiful face and settling on her lip, it made him dig deeper and go harder until she screamed, "Lord knows, Daddy, I'm coming . . . I'm coming home to you, baby."

After the best sex Isis had ever had in her life, she went to the bathroom to take another shower. Logic had turned on the radio; she began to sing every song that came on it while the water pounded against her skin. Once she finished washing up, she got out and dried off; she got a thick washcloth and soaped it up real good, and then headed over to the bed, where Logic was lying on his back with a rock-hard dick still in his hand, ready for round two. She thoroughly washed him up, causing the soap smell on his dick to mingle with the strong sex smell that was already lingering in the condo. *Goddamn, I must be high,* she thought, as the fresh soap scent started pulling her closer and closer to his dick. She was drawn to the dick like metal to a magnet. She didn't hesitate to wrap her hand around the base of his dick with one hand and cup his balls in her other as her head bobbed up and down on his prize. The blowjob she was giving him had Logic seeing colors: blues, reds, greens, and yellows.

After about twelve straight hours of fucking, Isis was still at full throttle, thanks to the pills, but Logic had dozed off. Once again, she had been singing every song that came on the radio, even the ones that she didn't know the words to. She nudged Logic and asked, "Are you asleep?"

He never opened his eyes. The performance that he'd put on had exhausted him. "Not anymore," he did manage to say.

"I need something to help me to go to sleep," she begged. "Do you have any sleeping pills?"

He did have some sleeping pills, but he wasn't about to let her put anything else into her system. "Oh, no you don't. It's not good to mix the two together," he said. "You wanted to roll with the big girls, you gonna have to ride it out like a big girl."

After three more hours of pretending to be Janet Jackson, Mary J. Blige, Diana Ross, Betty Wright, and every other singer whose song was played on the radio, she finally wore down and fell asleep—just about the best she had slept in her life.

Chapter 14

No Witness ... No Crime

When Isis woke up, a day and a half had passed. She wasn't even sure where she was. *Logic? Where is he?* She looked on the other side of the bed, and there he was.

"How you feeling?" he asked. He was holding a cup of tea that he had prepared once she began moving around in bed. He knew she was about to wake up. "Drink some of this, it will make you feel better."

"How bad was I?" she asked, afraid that she might have done something to turn him off.

"You don't do a good Whitney Houston imperson-ation." He chuckled.

"What else?" she asked. "I'm embarrassed."

"Don't be," he said. "I fucks with you because you are

not afraid to be you. I'll take you however you are over a fake bitch any day, throwing up, drunk, high, or at your best."

"Well, damn. I mean . . . thank you," she said. "I fucks with you too." She wanted to give him a kiss, but she knew that her breath was truly stinky, so that would have to wait.

Logic allowed her to rest a little longer before he demanded that she eat something. He didn't have to do much persuading. She was famished.

They were sitting at the table, almost done with lunch, when Logic's phone rang. He had gotten four calls back to back before he said, "Let me see what this mu'fucka want." He hit the green phone button to see what Jacob was being so persistent about. "What, nigga?" he spat.

"I managed to catch up with an old friend of ours," Jacob informed him. "Found him trying his luck in the casino."

"Word?"

"Yeah. I got 'im wit me right now." Jacob knew that there would be a sizable reward for his deed.

"Where're you at now?" Logic asked, with a tinge of excitement noticeable in his voice. Although this sack of shit had been off the radar for a while, Logic had known that it would only be a matter of time before he would resurface.

"You can meet me between the glades and the wood." Jacob was referring to a fairly secluded area commonly used to dump trash.

"Naw," Logic said. "Make it that spot right off of the Florida Turnpike."

Jacob knew exactly where he was speaking of. "Okay, we'll be waiting."

After ending the call, Logic looked to Isis and said, "Bring that tea with you; we got some business to take care of." And on that note, the two prepared to leave the house.

Isis rode in the front seat beside Logic, admiring the brilliance of the orange-red sun as it set until it was ready to surface again at dawn the next day. It was beautiful. The days in Miami were moving so fast; she had just gotten out of the bed, and now it was dinnertime already. She marveled at the lights shining from the Hard Rock Hotel & Casino as Logic took the Griffin Road exit off of the turnpike and navigated to the spot where he had arranged to meet with Jacob.

The meeting place was an alligator-infested swamp. It didn't take long for him to spot Jacob's car even though it was parked out of sight. Jacob had Donnell at gunpoint, but once he saw the headlights of Logic's Aston Martin peek around the bend, then saw what had to be Isis riding shotgun, he knew that Logic was only going to talk to him. He pulled Donnell out of the car. As Logic put the car in park, Isis's phone began to vibrate. It was her sister. For a minute she thought to ignore the call, but she hadn't spoken to her sister in three days, so this would be a good time for her to catch up while Logic was talking to his boys.

"Sit tight, Princess," Logic said as he opened the car door. "I'll be right back."

After he was out of the car and looked back to make sure Isis was okay, she replied, "No problem. My sister is on the phone anyway."

"Tell her I said, 'What's up.' "

Isis smiled as he walked away from the car, and then she turned the volume down on the CD that had been playing. Before she could greet her sister and begin to tell her about what had been going on for the past three days, she heard Phoebe say, "Can you talk? I really need you for about thirty minutes."

Isis knew that Logic wouldn't be out of the car for thirty minutes, so she promised her sister she'd call her back just as soon as she got back to the condo.

"Okay," Phoebe said, "but please, don't forget."

"I won't." Isis hung up the phone wondering what it was that her sister wanted to talk about. She would just have to find out tonight when she called Phoebe back. Meanwhile, less than twenty yards away, she could see Logic and Jacob. They had another guy with them, but he had his hands taped behind his back. Isis rolled her window down and strained to hear what was going on.

"Look what we got here," Logic said, walking over to the two men. "You've been MIA for a minute."

His once-trusted friend didn't say a word. He had been around Logic long enough to know that regardless of what he said, things would more than likely lead to the same results.

"Me and Jacob was just talking about you the other day," Logic said. "Thought you had joined the army and was hiding out over in Iraq. Jacob figured that you were too scared to enlist in anybody's army and fight." Logic smiled. "But I told 'im you would be safer in the Middle East fighting sand niggas than running off with five hundred thousand dollars that belonged to me without so much as a note to let me know what was going on." Logic shot spit between his teeth and onto the ground.

"Logic, man, I know it gotta look fucked up right now, but please be patient with me. I was gonna call you. On my grandmother's grave," Donnell swore. "I'm just having a string of bad luck."

Logic didn't respond to Donnell's begging. This was a method he had learned a long time ago: The less you said, the longer a scared motherfucker would beg. And Logic was enjoying this.

"Man, I know you invested a lot of money in me," Donnell continued, "but you know as well as I do that you can't get blood out of a turnip. Think about how far we go back. You know my mother and father, my kids. It's only money! But us, we're like family. For God's sake, man. What you gon' do? You gonna kill your family?"

Logic noticed that Donnell had gotten braces. He hadn't noticed them until right at that moment. "That might not be a bad idea, now that you've mentioned it."

Jacob raised his gun. "Shall I?" He spoke to Logic but glared at Donnell.

"Wait." Logic put his hand up, lowering his head as if he was some gangster out of a movie.

"I know yo' grandmother, yo' sister, yo' whole family—come on, man," Donnell pleaded one last time.

Although he hadn't intended for it to come off that way, Donnell's last effort sounded too much like a threat for Logic to stomach. "Kill this fucking coward, man."

Jacob did as he was told, and the two bullets that chased each other out of the barrel of Jacob's gun, through the front of Donnell's forehead, and out of the back of his skull left him speechless, useless, and lifeless.

Isis witnessed the entire thing. It had all happened so quickly. She was in shock but didn't scream. There was no need. It wouldn't have helped anyway. In her eyes, it was inevitable. What's meant to be is meant to be, and none of us can change that, so there was no need for her to fret.

Besides, it wasn't the first time in her life she had seen a man die. After all, this man who was just killed was a stranger. She had loved Dave with all of her heart and soul when she'd watched the State of Virginia kill him. He had died right in front of her eyes, and she hadn't shed a tear. Isis kept her cool and, once again, removed herself from the situation, as she had done before. It was something she was getting used to doing.

Jacob looked up from Donnell's dead body and looked directly at Isis. "What about her?" he asked Logic.

"What you mean, 'what about her'?" Logic glanced over toward his car. Isis was sitting there picking her nails as if she didn't have a care in the world about what was going on outside of the car she was in.

"What do you always preach?" Jacob asked. " 'No witnesses, no crime.' "

"That there ain't no witness. *She's* my future."

Isis tried to pretend she didn't hear Jacob trying to convince Logic of the need for her end. Hearing those words flow from Logic's mouth put her at ease, but it also made her think about what the psychic had told her when she was in Las Vegas: *The man who will love you will address you as his princess. . . . Everything thirteen will forever be a bad omen for you. . . .* She was in a daze. Seeing the brains of another human being blown out in front of her very eyes, the psychic's words' becoming reality, what Dave had said in his last letter, and the fact that this was indeed the thirteenth day she'd spent in Miami with Logic sent her mind to another place. Her physical body was sitting in the car, but another part of her was a million miles away. But this wasn't the time to be drifting off. She needed to be concentrating on the right here and right now. Although scenarios in her life had changed, she hadn't.

Jacob had a wild look in his eyes. "You got to be kidding me, man! Tell me that you're joking. . . . We got too much at stake," he said. "Don't let your dick get us life in the joint." Then Jacob made the most profound statement he'd made all evening. "Three people are way too many people to keep a secret of this magnitude. Our lives are at stake."

Dropping his head, Logic replied in a quieter voice, "You are right. I don't know where my mind was at." Logic took out his gun and started over toward his Aston Martin.

"That's why we call you Logic, my nigga," Jacob said. "Leave nothing to chance. Handle yo' business." Jacob smiled.

As Logic walked to the car, he had thoughts of Isis: how calm she was, how she trusted him, the intimate moments they had shared together, the blunt, the E, the laughs, Vegas and their intimate talks. Although Isis had seen and done a lot, there was something about her innocence that he genuinely liked, that he was drawn to. Logic was three steps from the car when Isis realized what was about to happen. She began silently saying the Lord's Prayer, while gazing into his eyes.

But then Isis watched in disbelief when Logic turned around and called out, "Jacob?"

Jacob's eyes grew wide with a look of pure terror. The three bullets flew out of Logic's gun and found their target, and Jacob's body crumpled to the ground. The sound of the shots was muffled by the silencer he had had specially fitted for the Glock .40-caliber. Now there were two dead bodies to dispose of.

Logic never checked to confirm that Jacob was dead; he knew that the powerful weapon had done its job. And if he was wrong, by the time someone found Jacob in this deserted swamp area, both he and Donnell would be stinking.

Without saying a word, Logic got into the car and started it up. He then looked over at Isis, whose only response was "I never liked him anyway."

Logic chuckled, then kissed her on the cheek. "That nigga must've been crazy, suggesting that we kill my baby. Shit, I just found my baby."

I can't believe he just killed for me, Isis thought. She leaned over and returned Logic's kiss to the cheek.

He then gazed into her eyes. "I know this is short notice and will probably go down as one of the craziest proposals in the history of marriages, but will you marry me . . . tomorrow?" Logic had fallen in love with Isis, but he also knew that the court couldn't force one spouse to testify against another. If she said yes, he would be killing two birds with one stone.

"Why so soon?"

"Why not?"

She thought about his question and then gave an ultimatum of her own: "I'll marry you right now, but on one condition."

"What is it?"

Isis took a long look into his eyes. "You have to make sure my sister is at the wedding."

"Where is she? I'll have her flown in tonight."

Chapter 15

Wedding Bells

The next morning, wedding bells were ringing. Isis and Logic had a suite at the Ritz-Carlton and had pulled together a makeup artist, a hairstylist, and a photographer to make the day as memorable as possible. Lola brought over a rack of dresses for Isis to choose from to wear to the city hall, where the justice of the peace would perform the ceremony. A florist showed up and helped Isis choose the perfect bouquet. The ceremony's being held in city hall didn't mean that they couldn't do it in style.

Before 10 AM, the most important guest had arrived—Phoebe. She came through the door with a cart full of luggage, as if she was going to be staying with them for months.

The sisters greeted each other with a huge bear hug. Isis looked toward her sister's bags. "How long you gon' stay with us?" Isis wore a white Ritz-Carlton terry-cloth robe.

Phoebe hadn't seen her sister in a while. She gave her a once-over and welcomed the glow she saw on her face. "Sis," she said, "you getting married! I didn't know what you might need, so I brought some of everything. I packed one suitcase with things new, one with things old, and one with things borrowed. You caught me with my panties down, you know; I had only about six hours to prepare, pack, and get here."

"Thank you, sis, but all I needed was for you to be here." Seeing Phoebe's effort to make her day right had Isis one slow song away from being teary-eyed. "Let me introduce you to Lola. I told her your size, and she has a couple of dresses that you can choose from."

After picking a dress, Phoebe turned her attention back to Isis. "So, what time is the wedding?" Phoebe asked.

"Maybe three-thirty," Isis guessed.

The fact that Isis didn't know the time of her own ceremony wasn't a good sign to Phoebe. "Sister, you sure about this? I mean, you know I'm down for whatever, as long as it makes you happy." Phoebe shot from the hip. "So are you?"

"Am I what?"

"Are you happy?"

Isis's answer was delayed by the ringing of her phone. "Hold on, sister, it's Logic." She pushed the button to answer the call and put the phone up to her ear.

"Hello, Princess." When Isis heard Logic's voice, her face lit up like Times Square on New Year's Eve. Phoebe had never seen Isis that happy in her entire life, not even with Dave.

"Hello to you, baby," she said, smiling.

"I just called to see if your sister was in yet," he said. "I want to talk to her."

"She's right here." Isis handed the phone to Phoebe. "He wants you."

Phoebe was surprised, but she took the phone anyway. "Hello?"

"How was your flight?" her brother-in-law-to-be asked her.

"It was good. What could be better than first class?"

"A private jet, but that's not why I called. Your sister kicked me out of the suite because she said something about it being bad luck if I see her before the wedding. I don't know about all of that, but I do know that it wouldn't be right for me to wait to meet my only sister-in-law until after the wedding. So how would you feel about meeting me for a drink? Or a cup of coffee, if you feel it's too early for alcohol."

"Too early?" she said. "I've been up ever since last night when I got the phone call from you and my sister and I'm so excited. Actually I need something to calm me down." Phoebe wanted to see, firsthand, the man who had her sister beaming like a child at Christmastime.

"Meet me in the lobby. You'll recognize me by my good looks," Logic joked.

After meeting Logic, it didn't take Phoebe long to discover why her sister wanted to marry the man. What wasn't there to like about him? He had charisma by the pounds and he was good-looking; the man was simply marvelous. Before they even left the hotel restaurant, Phoebe was already referring to him as her brother.

The wedding ceremony was quick and sweet. Afterward, they had a small dinner party with Phoebe and a few of Logic's friends and family. The next day, Phoebe said she needed to get back to Texas, but not before making Isis a promise that she would come out to visit them again soon after they got back from their honeymoon in St. Tropez.

Isis looked forward to her sister's return visit, but for the next seven days, it would be just her and her husband, creating their new lives together as one. If only the psychic had told her how wonderful that was going to be . . .

Chapter 16

The Call

Once Logic and Isis returned from their honeymoon, they started looking for another place to call home, a place that wasn't like the bachelor pad he had been occupying but something they could furnish together. Meanwhile, they were still staying in the condominium. They were at the table having breakfast, one day short of being married for two weeks, when they received a call that they would both remember for the rest of their lives.

The call came from Jimmie, the downstairs doorman. "Mr. Wiseman, federal agents are on their way up to your place." Jimmie lowered his voice to a whisper as he said, "While they were waiting for the elevator to come, I think I heard one of them say something about having a warrant for your arrest. I told the elevator butler to stall them the best he could, but I'm sure they'll be taking the stairs as well. That's all I know. I wish I could be more of a help."

Logic had been more than generous when it came to tipping Jimmie over the past two years for keeping an eye on things when he wasn't in town; that generosity had just bought him a few extra minutes. Before Jimmie hung up, he also pulled Logic's coat to the fact that when he saw the warrant, it had the wrong address printed on it—unit 2771 instead of the correct address, which was 2717.

The twelve FBI agents were dispatched to execute the arrest warrant for one Logic Wiseman for an assortment of charges, including money laundering, loan-sharking, and murder. It had taken the government a while to find someone who was willing to speak out against him. Logic was usually very careful with the people whom he chose to deal with, and between his more-than-fair business practices and his ruthless tendencies when crossed, no one wanted to go there with him.

Officer Stephen Newman was in charge of the investigation and had prayed on many a night that there would be a break in the case. Then one day, about two and a half weeks earlier, the answer to that prayer walked into his office and said, "I was told that you're the one that I needed to speak with if I had information to give on Logic Wiseman." Followed by "Oh, by the way, my name is Tre Wilson, the film director," the informant said vainly.

When Logic hung up the phone with the doorman, his eyes rested on his wife of thirteen days. He wasn't afraid or nervous for himself, because he'd known for a long time that this day could, and would, eventually come. But a federal indictment didn't automatically equal a prison sentence. Some people say that the party isn't over until the fat lady sings, but Logic's saying went a little different: the party isn't over until the fat lady shits. Right then, there was no room for her because he was still on the toilet. And as far as Logic was concerned, he had a lot more shitting to do. But he did need to get Isis as far away from shit as possible.

"You gotta get out of here," Logic said to his wife as calmly as he possibly could. "The alphabet boys are on their way up here with a warrant for my arrest and probably a warrant to search this place."

Isis digested his words and then stood up quickly. "If I have time to get out, then you do too. I'm not leaving without you, Logic."

"I knew you would say that. That's one of the reasons why I married you," he said. "They probably have all the exits to the building covered by now, but they won't be looking to stop a woman by herself. So I'm not asking you, I'm telling you to get out and save yourself. Plus, I need your help."

"Anything, Logic. Just tell me what to do."

"Okay, Princess, but we have to move fast." Logic proceeded to give Isis instructions. "I got a suitcase in the closet with $1.5 million in cash in it; it weighs about thirty-five pounds. Do you think you'll be able to carry it?"

"To where?"

"There's an all-black '85 Riviera parked on the parking deck." He handed her a slip of paper after retrieving it from an end table drawer. "This will tell you exactly where to find the car. Just drive to a hotel and wait for either me or my lawyer to call. I'll be in touch as soon as I know what the damage is."

Isis threw on some sweats while Logic pulled the suitcase out of the closet and something from the safe. "Don't let anything happen to either of these." He passed her the suitcase, a ledger that listed everybody who owed him money, and a ring of keys. "If for some reason you're forced to have to make a decision to leave either the money or the keys behind . . . let me make this absolutely clear: Guard the keys with your life. And remember, regardless of what happens to me, I love you. Now give me a kiss and get out of here."

Isis was nervous when she stepped out of the door. She didn't want anything to happen to Logic. The suitcase was heavy but manageable. She hadn't known that money weighed so much. She strolled to the elevator and pushed the button to go down.

It arrived within seconds. Isis stepped into the elevator and transformed, removing herself and replacing herself with Wonder Wife, finding the guts to be strong and carry out the plan for Logic.

Just before the door closed, two men came around the corner. "Hold that door!" one of them shouted, running toward her. Isis's heartbeat quickened until it was pounding as fast as a drummer at a college football game after his team had just scored a touchdown. "Do you mind if I ask what apartment you just left from?" The man doing the talking flipped out his ID and badge.

"Not at all," she said. "I was coming to bring my son some more clothes over to his grandmother's house, but she wasn't there. She got some nerve. She always does that, you know. Call me all morning asking me to bring more clothes, like I have nothing else to do. You would think the boy was running through the house buck naked or something, as much as she called. Now I'm going to be late for my appointment at the gym. Who's going to pay my personal trainer? Don't get me wrong—I love my mother and all. She's the only one I got, but—"

"That'll be all, miss." The agent cut her off before she rambled on all day. "You have a nice day."

When the door closed, Isis let out a huge sigh of relief. *Thank you God,* she said to herself as she looked up. *So far so good.*

Once the elevator reached the underground parking deck, she started to breathe a little better, until she saw three more agents standing around. Watching! She tried telling herself that there was nothing to worry about; they were looking for a six-foot-two-inch bald man, not a five-foot-seven-inch woman with hair down her back.

You can do this, Isis.

There it was. The old-school car was in mint condition and parked exactly where Logic said it would be. She walked over to it, put the key into the door, slid behind the wheel, and then turned on the ignition.

Vrrooom.

It started right up, and Isis was on her way. But where the road would take her, she had no idea.

Chapter 17

Logically Speaking

Logic was being held in the county jail. It had 1,500 prisoners, but one floor was reserved to keep only federal detainees; that was the floor where Logic had been housed for five days. According to his lawyer, the case they had against him was bad—but not insurmountable. They had two witnesses who were going to testify against him. He didn't have a bond, and a bond hearing was laughable. So he had plenty of time to sit back and think about his future, Isis, and their future together. He decided to give her a call to share his thoughts.

"Baby," Logic confessed, "you know I love you with all my heart. A lot has happened in these two short months since we met. I never in my life thought I would've ever loved anybody as wholeheartedly as I've loved you. But the truth of the matter is I'm no good for you. Some might go as far as saying that I'm a no-good muthafucka, and they might be right."

Isis had been laying low in a Ritz-Carlton suite for five days, waiting to get a call from Logic, but she never would have thought he would talk that way. That was the last thing that she needed to hear. "Don't say that," she said. "That's not true."

"It's true. I'm old school. My morals and tactics run totally against the grain of the way cowards live nowadays, and there are one thousand times more of them than there are guys like me."

"I agree," she said. "Your principles may be different from others', but I'm talking about us."

"If I'm not able to protect and take care of you, what good am I to you?"

"Then let me take care of you," she said.

"A lot of coward niggas out there would love to harm or disrespect you, thinking it would hurt me. And you know what? It would hurt me. It would tear me apart."

"You're talking crazy, Logic. It's not that easy, and I will not disconnect from you. Not for those reasons. I'm tired of letting other people control my life." She had her mind set.

"Listen, baby, you got a career to babysit. Devote your time to being the next Jacob the Jeweler, Harry Winston, or David Yurman, not to me." Logic went on for a few more minutes trying to reason with Isis, talk her into annulling their marriage, but she wasn't going for it. "Look, this is what I'm going to do, since you are hell-bent on fucking with me, I might as well make it worth your while. I'm going to plug you into a few influential people who, by wearing your jewelry, can jump-start your career. People that owe me favors: rappers, actors, and ball players."

Isis listened, trying to take in everything that her husband was sharing with her. His wisdom could prove to be priceless.

"These . . . associates, let's call them, are not to be trusted, but they can be counted on to some extent, because I have what you call a love-hate relationship with them. They love me when they are borrowing my money, but they hate me when it's time to pay up. They hate even more the damage I'll do to protect my investments if they don't. I've helped a lot of these people get their start or make it through troubled waters. I've also fucked up a lot of mu'fuckas who ain't play fair in return. This is why you must be selective as to who you let know of our relationship. Sometimes it's going to be better if I can just get you the meeting with certain individuals but no one knows that I'm your husband. That way we can tag-team these clowns without them knowing who was in the ring."

Isis listened to Logic's way of thinking. Deep down inside, she agreed with most of what he said, but it still hurt her heart that once again she would be left to endure the heartless streets alone. Not to mention being a woman trying to come up in a male-dominated field. "So, no more talk about you leaving me, then?" she said.

"Okay, baby, but there's one more thing."

"You'd better not say you have another wife."

Logic laughed. "Not exactly. But I need you to promise me that you won't ever sell the Riviera, at least not without my permission."

"Is that all?" she said.

"That's all. Park it somewhere safe."

"Okay. Do you have anywhere in Miami that you can suggest?"

"Put it on the auto train and send it up north to a storage in Virginia somewhere where you can put your hands on it if need be."

"No problemo, but do you mind if I ask why?"

"Yes, I do. But what I don't mind telling you is to call Smooth Breeze as soon as we get off the phone. He's good people; plus, he owes me a lot of paper and pays faithfully."

"No disrespect to your gangsta, but for how long do you feel that he will continue to pay you?" Isis had been through the jail thing a few times. And she knew that once a man goes to jail, people start to show their true colors.

"Well, you are going to tell him that I said he needs to escalate everything I told him in the club about letting you make something for him. As a matter of fact, wait until I call you tonight and we'll call 'im on the three-way together."

"Anything else, baby?"

"That's just the beginning. There's this Al B. Sure-looking muthafucka that boxes and shit. I'm going to have him shout you out and wear your Web site address on his shorts when he fights, and wear your T-shirt and jewelry when he's getting interviewed."

"That'll be real good publicity if you can make it happen." Isis was getting really excited.

"Eventually, I'll plug you with this gay-ass NBA joker and a couple of football dudes too."

"Those people make so much money," she said. "How come they owe you those types of favors?"

"Everybody doesn't make the super payday, and regardless of how much money you make, if you spend more than you take in, guess what?"

"You get broke," she said.

"Worse. You end up owing a muthafucka like me."

* * *

Later that day while Isis was trying to figure out things at the hotel pool, her Aunt Samantha called.

"Ice, are you behaving yourself?" she asked. "Well, never mind that. Of course you aren't . . . you're a newlywed. Ty and Anthony are having a christening for little Abigail and they want you to be there."

Isis took family very serious, and she already felt guilty for not inviting Samantha to her wedding. And she really had only one good reason for not doing so: She hadn't wanted Samantha to try to talk her out of it. Even though Ty and Anthony weren't blood, they were family. "When is it?"

"It's next Sunday."

Isis thought about all the things that she had to do, and then said, "Tell them that I wouldn't miss it for the world."

After soaking up plenty of rays at the pool, Isis went and stopped by the mall and did a little shopping. Logic had been on her mind all day, ever since she had spoken to him earlier. She knew Logic was going through a lot. Two people were supposed to take the stand against him. One was that guy Tre, from whom he'd taken the Ferrari at the club. Although that was disappointing, it didn't worry Logic too much. Tre could be touched before he ever stepped foot in a courtroom. But the second witness was a problem because no one knew his identity. The only thing that Logic's attorney, Michael McGetty, could find out was that the person was a reliable informant. Aren't they all?

As promised, Logic called Isis later that evening. "I've been waiting for you, handsome," she told him after accepting the collect call.

Logic spoke quickly. "I don't have long, because they gonna lock us down early for some bullshit. I need you to call three people."

"I'm ready when you are."

"Peace. First dial 555-4307. That's Breeze." She clicked over and did as she was told.

After she got Smooth Breeze on the line, she clicked back. "Here you go, Logic."

"Breeze, what up?" Logic said.

"The sun, moon, stars, and modern-day slavery, but what else is new?" Breeze said.

"What's the soonest you can see Isis about what we talked about?

"I got a concert tonight at the arena in Ft. Lauderdale. I can leave her tickets at the door with backstage passes."

"Nigga, you smoke so much weed you may forget you talked to me tonight," Logic said, half joking. "Have the tickets sent to her hotel with the passes in an envelope and leave them at the front desk with her name on it."

"Done," Breeze agreed. "Anything else?"

"If one of us comes up with anything, Isis will give you a call." Logic then told Isis, "Kill that line." The line went blank. "Now dial 555-6369."

The second person she got on the phone for Logic was an NBA player named Fonz. Logic shot a few quick words, and Fonz agreed to meet Isis within the next hour to discuss purchasing a few pieces of jewelry.

"Okay, now that we have that part straight, I need you to make one last call: 555-2106. Her name is Sly."

"Her?" Isis asked, with a tinge of jealousy in her voice.

"Yeah, she's a bitch," Logic said. "A loyal bitch at that. I need to get her to make sure that your transition is smooth to my world and Miami, being that you're fresh to the ways of the city."

Isis took offense. "I can handle myself." Even through the phone, Logic could tell that she had her hands on her hip when she said it.

"I know you can, Princess, but let's do it my way this time. Besides, Sly is like a sister to me."

Logic spent about seven minutes on the phone with Sly explaining to her how Isis was new to the area and how he needed her to watch out for her and make sure that she had everything she needed and or might think that she wanted. Sly agreed without hesitation, knowing good and well that Sly the Spy was going to be on her ass.

Chapter 18

The Fonz

Isis entered the luxurious lobby of the Loews Hotel with her leather show bag on her shoulder securing the pieces and designs that she was going to use to seal a deal with Fonz; a deal that would require him to wear her custom-made jewelry exclusively using his name and fame. This favor was exactly what she needed to launch her career, and Isis was confident that the danger she was putting herself in by tiptoeing across the lobby's slippery, marbled floor in four-inch Roberto Cavalli pumps would not be in vain. She was determined that the result of her meeting with Fonz would be her designs getting the attention they needed to catapult her into becoming the most sought-after jewelry designer on the East Coast.

Move over, Jacob the Jeweler . . . Ms. Ice is after your crown.

She had just stepped out of the women's bathroom, which seemed more like a personal dressing room for a superstar, after touching up her makeup. And now she was standing in the lobby where Fonz was supposed to meet her, trying to search him out. After a few minutes passed and there was no Fonz in sight, she whipped out her cell phone and dialed his number. How hard could it be to spot a six-foot-eight-inch basketball player in a hotel lobby?

Fonz was at the bar throwing back shots of cognac with a couple of his friends when his phone started vibrating. "Damn, who da fuck this?" Fonz spat as he pushed back a double. Glancing down at the screen he said, "Oh, shit, Logic's bitch. I forgot I was supposed to meet that ho about some damn jewelry."

"Fuck that bitch," one of his drinking partners riffed. "Who the fuck she think you is, Shaq or some shit? You supposed to front-man a jewelry line?"

"I'm feeling so lovely off this 1738 right about now, I just might." Fonz pushed the reject-caller button. "Fuck her." Then he called out to the bartender, "Hit me wit one mo', Joe."

Isis was only a few feet away from Fonz. If she'd turned around and looked behind her from the couch she had gotten comfortable on, she would have seen him and his entourage at the bar.

"You're kidding me, right?" Isis said to herself, staring down at her phone as she got Fonz's voice mail. *Calm down and take a deep breath, girl,* she coaxed herself. *He probably just didn't hear the phone ring or couldn't make it to the phone. He'll call my number back once he sees it on his caller ID.* After a few moments passed and Fonz hadn't called Isis's phone, she decided to try calling him again. *Remember, this is your dream. Other people don't make dreams happen. You got to make it happen.* Isis replayed Logic's words in her head

"Damn, this ho is relentless," Fonz stammered, after looking down at his vibrating cell phone at Isis's number showing up again. "Let me send this bitch on her way, 'fore she fuck 'round and blow my buzz." Fonz accepted the call, "Yeah, what's good?"

Isis was expecting a warmer and more welcoming greeting than the one she got. She didn't trip, though, because with him being an athlete, she figured he was used to groupies puffing him up. Chances are he had mistaken her for one of them. Not taking it personally, she returned his greeting. "Hello, Mr. Cottle, this is Isis, Logic's girl," she said in a professional tone. "I'm supposed to meet you today at eight PM to discuss the jewelry proposal."

"And?" he replied.

Shaking off his still nonchalant tone, Isis continued, "*And* I'm here."

"Is that shit so?" Fonz was talking to Isis as if she were a trick. In his inebriated mind, that's exactly what she was—Logic's trick.

"Yes, that's so, Mr. Cottle." Isis remained passive and professional, the same way she had been her entire life.

"Then where are you?" Fonz said, downing another shot and rising up out of his seat scanning the area. "I get wit y'all niggas in a minute," he said to his entourage, and then headed out of the bar and toward the lobby.

"Right here in the lobby," Isis answered, standing up from the couch, searching for him as well. Then when Fonz saw her, his entire demeanor changed.

Isis stood there in her Roberto Cavalli white jeans hugging her in all the right places, a matching blinged-out wife beater, and a pair of funky four-inch stiletto heels. Her hair was up in a big Chinese bun with one piece of hair dancing over her right eye. She looked like a superstar.

He looked her over a couple of more times, thinking that liquor was playing mind games with him; she couldn't be this fine. When he looked into her face, he became mesmerized by her beautiful round eyes and thick eyelashes. Logic's having sent her didn't change the asshole that Fonz was. He planned on keeping his word, letting Isis use his name to pilot her line. But just as with any other ho who got what she wanted out of him, he was going to fuck her first. "I see you, mamacita," Fonz said, hanging up the phone and walking toward her.

"So you want to design some jewelry for me, huh?" Without waiting for a reply, Fonz walked around Isis and boldly checked out her ass.

"Uh, yeah," she stammered. All of a sudden that confident stance she had used to strut across the lobby floor in hopes of fulfilling her destiny began to melt into a messy puddle at the feet of her Cavallies. "Yes." She feigned confidence and control as she turned around to face him. "Actually, I have a few things that I brought for you to look at." Isis cleared her throat and tapped her bag, indicating to him that that was where the pieces of jewelry were.

He smiled, licking his lips this time. "How bad?" he said.

"Excuse me?" she replied.

"You heard a nigga." Fonz took his index finger and gently rubbed the bottom of Isis's chin. It was gross, almost like he was caressing a woman's clit. "How bad you want it?"

Isis could smell the liquor on his breath, he was so close to her. "Look, Mr.—"

He cut her off. "Fuck all that formal shit. Call me Fonz. I know you here about business and trying to be all professional and shit." He pressed his lips against Isis's ear, "But I know what's up in those jeans of yours; the same thing that's up under every other bitch's suit that want a piece of the good ole Fonz-A-Freak."

Isis could have sworn that on completing his sentence, he quickly slithered his tongue in and out of her ear like a snake's. She'd had enough of the Fonz. She felt as if she were standing in the hotel lobby butt-ass naked and Fonz was the culprit who had torn her clothes off of her. And although Mr. Cottle was displaying the decorum of a potbellied pig, she still tried to remain professional. She stepped away from Fonz. "Listen, I think we should reschedule this meeting for another time, when you haven't had so much to drink." She gripped her case tightly and stormed out of the hotel, barely making it to the door before tears of anger flooded her eyes.

She was crying hysterically as she sat on the bench outside. She felt the same way she had felt that day in the courthouse when she stumbled on Bam's double life, as if she was having a panic attack. The deep breaths she was taking made her choke, causing her to feel as if she was about to vomit. Racing over to the trash can, she did just that. After she had thrown her guts up, one of the bellmen handed her his handkerchief. "Thank you," she said, just then realizing that some of the vomit had gotten on her shoes. *Fuck!*

Isis took off her shoes and left them right there in the puddle of puke. After all, they were no good to her in that condition. The thing that pissed her off the most about the shoes was that she wasn't going to get the chance to wear them when she went to visit Logic. He'd bought them for her before he got arrested. Maybe she would buy another identical pair.

Sitting there waiting for the valet to bring her car around, Isis began to think how Fonz made her feel, how much of an asshole he was. When the valet arrived with her car, she put her designs in the trunk. The bellman said, "Ma'am, we can refer you to a really good shoe place right here on the beach. They're amazing. Would you like for us to put your shoes in a plastic bag?"

"Sure," she said. "Can you watch my car for a couple of seconds, also? I'll be right back. I forgot something really important." And that she had. This would be the first time in a long time that she didn't remove herself from the situation.

Isis rushed back in to the hotel barefoot. Once the sweat on her feet made contact with the already slippery floor, she almost fell, but that didn't stop her from storming into the lounge, heading right for Fonz, who was standing up telling a story to his friends and some bystanders. He spotted Isis. "Oh, baby, you changed your mind, huh?"

Everyone turned their attention to her as if she was putting on a performance, so she didn't disappoint. She walked straight up to Fonz with as much grace as she could muster in bare feet, and then leaned in as if she wanted to whisper something in his ear. When he leaned his long torso in her direction to meet her halfway, he got something he wasn't looking for. Isis caught him square in the nuts with a hard knee lift. It folded him in two. "You fucking asshole," she screamed as she picked up a drink off the table, dumped it over his head, and stormed out of the hotel to her car.

"Miss, I managed to get some slippers for you as a courtesy of the Loews Hotel," said the guy whom she'd asked to watch her things.

"Thank you again," she said calmly, reaching into her pocketbook. She came out with a twenty-dollar bill. "This is for all your troubles."

As she pulled onto Collins Avenue her mind began to race. *What am I going to tell Logic tomorrow when he asks how things*

Chapter 19

Smooth Breeze

On Isis's drive back to her hotel, she wondered if Smooth Breeze would do what he said he would do or if he would be a jerk too and bullshit her because Logic wasn't there. As soon as she made it back to the Ritz, she went straight to the desk. "Do you have something for Isis Tatum?"

The young lady who was working the desk checked her notes and looked around. "I don't see anything. Can you tell me what I'm looking for?"

"It should be an envelope. Someone was supposed to drop it off just a little while ago."

"Do you go by any other name, Isis?" the clerk asked, trying to be helpful.

went? That I acted like a placekicker and used his homeboy's nuts for the football?

While she was still stuck in thoughts of the day's encounter, her cell phone rang, startling her. It was one of Smooth Breeze's boys, Tony, confirming that her pass was at the hotel. She was so frantic that she didn't know what to do, but there was one thing she knew, if she hadn't learned anything else, and that was that she wasn't going to allow herself to be in that situation again. On that note, she programmed her car's navigational system to the nearest Best Buy. From that point on, she would record every conversation that she had with any of Logic's people in case she needed to play it for him to analyze it or in case someone was lying on her to him. She would always be protected and have all the evidence she ever needed.

"Well, some of my friends call me Ice, but"—and then it hit her that her name was no longer Tatum—"Wiseman," she said. "Isis Wiseman. I was just married a few weeks ago. It takes a little getting used to."

"I understand," the clerk sympathized with her. "We do have a package under Wiseman, but I'm going to need to see some ID that at least has your first name on it."

After the woman was satisfied with the identification Isis had given her, she handed over the package. Just as Smooth Breeze had promised her, it contained an all-access VIP pass for the event. It didn't take Isis long to head up to her room, shower and change clothes, and then make her way to Ft. Lauderdale.

Once she got there, she saw that the arena was packed. People were everywhere: some just hanging out, some with tickets waiting to get in, but most of them were trying to get tickets to the sold-out event. People were looking so desperate, Isis was afraid to pull out her VIP pass. It felt like all eyes were on her when she strutted to the front of one of the lines.

When she reached the door, a security guard asked, "Who do you think you are?"

She flashed a Hollywood smile and pulled out her all-access pass. "Ms. Ice, darling" was her reply.

"Oh, I'm sorry," the guard apologized, "just doing my job."

Before, it had *felt* as if people were watching her; now, she was sure—people were staring. The groupies who stood around wishing that they were her rolled their eyes as the red-carpet treatment was given to her.

She pulled out her phone to call Tony, as Smooth Breeze had asked her to do when she arrived. Tony showed up and escorted her back to Breeze's dressing room—or dressing rooms, because he occupied three of them. One just had a few folding chairs set up in it, and to get into the next room, one would have to go past a 300-pound bouncer. As the bouncer moved to the side, Isis noticed that the room contained refreshments: Hennessy, Grey Goose, Patrón, orange juice, sodas, and ice. There was a table in the corner that must've been designated solely for rolling, because the punch bowl that was sitting on it was filled with strong-smelling weed. And there were two guys sitting at the table methodically wrapping the trees up in cigar paper, along with about seven more dudes sitting around shooting the shit at a room full of groupies. The chicks laughed at the corny jokes, trying hard to be noticed.

"Breeze will be out in a minute to get you," Tony said to Isis. "Meanwhile, just make yourself comfortable."

Two chicks in particular were giving her more eye attention than was required. "You here for Smooth Breeze?" one of them asked Isis, while the other looked on.

"Yes. Actually we have a meeting set up," Isis informed her.

"What kind of meeting?" the other skeezer asked.

She could still feel the ice daggers that they had been giving off at her since she'd stepped foot through the door. "Business," she said.

The first one spoke up again. "Chrissie, leave that girl alone. Look how she's dressed; you know good and well Breeze don't want her ass no way."

Isis looked down at herself. She knew that she looked cute. She was now wearing blue jeans—designed with pink stones—a white halter top, and $700 Emilio Pucci shoes. No, she wasn't dressed like a hoochie, but she definitely had her grown and sexy going on, unlike Chrissie, who was rail thin and dressed like a hooker trying to get a come-up on dollar day. Her friend really wasn't a bad-looking girl. She was actually rather cute with the one dimple and beauty mark on the left side of her face. But the outfit she wore was a different story altogether. The short, black spandex micro-miniskirt with no panties underneath was a bit over the top *and* tacky. And she had the nerve to sit with her legs gapped wide open. *She could have at least invested in a razor,* Isis thought.

"Well, boo," Chrissie announced to Isis, "I'ma tell you like this: I've been here since six o'clock waiting to give him some of the best brains south of the motherfucking border, okay?" Then she stood up so that she could look down on Isis. "And you or no other bitch gonna fuck that up for me, 'cause once I put my lips around his dick, baby, you gon' see my face in the tabloids with the words *Mrs. Smooth Breeze* printed under my shit."

Most of the dudes in the room started laughing. "Y'all bitches is crazy as shit," one of them said.

"Ladies, ladies," another said, "no fighting backstage."

Just then Smooth Breeze's boy peeked out the door and called Isis to the back.

"Remember what I said," Chrissie snarled as Isis stood up to walk in. There was no need for Isis to respond to the trifling ho, because *she* was where Chrissie wanted to be—in the dressing room! And she didn't have to get naked to do it.

The thick cush smoke gushing out of Breeze's dressing room almost knocked Isis down as she entered. He was sitting in a leather love seat sipping a drink with an ashtray close by. His dark chocolate complexion, black wife beater, diamond rings, and necklaces blended in with the black furniture like a chameleon.

"What's cracking, Ms. Ice? You want something to smoke?" Smooth Breeze asked, his bloodshot eyes beaming in on her as he patted a place beside him for her to sit.

She shook her head. "I don't smoke," she said, declining the marijuana and getting right down to business, just in case his attention span wasn't very long. "But I do want to help you step your jewelry game up."

Breeze took a long pull off one of the blunts, held the smoke in for what seemed like forever, and then exhaled. "You don't like my jewels?"

"They're"—she looked at them again, trying to find the right words to use so that he wouldn't feel insulted—"beautiful . . . for an upcoming rapper. But surely not for a big star like you."

He defended his style. "I paid a nice piece of change for this shit."

"The most expensive isn't always the best quality," she explained. "I can get you more bang for your buck; plus, the pieces will be one of a kind. A man of your status shouldn't have to share the same jewelry options as a kid on the block moving work." Isis knew that she was giving his overweight ego a lightweight workout, but he needed it. Or maybe she just wanted some get-back on somebody for the way Fonz had treated her earlier that night. "Your jewelry should say to your fans, 'I'm that nigga,' and to your peers, 'Step your game up or step out the game.' " She could tell by the gleam in his eyes that she had him interested.

"That's what's up!" He smiled. "If your work is as good as your sales game, I'm one lucky mu'fucka."

Now it was her turn to smile. "Then let me show you some of my work."

"Ain't no need." He put up his hand. "I believe you can turn straw into gold, or else Logic wouldn't be allowing me to spend some of the interest on his money with you to set it in motion." Somebody knocked on the door.

"We out of yak," one of the guys from the other room announced.

She reached for some of her designs, and just then, Breeze began to try to straighten out the situation.

"Yo, Tony, call that bullshit-ass promoter and tell him to get some fucking Rémy in this bitch or we're leaving." He then looked to Isis. "Work on something real fire for me and call me when it's ready." Then he noticed the wedding ring that she had designed for herself. "Goddaaamn." He covered his mouth in awe. "I see why they call you Ms. Ice." The ring was at least ten carats. "Yo shit is cold, Ma."

She laughed. "Thank you. Now, you want to see what I had in mind for you?"

He waved her off. "Surprise me when it's done. But I hope you stick around for the show."

Tony interrupted by poking his head in the door again. "Breeze, you got a couple of these groupies that's stuck on stupid until they see you. Ms. Ice, do you mind waiting in the other room for a sec?"

While she was getting her bag, Breeze went on to say, "I ain't really trying to see nobody else. I just want to do this performance and bounce."

"These bitches been out here since the doors opened," Tony said. "They beat the sound man here."

"I can give those hos an autograph and a picture, but after that, they got to get the fuck out of here."

Tony opened the door for Isis to leave, then called Chrissie in. "But my girlfriend is in the bathroom," she informed Tony.

"Well, you can go help the bitch wipe herself or you can go in and take a picture with Breeze."

"I'm going in." She looked back at one of the other guys to whom she had been talking. "Can you tell my friend to knock on the door when she gets back?" Then she rubbed the palms of her hands down the front of her outfit, trying to smooth it out, and waltzed in like a Naomi Campbell on crack.

Isis looked at Chrissie and chuckled to herself at the thought of Chrissie actually thinking that Smooth Breeze would marry her. *Wishful thinking, I guess.*

Chapter 20

Embracing Who You Are

Samantha was there to pick up Isis from the airport thirty minutes before the flight was due to arrive. Isis had told her that that wasn't necessary, that she could have taken a cab or rented a car, but Samantha wasn't having it. She hadn't seen her only niece in two months. The least she could do was pick her up.

Isis looked stunning walking down the corridor from the plane. Samantha was impressed with what the Miami sun had done for her. You couldn't get that out of a bottle or anybody's tanning salon: Her skin was almost flawless. And there was something else about Isis that Samantha couldn't quite put her finger on. She was glowing. That was it—Isis had an unmistakable glow.

For the first time, Samantha really grasped the fact that Isis was a full-grown woman.

She greeted her niece with a giant hug. "You look so sophisticated. That couture is definitely working for you, baby." Samantha was proud of the woman she had helped to raise.

"Thanks, auntie." As they walked down to the baggage-claim area, Isis said, "Take a look at this." She handed her a photo from the wedding.

"Oh, my goodness, chile, you all look so happy. I'm furious that you didn't include me."

"Don't be," Isis said. "I just didn't feel like hearing your mouth." Then she proceeded to imitate Samantha. " 'Are you sure about this? Do you know what you are getting yourself into? You know marriage is a big step and has to be taken seriously?' "

"Stop!" Samantha demanded. "You've made your point."

"I'll always love you, Samantha. But I'm grown now and I've gone through a lot. Sometimes I'm going to need your support, not your criticism."

Big bad Samantha shed a tear. "All I want to do is protect you."

"I know." Isis put her head against Samantha's arm.

Samantha changed the subject. "Well, I'm glad I didn't run into traffic on the way here, because I kinda got sidetracked getting the house together before I picked you up. I put clean linen on your bed just in case you are going to stay with me."

"Thanks a bunch. I really appreciate it."

A loud buzzer sounded off, alerting everyone that the luggage was about to start coming down the beltway to the carousel.

"That's my luggage right there," Isis pointed out. "The Louis Vuitton."

Don't get it twisted, Samantha was dressed in drag, looking nothing less than the glamorous woman that she had strived to be for over thirty years, but she hustled over to that luggage carousel and snatched those suitcases as if they were nothing more than feather dusters. In pumps, she still managed to man-handle the heavy bags and not let a piece of hair get out of place as they headed to the car.

"Damn, baby, you leave with no bags at all and return with two Louie suitcases and a Louie carry-on." Samantha got excited and started rolling her neck when she said, "And that Louie pocketbook is fierce! I hope your auntie can borrow it?"

"That's not a problem at all." Isis smiled while watching her aunt from behind her Gucci frames.

"It just shouldn't be—all that shit you used to sneak-borrow from me without my permission."

"I always put it back, though."

"You did," Samantha agreed, tossing the bags in the trunk. "But I don't know if I'll be able to say the same about that Louis." She winked as they headed home.

• • •

The christening was beautiful, but the after-party was even bet-ter. How could it not be? A bunch of gay men and women who used to be men, or still might have been men, were all there dressed to kill, all carrying presents to die for. The pink diamond earrings that Isis and Logic had gotten for Abigail were a big hit, prompting some of the guests to order a few pieces from her.

Isis could only imagine what Little Abigail's sweet-sixteen birthday party would be like, judging by the way her parents went all out for the christening. They had a full, open bar, and bite-sized caviar, stuffed shrimp, lobster, and crab cakes being served by model-thin women. All of this for a little baby girl who slept through the entire party.

Once the celebration was over, and as Ty and Anthony said good-bye to their guests, Isis and Samantha volunteered to stay and help the doting new parents clean up the mess.

"You know we must love you because, honey, we don't clean for anybody," Samantha said.

"We wait to be waited on and served." Isis plopped down on the plush sofa.

After everything was done, Abigail woke up crying, ready for her feeding. Isis held a screaming Abigail while Ty warmed up the bottle. Isis sat in the nursery with Ty as she fed the baby to get her back to sleep. Once Abigail was asleep, Ty and Isis went into the den while Samantha and Anthony drank and talked shit to each other.

"So," Ty said, pouring Isis a drink, "I haven't been able to sit you down and chitchat with you in over three or four years. Now that you're all grown up, you be on the move. You remember when I used to pick you up from school?"

"I do, and I miss talking to you too! I never told you this, but our talks used to mean so much to me."

"Remember, I used to always call you the chosen one? Well, I'm still always here for you."

"Yes, you always said that," Isis said. "But how come I feel like I am the cursed one?"

"Cursed? Why do you feel like that?" Ty asked as she got up to shut the door so that they could talk in privacy.

When Isis was growing up, Ty was always the person she ran to when Samantha got on her last nerve or when Isis couldn't have her way. She was always comfortable talking to Ty and knew that Ty always had her best interests at heart and wouldn't go running her mouth to her aunt.

She sighed, focusing on the long piece of hair that always

seemed to find a home over Ty's left eye, and just blurted it out: "It seems like every man I love has their life taken from them one way or another."

Ty took a sip from her drink. "How so?" she asked.

"Every man I ever loved either is killed or has life as they knew it taken from them. I feel like I have the curse."

"That's kind of extreme. Don't you think?"

"But true."

Ty moved the hair from her eye. "Can you give me an example?"

"Well, it started with my father," she said. "He was the first man I ever loved, and my mother killed him when I was thirteen years old. Then there was Dave. I know a lot of people say that I wasn't old enough to love like that then, but I did. And we both know what happened to him." This time Isis took a sip of her drink. "The state executed him."

"None of that was your fault, Ice."

"There's more. I lived with this guy name Bam for two years before he was sentenced to life in prison. He was a no-good piece of shit, but that don't change the fact that I loved him, and now he has to spend the rest of his life in prison."

Ty raised one of her eyebrows and continued to listen.

"But I didn't really start paying attention to it until I met this psychic."

"Psychic?"

"I met her when I was in Vegas. She told me that someone in my family would have a child named Abigail. That I would be married very soon, and my future husband would call me Princess. She also told me that everything about the number thirteen was bad luck for me. And guess what?"

"Sometimes those psychics are nothing but fakes," Ty said.

"And sometimes they're not. I got married to a man that called me Princess from the first day that he met me, and he was arrested—facing life—thirteen days into our marriage."

"Okay." Ty stood up. "Since you are listening to perfect strangers who call themselves psychics, do you want to hear my take on these things? Someone who loves you, someone who has known you since before you were born and watched you grow into a woman?"

"I've been waiting all night to hear it," Isis admitted.

Ty cleared her throat first and then said, "I honestly felt like you were one of the chosen ones ever since you were a little girl. There was, and still is, something special about you."

"Probably because I was the only one in the family with a curse. I feel like the Black Dahlia or something. Maybe Dave put it on me?"

"I don't think so, Ice."

"You should have seen the execution—how his expression *changed* on his face once he was dead."

"Maybe when they pronounced him as dead, he wasn't really dead," Ty shot back quickly.

"But I got this deep letter from him the morning after he was put to death."

"Dave probably mailed that letter out the day he was executed. Ice, all he probably wanted was to just *rest in peace*."

"Well, I have my own feelings. I think that all of these men are all somehow connected."

"Yes, they are, through you. You connect them."

"But it has to be more. Bam told me I would be cursed for taking his money. He said it was blood money. And guess how much money it was, Ty?"

"Thirteen dollars?"

"No," she said. "It was $313,000. And the bad part was that

he had someone break into our house and stole most of it back from me."

"Bam is a crazy son of a bitch behind bars that'll do anything to make your life as miserable as his is. And you let him get under your skin like that?"

"No, I don't."

"I don't know what to believe, but I know what I would do."

Isis looked at Ty. "Okay, I'm waiting."

"I don't want you to think I am trying to be mean, but I feel that maybe all this is a sign. Maybe . . . let's say maybe you *are* a black widow."

Isis didn't like the connotation of the words *black widow*. "A black widow kills men. I don't kill; their life is just taken in some kind of way."

"Well, listen; just hear me out." Ty rubbed her temples so that she could begin to explain what her thought process was.

"Okay."

"Well, let's say that you are the black widow."

Tears filled Isis's eyes.

"Listen to me before you get all emotional," Ty warned.

"It's hard not to get emotional."

"Why? What does being a *black widow* mean to you?"

Isis answered slowly and sadly, "That happiness will never come to me."

"I disagree." Ty put her hands on Isis's shoulders. "Get all of that stinking thinking out of your head and focus on what I am trying to say to you, nothing else. There's a difference between hearing and listening."

"I know. I'm listening to you," Isis said.

"When I realized that I was a gay man, I spent years pent up, suffocating in the closet. I was lying to everyone, including myself. But the minute I realized who I was, a woman trapped inside of a man's body, everything got clearer. I knew that and understood that the universe somehow had made a genetic mistake, but I was no longer afraid to announce it to the world. I embraced who I was! And no matter how much money Anthony brought home to me or how many diamonds and furs I had, I could never be at peace until *I embraced who I was*."

"So . . . what are you saying to me?"

"I'm saying, if you feel you are the black widow, then admit it to the world, embrace it . . . and most of all, profit from it. Make it your trademark. Make other women wish they could be you. Make them wish they had the balls to be you."

"Profit from it?" Isis was puzzled.

"Girl, if you know the niggas gon' die, at least start taking life insurance policies out on 'em," Ty joked.

Isis smiled.

"You need to be in power," Ty said. "Don't worry about men! They don't run shit. Make your mark doing whatever it is you want to do and know that we are all rooting for you!"

• • •

That night Isis couldn't sleep thinking about the pieces that Ty had dropped on her. She lay in bed anxious about what life had in store for her. As the new day came in, Isis was reborn. And so was her new jewelry line: the Black Widow.

Chapter 21

Born with a Veil

Isis was booked on a flight leaving Richmond International Airport at 5 PM en route to Miami, but before she headed out, she went to the prison to visit her mother again. Sandy had been locked up for ten years, and this would be only her second visit from her daughter, but it wouldn't be the last. The process she had to go through at the prison to see her mother went a lot smoother than it did the last time she was there, which was odd because there were a lot more people this time. She didn't even have to wait as long for Sandy to come out, which was great because Isis couldn't wait to put her up on all of the crazy stuff that had been going on in her life since the last time that she saw her. Well, maybe not everything.

Sandy listened to her daughter intensely and enjoyed every moment of it. She offered a little advice here and there but mostly listened. Sandy did tell Isis that she had gotten a few more letters from her ex-lover Ruby and that it would mean a lot to her if she called Ruby one day just to say hi. Isis said that she would.

Thirty minutes into their visit, corrections officer Wilma Buster walked up to their table and announced, "I'm sorry, but because of the overcrowding, all visits have been cut in half. I'm going to have to terminate your visit."

"Buster," Sandy said, "I'm not in the mood for your stuff today." All the prisoners knew that Buster could be a real a-hole when she wanted to be.

"Sandy, I know you don't see your daughter very often, so I wouldn't disrespect you like that. I've already put a couple of people out ahead of you." The guard looked at Sandy, at Isis, and then back to Sandy. "The best I can do is give you an extended visit the next time," she promised.

Isis cut in. "Ma, I need to get out of here to make sure I don't miss my flight back to Florida anyway. Call me sometime tonight, after eight, so that I can finish bringing you up to speed, okay?"

Sandy agreed, they hugged, and Isis hit the highway.

Besides the little boy who was sitting behind her making noise, Isis's flight wasn't that bad. The minute the plane landed and she powered her phone, it rang. She didn't recognize the number, but she answered. She didn't want to take the chance of missing a call from Logic just because she didn't recognize the number—maybe he was calling from somebody's three-way. "Hello?"

"Hey, Isis, this is Sly," the voice on the other end said.

"Girl, don't let me find out that you and Logic got a monitoring device on my ass somehow. I just got back in town."

"I wouldn't be surprised," Sly half joked, "but if your *ass* is bugged, I'm not privy to it."

"I was joking," Isis said.

"Well, I spoke to Logic earlier today. He wants me to meet with you."

"Meet with you for what?" Isis said, offended. "And why do I have to get messages from my husband through you?"

"First of all, the tier Logic is being held on had some type of riot or whatnot. Now the whole building is on lock, so he can't use the phone. Well, he's not supposed to use the phone, anyway, but he snuck to use the phone to call me," she said. "I know you don't know me from an ant on the sidewalk, but Logic and I have been friends for a long time. He's like a brother to me. He's really worried about you, and he's on my butt, hard, to make sure you're okay. So I beg of you to please let me help you out in some way: run some errands, drop some clothes off at the cleaners, watch your back 'round these shady-ass niggas . . . whatever."

Although Isis wanted to hear Logic's voice, she was also relieved that she didn't have to explain just yet why she almost turned his associate, Fonz, into a eunuch. Sly's plea touched Isis. "Okay, Sly, if you're like a sister to Logic, then you're my sister too." They made arrangements to meet in a couple of hours and ended the call.

Isis was happy to be at the condo again. Although she had been staying in first-class hotels, they were still hotels. She could never really feel comfortable at those places. People just stuck the key card—which no one but the assigned guest should have—in the door at all times of the day, asking if you wanted your room cleaned or the bed turned down.

This was the first time that she had been there since the police had arrested Logic. She was surprised that the place wasn't in shambles, but then again, they didn't have a search warrant—only a warrant for his arrest.

The first thing she did was forward all the calls from her cell phone to the house so that she could charge her cell phone. Then she started unpacking and separating clothes that needed to be washed from the stuff that had to go to the cleaners. She hit the power button on the television remote control and turned to the news to have a little background noise in the house. She hated when it was too quiet. In the movies, things got really quiet when something bad was about to happen.

The house phone rang. *Well, that didn't take long*, she thought. It was an out-of-area number. "Hello?"

An automated recording came on. "You have a pre-paid collect call from . . ." and then she heard her mother's voice say, "Sandy." The recording picked back up. "If you want to accept this call, press three. If you want—"

Isis hit the mute button on the seventy-inch television, and then pushed the number three button on the phone. "You got good timing; I just got in a few minutes ago."

"How was the flight?"

They laughed together when Isis told her about the bedeviled little white kid that kept throwing his toys at people and how he wouldn't stop crying when his mother took them away. They even found humor in the whole Wilma Buster thing, and how their visit got terminated early. Then Isis got quiet and changed the subject. "Mother, I need to talk to you about something serious."

Sandy was still envisioning the bad little boy on the flight, clunking people upside of the head with G.I. Joe men, or whatever it was the kids played with these days. "Okay, honey, what is it?"

Isis just put it right out there. "I think I'm a black widow."

Sandy hoped her daughter wasn't going crazy. "You think you are a spider?"

"No, not exactly," Isis said, and sighed.

"What's goin' on then, baby?" Sandy lowered her voice and said in a whisper, "You didn't murder anyone, did you?"

"Of course not, Mother." Isis explained all the things that had transpired in her life regarding the men she'd loved and the conversation she had with Ty. She told her everything, even the part about Ty thinking she was the chosen one—the whole nine.

Sandy was stunned by what she was hearing. "Baby, you are special, but that don't make you a bad person, nor does it mean that everything that has happened to those people is your fault," she said. "How can you blame yourself for what happened to your father? You were just a little girl."

"Of course you are going to say I'm special; you're my mother."

"Well, baby . . ." Sandy paused. "When you were delivered, the nurse at the hospital told your father that you were a baby born with the veil."

"What the heck does that mean?"

"It means that you are special."

"It means that I am possessed, that's what it means."

"No, it doesn't, but—"

Isis jumped in. "I mean, Mommy, it's like once I love a man with all my heart, giving him a part of me, it's his destiny: life in prison or no life at all."

"If you're going to convince yourself that you are cursed," her mother said, "at least tell me what you plan to do about it."

"For starters, I'm not going to run from it. It's like when someone's dog charges at you; the owner usually says that if you don't run, then it won't bother you. Well, that's how I feel about this," she said. "I'm going to embrace it. I'm not going to run."

"And how are you going to embrace it?" Sandy wanted to know.

"I'm going to make this thing pay off, that's how. From now on, I'm going to call all of my designs Black Widow Jewels. And in all of my pieces, I'm going to put a spider web where the gold stamp would normally go."

"That's a great idea, Isis."

"And from this day forward, I'm only going to wear all black or all white. I do wear a lot of black and white now, but I am going to not half-step on it—only black or white."

"Okay." Sandy smiled although she didn't quite think that this is what the person who created the old cliché "If life hands you lemons, make lemonade" had in mind. But at least her baby was creative.

"If I am feeling shitty or in a kick-ass mood, then I will wear black. But if I am in a good mood or whatnot, I'll rock all white."

"I get it," her mother added. "It's like a 'white reveals and black conceals' type of thing."

"I hadn't thought about it that way, but . . . yeah."

"I think it's a great way to flip something negative into something positive."

Isis was distracted by the television when she saw a conservatively dressed lady who looked very familiar to her walking from the courthouse. Then a mug shot of Smooth Breeze flashed on the screen. Next, they showed a small piece from one of his concerts. Isis searched for the remote. "Ma, hold on." She took the television off mute and turned the volume up.

The anchorwoman said, "It could be a while before the highly anticipated junior album from Smooth Breeze is released because of the startling charges filed against the Grammy award–winning rapper today. He's being charged with sexual battery and forcible sodomy of a college student named Chrissie Berry, who was interviewed earlier by Jaqueline Doss."

"He was my favorite rapper," she cried. "All I wanted was an autograph and a picture. He took my virginity!"

"Oh my God," Isis gasped out loud, recognizing his accuser. "I can't believe this shit! Ma, I gotta call you back . . . I mean you gotta call me back. . . . Just call me back later, Ma."

"Is everything okay?" Sandy was worried.

"No. I mean yes."

"Which is it, Isis? You're scaring me."

"Okay." Isis took a deep breath. "You remember the rapper I told you I went to see? I saw this little hoochie throwing herself at him, and now she's taking him to court for rape."

"Rape?"

"Look, Ma, just call me back tomorrow."

She hung up the phone and flipped the TV channel to another news broadcast. They were covering the same story. The reporter stated, "The camp that rapper Smooth Breeze sponsors for the underprivileged children of Dade County has canceled a banquet in his honor pending the outcome of these charges, and the parade scheduled for next week to give him the key to the city has been postponed until further notice. It looks like the only numbers that he is going to be counting if found guilty are the jail numbers stenciled on his state-issued jumper."

Isis was stunned. She ignored the ringing phone until she viewed the caller ID and saw that it was the number of Phoebe's mother's house. What was her sister doing back in Richmond? The last time Isis had checked, she was supposed to still be in Texas.

"Hey, sister," Isis answered.

"This isn't your sister, Isis. It's Brenda." This was the last person Isis thought would be calling her.

Hearing her sister's good-for-nothing mother almost made her teeth itch. Isis didn't have anything to say to that woman, and she didn't want to hear anything that woman could possibly have to say to her. Isis was about to hang up the phone dead smack in her ear until a thought entered her head: *What if something has happened to Phoebe?* Brenda had always hated Isis because she was Ice's child by another woman, and she was jealous of the fact that Isis had a stronger relationship with her own daughter than she did.

"What's wrong, Brenda?" Isis asked. "Has something happened to Phoebe?"

"Yes," Brenda replied. "Your sister has lost her mind, that's what has happened to her."

"Why do you say that?"

"You need to talk to her," Brenda said, ignoring Isis's question.

Isis was tired of Brenda jacking off her time. If something was seriously going on with her sister, she wanted to know. "Talk to her about what? Just tell me what's wrong."

"She's down there in Texas messing with that guy, and he's whipping her ass. That's what's wrong."

"W-whaaat?" Isis's voice got louder.

"I don't know what to do." Brenda broke down crying. "I think he's going to kill her," she said in between sobs. Although Isis disliked Brenda with a passion because of how she'd tried to keep her and Phoebe apart by hating on their relationship, it wasn't until Isis was older when she really understood that if Brenda hadn't been such a bitch that day Sandy had showed up on her doorstep, then that day might have turned out very differently. Even so, Isis almost felt kind of sorry for Brenda just then because she had never heard Cruella De Vil show any kind of real emotion except hate and anger. But not quite. Fuck Brenda. All she wanted to know was the business with her sister.

"Brenda, how do you know that this man is puttin' his hands on Phoebe?"

Brenda wasn't really feeling the fact that Isis was asking her all these questions. She smacked her lips and replied, "Because her cell phone called me by mistake last week and I heard it with my own ears, him fighting her, although I've suspected it for a couple of months now."

Isis couldn't believe that Brenda had withheld this information for an entire week. "Why did you wait this long to let me know?" Isis wanted to know. "What if he *had* killed her?"

"It's all my fault," Brenda said.

Isis thought, *You're probably right.* But she said, "No, it's not," trying not to make her sound as bad as she was probably already feeling.

"Yes, it is. I've nagged at her so much that it drove her away. I taunted her about everything: getting a career, going to college so she can meet a rich man, doing something with herself. And when she didn't make the cheering squad, I rubbed it in." She paused before continuing, "She'd rather stay there with that guy and get her ass whipped than come home and listen to me tell her 'I told you so.' "

Isis's jaw tightened and her eyes became moist with anger. Just the thought of her sister getting smacked around was enough to make her blood boil. And the fact that all this time she'd thought that her sister had made the squad.

Brenda continued walking down memory lane and blaming herself. "It's entirely my fault—if I wouldn't have been so greedy, Sandra wouldn't have killed Ice, and he'd be here. He woulda never let his two girls go through the shit y'all have been through. Ice wanted y'all to be strong black women. He didn't want y'all to be submissive to no man. He wanted y'all to stand up for y'allselves, not be tied up in the web of these menfolks that don't mean y'all nothing but trouble."

Talking about Ice made Brenda feel a little better about the entire situation, but it also gave Isis a little more insight about how her father viewed life and wanted things to be mapped out for his daughters.

"Brenda, I got to get off the phone. I'm gonna call Phoebe."

"She's not gon' come clean," Brenda said. "She knows how to play it off over the phone."

"Then I'll fly to Texas," Isis insisted. "She's wanted me to go there anyway. I promised her I would."

"Thank you." Brenda actually sounded appreciative. "Will you keep in contact with me, please? I am really worried."

"I will keep you posted," Isis promised.

Isis got Brenda's cell phone number, and then hung up. She sat on the edge of the bed wondering why she hadn't had any indication of what her sister was going through. She knew they hadn't talked lately as much as they used to, but she had chalked it up to the fact that they both were entering new phases of their lives. Isis picked up the phone and dialed her sister's number anyway, just to feel her out.

The call went through. It rang a few times, and then Phoebe answered in a soft, low voice. "Hello."

Her voice sounded a little pitchy, so Isis asked, "You crying?"

"No. I was umm . . ." Phoebe seemed to stall for a moment. "I was asleep."

She's never been able to lie to me worth shit, Isis thought. "I was just calling because I wondered what you were going to be doing over the next few days."

"Uh, why?"

"Sister, can you talk, or are you busy?" Maybe someone was listening or monitoring her calls, so Isis wanted to give her sister the benefit of the doubt.

"No, I'm not busy or anything like that."

"Then why you sound so distant?" Isis asked. Phoebe sounded more and more suspect by the minute.

"I'm just tired; told you I was sleeping when you called," she snapped.

"Well, you never answered my question. What are you doing in the next few days?"

"I'll be caught up doing a lot of stuff here," Phoebe said. "Pretty much housebound."

"Then call me back later once you're more awake. And sister . . . I love you."

"Me too." Phoebe quickly hung up the phone.

The entire conversation was very awkward. Something definitely wasn't right. It was final: Isis was going to the Lone Star State to see her sister, right after she took care of a few things in Miami.

As soon as Isis got off the phone with her sister, she called Tony. She hit his number three times; the first two times the calls went straight to voice mail, but he picked up on the third. She could hear in his voice that he didn't really want to talk, but she told him that she had some information that could save the day. This got his attention.

"Where y'all staying?" she asked him.

"We moved to the Sheraton in Bal Harbour," he told her.

"I'm going to send you a package with a few important things in it," she said. "Be sure to call and let me know as soon as you get it."

The next call was to Sly. Isis asked Sly to meet her at the Ritz-Carlton Hotel in South Beach.

Isis was sitting in the hotel restaurant when she saw Sly walk through the door. She recognized her by the white-and-yellow L.A. Lakers Kobe Bryant jersey she said she would be wearing. Sly looked nothing like Isis expected. For some reason she thought the girl would be some big burly chick. Sly was the total opposite, all skin and bones. She was light-skinned and looked sort of Spanish with long coal-black, curly, bushy hair. It looked like her hair might weigh more than she did.

Isis raised her hand in the air to get Sly's attention. It worked. As Sly walked over to the table where Isis was sitting, she understood why Logic was so head over heels for this girl. She was breathtaking, and the all-white Capri outfit looked marvelous on her. Sly sat at the table, told the waitress to bring her a glass of water, and then addressed Isis for the first time in person.

"Please tell me you got something for me to do," Sly begged. "I have to tell Logic something when I talk to him again. And I can't lie to him."

"I'm glad that you asked. First, I'm going to need you to take me to an Anne Fontaine so I can get some white shirts."

"No problem. That's in Bal Harbour."

"Good. Do you know where the Sheraton is from there?"

"Yeah, it's right across the street from there."

"What about a Hallmark store?" Sly had been twisting her hair between her fingers ever since she'd arrived. Isis wondered how long she'd had that habit.

"One of those shouldn't be far from there either," she answered.

"Okay. Then while I'm in the Anne Fontaine, I need you to deliver a package to my boy, Tony. He's staying at the Sheraton, and the package is very important, so you gotta make sure he has it in his hands before you leave.

"I'm going to Texas to check on my sister tonight, and I'm not sure exactly how long it's going to take. But for every day that I'm away, I want you to send Logic a card from me."

"That's not a problem either."

"I'll pick the cards out and sign them before I leave. That way all you'll have to do is drop them in the box so that Logic can get mail every day so that he knows I am thinking of him."

"He already knows that. Trust me, if he didn't, you would be just some miscellaneous chick. Believe what I am telling you. Logic has never been caught up over no woman before, and I've known him a long time." Sly took a deep breath and then said, "Anyway, though, mailing those cards are small things. Count it as done. Anything else?"

"Not right now," Isis said, "but thanks, girl."

"If there's anything that you think of while you're in Texas, please feel free to call me."

"Okay." She smiled, knowing deep down that she had just met a real live thorough chick. A lot of people made the mistake of underestimating Sly because of her small stature, but no one ever made that mistake twice. She was stronger than a lot of men twice her size, and she was a crack shot with a pistol. The latter was thanks to her father, who'd taught her how to shoot when she was only ten years old. Isis was happy to have her on her side.

Chapter 22

The King of Texas

Isis's flight had landed in Texas earlier that morning, so she had decided to stay at the Westin Galleria Hotel and start on her save-a-sister mission—if she needed saving—first thing in the morning. It was now a little after 10 AM. Isis had called Phoebe's phone several times, but she wasn't answering. Undiscouraged, Isis looked in the phone book for a car service. As her driver pulled the car up to the house for which Brenda had given her the address, they passed a couple of Mexicans working in the yard. They kept going around the winding road, up to the main house. Just when she was thinking that this might not be the right house, she saw a cute wooden sign with the name *Vanz* engraved into it. This was it. *Little sis is living large!*

Isis stood on her sister's doorstep and pressed the long chiming doorbell. Just like the phone, no one answered. She was about to turn around and leave when an older Asian lady opened the oversized front door with a blank look on her face.

"Yes?"

"Hello." Isis smiled at the lady. "My name is Isis Tatum; I'm Phoebe's sister."

The lady stood there holding the door, giving Isis a cold look. "And?"

"*And* I came to see her," Isis said calmly. "I'm not sure about how it's done in your country, but here in America, it's very customary for siblings to visit one another. Now is she here or not?"

Although Isis didn't raise her voice despite her anger, the lady saw something in her eyes that said, *I ain't to be fucked with today.*

"She no expecting you?" The Asian woman tried to look past Isis to see if anyone else was with her.

"No, she wasn't."

"She no say she expecting any company."

"That's because she didn't know. It's a surprise." Isis threw her hands up and said, "Surprise!" hoping the woman would catch on. Instead the woman just stood there with the same old blank face. "She does live here, right?" Isis said, while nodding her head. "Phoebe here? Phoebe live here?"

"Yes, but her not here."

"Do you know where she is?" Isis paused when she heard the grandfather clock inside the mansion strike noon. She and Phoebe used to always talk about getting an antique clock like that. "Do you mind if I wait?" Isis suggested, not giving up that easy.

"She back late. But I tell her call you."

She really wasn't satisfied with the outcome, but other than knocking the frail woman down and storming the place, what could she do? "Please do. Thank you," Isis said.

She went back to the Lincoln town car thinking that she had seen crack stash houses that weren't that hard to get into. Then she stopped. She had a strong feeling that someone was watching her from behind, but when she turned around, there was no one at the door or the windows. She disregarded the feeling and climbed in the car.

She told the driver, "You can take me back to the hotel." She was going to lie down, then get up and do a little shopping, and wait on Phoebe to call.

Despite the mall's being packed and her worrying about her sister, Isis felt that her shopping trip went quite well. She was carrying several bags from Versace, Ann Taylor, and Louis Vuitton when she stepped into the Gucci store. Before both her feet could cross the doorsill, a little blond saleslady walked up to her. "Hi. Welcome to Gucci. Is there anything that I can help you with?" The only other customers in the store were three guys, and it looked like only one of them was actually buying anything.

"Yes, I'd like to see everything you have in white or black," Isis stated.

"Everything?" the saleslady asked.

"Everything," Isis answered without batting an eye.

The saleslady was taken aback; it wasn't every day that someone came in with a request like that. "Uh, no problem. I'm just going to need your sizes; then give me a few minutes to go in the back to pull out some of the hot things that may not have hit the floor yet." Before she walked away she said, "Oh, my name is Sarah. Just call my name if you should need anything else." The saleslady headed to the back of the store, past the chattering guys who were trying on shoes.

Sarah whispered into the ear of one of the three salesmen who were in conversation with the male customers. The salesman immediately headed over toward Isis and started helping her pick out stuff from the racks and shelves. Sarah carried out some other items as well.

Isis tried on a few pairs of shoes, looked at them from different angles, took a couple of steps in each pair, and fell in love with them. "I'll take all three of these," she said. "Do they come with matching belts or bags, Sarah?"

"Yes." Sarah turned to the new woman whom she was training. "Sue, will you go get the two belts that I showed you earlier . . . the ones that match these shoes?"

Sue nodded and turned to do as she was asked.

"Oh, and, Sarah, I need a white baseball hat and white sneakers—the ones you have on display, I'm not loving. Can you call Karen at the Forum Shops in the Vegas store and see if they have any different ones?"

"I sure can," Sarah said, impressed by Isis's knowledge of their other stores and managers in different states.

Isis gave orders, and everybody in the store knew that today was their lucky day because they were dealing with a lady who knew what she liked and wanted. All attention was on Isis when she pranced around the store in a pair of brown stiletto sandals and asked, "Do you have these in white, Sarah?"

"I don't think we do," she said. "I know we have them in a reddish color."

"No. I need them in either white or black."

"What about blue?" the new girl jumped in. Sarah looked at her as if she was crazy. She would have to have a talk with her later.

"Either black or white, and with these," Isis looked at the shoe, "I would love to have them in white."

"I can try to make that happen," Sarah said, "but I may need a couple of days."

"No problem. I'll leave you my card."

One of the guys who had been trying on shoes was on his way to the register to finalize his purchase. He had been watching the attractive young lady buying everything in the two colors and was curious, so he stopped and asked, "What's up with all the black and white?"

Isis never looked up from Sarah, who was buckling up a pair of black sandals for her. "That's all I wear," she answered.

"Is there a reason for that?" he asked.

Isis looked up and noticed the guy's features for the first time. He was six feet tall and wore a long diamond necklace with a seriously blinged-out diamond cross pendant that rested on his beer gut. He wore long, neat, skinny shoulder-length dreads that really brought out his reddish-brown complexion.

"Yes." She answered his question while standing up to see how the sandals felt on her feet.

"Care to share?"

She walked over to the mirror. "The world is either black or white. You do or you don't. Will or you won't. There really is no gray area." She stared down at the mirror to see how the heel of her foot looked in the shoes. "So it doesn't make much sense to me to have color in my wardrobe."

"Makes a lot of sense." He nodded. "So your entire closet is in black and white."

"Every inch," she confirmed.

"Damn. You seem like a diva. So how do you manage with such limited choices?"

"If you've got it in colors," she said, "I've got it in white or black. If not, I can get it."

Sarah spoke up. "I think you've been through just about everything we have, and I'm going to check on the sneakers and the other pair of sandals for you. Will there be anything else I can do for you?"

"That's it for me, Sarah. I'm ready to get out of here," Isis told her.

Everything that Isis had chosen during the hour-and-a-half-long spree was taken to the front of the store and rang up by Sue. "That'll be $7,462.53," she announced. "Will that be cash or charge?"

Isis pulled out her credit card to pay for her purchase, and there was Mr. Beer Belly again. "I'm sure you're probably charging this shopping spree to your husband's account today, but when you're ready to shop with the real king of Texas, make sho' you call me, ya heard?" He handed her a piece of paper with his number on it. "Some call me the emperor of the South."

"Okay, *emperor*, I hear you." She took his number. "And I will call you. I'm sure we can discuss some business somewhere down the line. I design jewelry." Isis felt as if she might have landed a potential big-spending new client, judging by the looks of his chain. "I'm going to lock your number in my phone."

"You do that." He smirked.

Sarah cut in. "Did you use valet parking, ma'am?"

"No. I'm staying at the Westin."

"Then would you like for me to have your packages sent over?"

"That would be good," Isis agreed.

"Can I ask you a question?" Sarah asked.

Isis stopped in her tracks and looked at her. "What is it?"

"When you decided that you were not going to wear any colors, what did you do with all your colorful clothes that you did have?"

"Well, I took them to the battered women's shelter and dropped them off for the ladies in need. Brand-new stuff, some of it, because not too long before, I had just got an entirely new wardrobe. But it didn't matter. Someone blessed me with a lot of nice things, and I wanted to pay it forward."

"That's sweet. Well, have a nice day, and please come back and see us."

"I will."

She had left the Gucci store and was passing the ice-skating rink inside the mall when she saw the light on her phone indicating that she had messages. Her phone service wasn't working in certain parts of the mall, so some of her calls had gone straight to voice mail.

There were three missed calls and one of them was from her sister. "Hi, sister. I got the message that you had came by. I'm so mad at you because I wish you would have told me. Randy and I went to Seattle to meet with one of his endorsement sponsors, so I am not in Texas and I won't be back for another four days. However, you can hang around if you wish, or we can just see each other another time. Love ya. Call me!"

That was what she got for coming all this way unannounced. She tried dialing her sister back, but the call went to the voice mail. *Shit!* Sly was one of the other people who'd called, so she hit her back. She probably had a message from Logic.

"Hey, Sly, what's up girl?" While she was talking, she watched as the king of Texas made his way through the mall with his boys in tow carrying his bags. *Emperor?*

"Good. What about you?" Sly asked.

"Girl, can you believe my sister ain't even in the state?"

"What?!" Sly exclaimed in disbelief. "Where is she?"

"In Seattle. I went to her house, and the housekeeper wouldn't even let me in," she said. "Anyway, why did you call?"

"When I called, I had Logic on the phone. He tried calling you himself, but your phone went to voice mail. But you need to get back here quick."

"What did he say?" Isis became alarmed. "Is he okay?"

"He's cool. He's just worried about you. Cursed me out for letting you go OT by yourself. From now on, you can't travel alone anymore."

Isis brushed Sly off. "I hear you."

"Plus, that dude Tony called me and said he'd tried to reach you too. You know, when I went up there to meet him, I called him from my phone, and I guess he saved the number."

"Did he say what he wanted?"

"Yeah, he said that he needed you to have Breeze's jewelry straight by Friday because that's when he's having the press conference."

"Friday?" Isis said in shock. She'd figured that the last thing that would be on Breeze's mind was some jewelry. Guess she'd thought wrong.

"Yeah, Friday!"

"Sly, today is Tuesday." Isis thought fast. She could e-mail the idea she had come up with for Breeze to Ricco, one of her jewelers in New York. He could have the piece made in two days and overnight it back to her in Miami by Friday. She didn't have any room for error, and it would be pushing it close, but it was doable.

"Well, all I can say is that you need to be on the first thing smoking back to Miami or wherever you got to go to get that shit right." Sly switched gears. "Also, Logic said he's going to try to call back tonight, so make sure you pick up."

"Okay," Isis said. She then turned to walk the other way to

head toward the Westin. "I'm on my way back to my hotel; I'll call you back with my travel plans."

After hanging up the phone, Isis realized that she was lost. Finally making it to the Westin's entrance, she noticed a nice car, which was nothing unusual for Texas, especially at this hotel. She thought it was a Bentley Azure but couldn't be sure. Then *he* got into it, Mr. King of Texas himself. She watched from a distance knowing that one day she'd be driving one of those, and it would not be a present from a man. It would be from the success of Black Widow Jewels.

Chapter 23

The Black Angel

The following day, Isis caught the first flight bound for the sunshine state. Sly picked her up from the airport with all of Isis's dry cleaning in the car. She also had a list of questions that she wanted to ask to make Isis's life as easy as possible so that she could meet the deadline for Smooth Breeze.

As Sly was running off the questions, she suddenly stopped. "Why are you smiling?" Sly asked. "Did I say something funny?"

"No," Isis said. It's just that you remind me of my sister." Then the thought of Phoebe possibly being in trouble upset her.

"I can't wait to meet her. She sounds like a real cool girl."

"She is," Isis said, wondering what was really going on with Phoebe. Why was she shutting her out?

"Ice, you okay?"

"Yeah, just thinking about my sister, that's all."

. . .

Sly took Isis home to change clothes and get ready to go visit Logic. When Logic walked out and sat in the chair behind the glass, Isis lit up. His muscular body was even more toned than before he'd gone in, and he looked genuinely happy to see her. He picked up the telephone that was used to talk through the glass. She picked up hers.

"So how are you?" he asked.

"I'm fine," she said. "Things are moving along pretty much like you said they would."

"Have you spoken to Breeze since they hit him with the charges?" he asked her.

"He didn't do it, Logic."

"How do *you* know he didn't?"

Isis told him about how she had met the girl who was pressing the charges—in Breeze's dressing room the night she'd gone to talk business with him at the arena. "They were in there talking about how they planned to suck and fuck the man all the way to the altar," she went on to say. "I got the whole conversation on my digital recorder."

"Digital recorder?" he asked. "When you started playing PI?"

"After meeting your friend Fonz, actually." Isis then told him about how she had had to knee the man for acting like a complete asshole and how she was afraid that he wouldn't believe her version of what happened, so she'd made the decision to record everyone she spoke to from then on. "I sent the recording to Smooth Breeze's people, so he should be all right. He's supposed to have a press conference on Friday, and he wants to wear one of my pieces."

"That's what's up, Princess," Logic said, congratulating her. "The other thing was my fault. I should've warned you about Fonz . . . he can be a piece of work. I thought he would know better than to try that shit on someone I sent, but maybe I forgot to mention that you were my wife. Don't worry, though; I'll get someone to handle that." He changed the subject. "What about my car? Is it somewhere safe?"

"I had it transported to Richmond like you asked, and my Aunt Samantha is going to put it in storage and send me all the paperwork."

Logic smiled. "Nothing rattles you, huh?"

Isis thought about the first day Logic had called her when she had just found out that Bam had taken everything that she owned aside from the clothes on her back, the suitcase she took with her to Las Vegas, and the twenty thousand dollars that was left over from the trip. She had thought it was the end of the world. "Yes, I rattle," she said. "But I try not to let it shake me apart."

They talked about a few other things before one of the guards walked up behind Logic and said, "Time's up." The hour had flown by, and it was time for Isis to leave.

• • •

It was 10:52 Friday morning, the day of Smooth Breeze's press conference. Isis had been on the phone and e-mailing back and forth with Ricco the previous night to get the piece of jewelry ready for her client. She wished that she would've had a little more time to do the thing herself, but that was not the case. Her heart was beating pretty fast as she knocked on Smooth Breeze's hotel room door.

Tony answered the door with a smile and a big hug, then he invited her inside. "Thank you, Ms. Ice, for everything."

Isis checked out her surroundings. Smooth Breeze and his crew were staying in a three-room suite that contained two bedrooms and a large conference room. The ever-present weed smoke was thick in the air, and the same guy who'd been doing the rolling the night she'd met them at the arena was still taking care of his business. She wondered if he ever stopped rolling blunts, or was it a never-ending job?

It was apparent that they had been staying there for a while because tags from new clothes, liquor bottles, and food containers were all over the place—the floor, the coffee tables, and all points in between. The maid would definitely have her work cut out for her—*if* they ever let the poor lady in to do her job.

"I thank y'all for allowing me to show the world my talent," she said. "You are welcome. I don't know if I told you or not, but my business's name is Black Widow Jewels. Smooth Breeze will be the first to wear a piece from the Black Widow collection."

Smooth Breeze walked in from the main bedroom, and his face took on a humongous grin. "Is this my favorite jewelry designer or my lead defense attorney? I'm going to have to write you two checks."

"It's me," she said, "the Black Widow, in the flesh."

"Well, I just want to tell you thanks again and to suggest that maybe you should change your name from the Black Widow to the Black Angel." Breeze talked more freely to her today than he had the first couple of times they had met. "I don't think you fully understand how you went on some Janice Cochran shit and saved the goddamn day."

"For real, I'm just glad I had what you needed to clear your name. Hos like that give real women a bad name," she admitted. "Then people want to know why you make a record calling a bitch a bitch. It's self-evident."

"You know what's crazy, though?" Breeze asked.

Isis was almost afraid to ask. "What?"

"I don't normally even fuck with them groupie chicks like that." Isis gave him a "Nigga, please!" look, so Breeze looked toward Tony, and Tony shook his head, acknowledging that he was telling the truth. Breeze continued, "I break my rule and give it to this chick like she wants it. Excuse my lack of modesty, but it is what it is, and this is what I get in return. And you want to know why she told Tony she was gon' send my red ass to prison?" He looked toward Tony. "Tell her, T."

Tony looked Isis directly in the eye. "She said that she almost choked sucking and drinking all the cum from that skinny red nigga's big-ass dick, and he didn't even ask for her phone number when she was done."

"Yeah, she came at me like a ho, so I treated her like one," Breeze confirmed. "Then the bitch tried to Tupac me. And you see how fast the media jumped on it: like an alcoholic to a fifth of Seagram's Gin. Innocent until proven guilty, my ass. Before the ink was even dry on the allegations, the whities started pulling the plug on my endorsements." He poured himself a drink. "It was only one thing that bitch said that wasn't a lie."

Isis was curious. "What was that?"

Smooth Breeze smiled. "She said that she was going to give me the best mother fucking brains I ever had in my life."

"If you wouldn't have come forth with that tape, he would've been fucked up in the game for sure," Tony added.

"I am glad I could be of help. Just do me one favor?" Isis said.

"Anything," Tony said.

"Don't let it leak that you got the evidence from me. People might not want to talk to me if they think they might be recorded."

"Fair enough."

"Well, let's lighten the conversation some," she said. "Let me show you what I have for you." She pulled out a medallion laced with black and yellow diamonds. It had the word *Bitches* with a slanted bar going through it. The word was spelled out in yellow diamonds, and the bar that ran across it was in black diamonds. The necklace itself was constructed of the same color diamonds. And of course there was a twenty-two-carat diamond ring to match.

No one spoke as Tony and Breeze looked over the pieces. Isis was afraid that they didn't like them. Then Breeze broke the silence. "Daaamn! You ain't playing with this shit, are you?"

"And neither should you." Isis smiled.

"You are my exclusive jeweler for now on," he said.

"Good. Then I can give you this as my gift." She pulled a fifteen-carat bracelet of black and yellow diamonds from her pocketbook and handed it to him.

"Ice. I mean, Black Widow . . . you outdone yourself. It's a good look. The glare from these bad boys might crack the damn TV camera lenses at the news conference."

"That's the idea."

"When can you have something for my boys?"

"I thought you would never ask. I'm going to leave these pictures." Isis laid down a rhinestone photo album containing photos of jewelry designs. "Just have someone give me a call and let me know what they like," she said. "And good luck at the news conference. Now I have to be leaving."

Breeze went to his press conference, which turned out quite successfully. He was later cleared of all allegations concerning the incident with the alleged victim, but a new controversy arose over why he would wear a necklace that described women in such a degrading manner. Breeze told the press that the necklace didn't have anything to do with women. Women never did anything but show him love. He said his beef was strictly with bitches, and he would appreciate it if the bitches would stop putting real women in their fight. "And for the women," he said, "you know who you are. Shout-out to my jewelry designer, Ms. Ice, icing me out with an exclusive Black Widow original. If it ain't got the spider stamp, it ain't original—ya heard!"

That was the jump start that Black Widow Jewels needed. Isis got a lot of calls about her jewelry, and the media went bananas wanting to know why she'd named herself and her work after a deadly spider. The press wanted to talk. But as it always does, the fame came before the fortune.

Chapter 24

A Sister's Cry

Phoebe and Randy Vanz had met while she was trying out for the Dallas Cowboys Cheerleaders. They had gone out a couple of times, but it was nothing serious. Cheerleaders weren't supposed to date the players anyway. But after Phoebe got cut from the team, it was a different story altogether. Her self-esteem was bruised, and she needed a man's attention to soothe the pain.

Randy was supposed to have been the number-one pick when he came out of the draft, but he broke his leg during the last game of his college career. He ended up being picked in the fourth round and was the third-string running back. What should have been a multimillion-dollar contract ended up being a $600,000 a year blow to his ego. He was mad. And he took his frustrations out on his new girlfriend.

Phoebe and Randy had had dinner earlier that evening. They were back at home, and Randy watched as Phoebe undressed in front of the mirror. He was always watching. Phoebe noticed that she had put on a few pounds over the past few months. How could she not? Randy's controlling behavior kept her cooped up in a four-million-dollar house that he couldn't afford but had to have. There was nothing for her to do all day except watch movies and eat. Her only opportunity to get out alone was during the day while he was at practice. Even then, she knew he had people watching her. Whenever she did something outside of the perimeters he had set for her, he corrected her in that good old Ike Turner way. And recently the beatings had gotten so bad that she didn't want to go out anyway, because she could barely hide the bruises that she was constantly nursing.

"Why did you order that cake tonight at dinner for dessert?" Randy asked.

She knew that he was looking for a reason to hit her, as if the verbal abuse wasn't enough. She chose her words carefully. "I only did what you asked me to do. You insisted that I have some-thing."

Before she knew it, her face met his hand, and once again he was using her as his personal punching bag. She tried to fight back. She always tried to fight back, but that seemed only to make him more hyped. Somehow in his twisted rationalization, it justified his fucked-up actions.

"Oh. You want to fight, huh?" he taunted, hitting her so hard with one blow that she stumbled and fell on her back on the cold, hardwood floor. He got on top of her and continued to hit her as if she was some practice toy. She reached for the ceramic cat that sat by the fireplace in the bedroom and managed to get hold of it. She cracked him upside of the head as hard as she could. It did the trick. He let her go and grabbed his head. But the effect lasted about as long as a two-dollar watered-down drink in an after-hours spot.

"Bitch," he screamed, and before she could escape, he had grabbed her by the leg. She kicked him in the face, which bought her just enough time to slip her foot out of his grip and run for the bathroom. She would lock herself in until he cooled off. But before she could get the latch on the door, he came charging toward her. He was still a little drunk from the liquor he had at dinner and disoriented from the blow upside of his head, so she managed to make him trip over her vanity table, and she slipped out of his grasp. While running out of the bedroom, she picked up the chair to the dressing-room table and then scooped up the remote that worked every lock and appliance in the house.

She closed the bedroom door and slid the back of the chair underneath the doorknob, and then ran down the hall, hitting buttons on the controller. One was to get into the laundry room to grab some sweats and sneakers. Luckily for her, she kept her pocketbook downstairs. She grabbed it, got the keys to the Lexus LS 400 that Randy usually let her drive, and burned rubber.

She pulled the car into a gas station down the street from the house. She went to use the restroom to clean herself up a little. When she looked into the mirror at herself, she started to cry. She had had enough. She looked a mess. She no longer had that soft, beautiful glow; she was beginning to look hard from all the beatings. She knew she had to get out. This time she wasn't going back.

She called Isis. "Sister, I need help."

"Phoebe? Where are you?" Isis said, relieved to finally hear from her sister.

"I'm at a gas station around the block from my house. I can't take it anymore; that nigga been puttin' his hands on me. I got to get outta here before somebody ends up dead."

Isis was furious. "Just tell me what you want me to do right now, sister. You need money? You need me to book you a flight? Do you have your ID on you? You want me to come get you? Just let me know."

"I have ID. Just get me a flight, but I don't want to go home to Momma. I want to come with you," she said, crying.

"No problem. Will you be okay while I make the arrangements? I promise I'll call you right back as soon as I get off the phone with the airline. If there's nothing leaving out tonight, I'll get you a hotel until morning." Isis heard a banging sound coming through the phone, followed by a male voice yelling her sister's name.

Phoebe panicked. "Sister, it's him. He's at the door."

"Don't let him in," Isis warned her sister. "I'm going to call the police."

"No—no police. I don't want his business to be in the media like that. He already got enough issues as it is."

"Fuck him! I'm only worried about you."

Isis could hear Randy's screaming through the phone. "Fee, open up the door. I don't want to have to kick this motherfucker in," he threatened.

"Randy, go away. Just leave me alone," Phoebe pleaded.

As Isis listened, she couldn't believe that this was the type of thing her sister had been dealing with. How had she hidden it so well?

"I'm not leaving without you, baby." This time he sounded calm and sweet like a pussycat.

"Don't fall for his bullshit," Isis yelled into the phone. "Don't open the door."

"Don't worry, I'm not." Phoebe wasn't crying as much as she was before.

A man walked up to Randy and tapped him on the shoulder. "Mr. Vanz?" the man ventured to ask. "Is that you?" The man had a strong Texas accent. "You're my son's hero. He's over there in the car and wants your autograph. Please, let's not disappoint him by letting him see you out here banging on the ladies' room door."

Knowing that he was drawing attention to himself, Randy got a grip. "Where's the kid at?"

"Right there in that there truck," the stranger said. "Won't you slide on over and say howdy to him? It'll mean the world to 'im."

Once Phoebe heard Randy leave to speak to his little fan, she slowly opened up the bathroom door and made a dash for her car, making her second escape from him in that night.

Isis screamed in the phone, "Sister, you there?" She was frantic. "What's happening?"

"I'm in my car, heading toward the airport," Phoebe said. "There's a Western Union there, but I want to go back and get my clothes. I look a mess. They'll think I'm some crazy maniac trying to board the plane, looking like this and with no luggage. I look like a suicide bomber with nothing to lose."

"Fuck your clothes! We'll get you more when you get here," she told her. "And fuck what other people think. You need to get out of there."

"Okay. I'm going to call you once I'm pulling into the airport parking lot."

Isis hopped online to send her sister money through Western Union and an airline ticket. About twenty minutes had passed since Isis had last spoken to her sister. Then the phone rang.

It was Phoebe. "Sister, a nice police officer was kind enough to let me call you before he took me in. He's taking me to jail for grand theft auto and a few other charges. Randy reported the car stolen. Please come out here and get me. I got to go."

"I'm on my way" was all Isis said as she prepared to make it happen.

Isis needed to get her sister a lawyer, a bond hearing, and a bond to get her out of jail, but she didn't have those types of resources in Texas. She wished she could talk to Logic, but she had to move now. She didn't want her sister to stay in jail one minute longer than she had to. Whom could she call?

Then she ran to the front room of the condo to get her pocketbook. She held it upside down, emptying it, looking for a piece of paper. If he was anything remotely close to what he claimed to be, surely he would be able to help her. There it was. She found it: It was a small piece of paper randomly torn in the shape of a trapezoid, and above the number, it read: The King of Texas.

She didn't waste any time before dialing his number. Someone answered on the second ring. "Talk to me."

"Is this how the king of Texas answers the telephone?" Isis asked.

"Who is this?" the same voice asked.

"It's the lady you met at the Gucci store," Isis said. "I never got your name."

"Larry Love," he joked. "And yours?"

"Isis."

"Pardon me, Ms. Isis. I didn't mean to answer the phone so rudely, but I know a few people from the 804 area code."

"Oh. Who might that be?"

"Just some folks," he said. "Where do *you* live—St. Petersburg or Richmond?"

"I'm actually from Richmond, but I live in Miami."

"MIA, huh?"

"Yup."

"So when are you coming back to my kingdom?"

"Well, actually that's why I was calling you. My sister lives down there, and her man beat her up. When she tried to leave him, he reported the car stolen, so now she's locked up. I'm going down there tomorrow to get her a lawyer and hopefully get her out, but I know nothing about Texas. So I'm going to need some advice. I figured who better to call than the Emperor of the South."

"No doubt, darling, I got you covered. When does your flight land?"

"Tomorrow," she said, "at eight in the morning."

"Then I'll pick you up from the airport."

She graciously thanked him and then added, "While I'm there, I also want to talk to you about possibly doing business together."

"What type of business?" he asked. "What do you do?"

"I design the hottest jewelry that money can buy."

"What a coincidence."

Larry "Lootchee" Fonzworth

"Make no mistake
about it, I always gets
whatever I wants."

Chapter 25

The Man

Larry "Lootchee" Fonzworth returned from Texas approximately six months ago after an extended stay in South America. Initially, Lootchee had fled to the border against his will. He was tricked by his then girlfriend into believing that the Feds had been asking questions and were hot on his trail, leaving him no choice but to take flight. However, he later found out it was a lie. After finding out that Lootchee had been using her name to ship illegal goods through the mail, his girlfriend, Bambi, concocted the entire story about the F.B.I., stole all of the merchandise and money he had stored at her house, and went back home to Richmond, Virginia. Lootchee stayed in South America for more than three years. Sure, he could have come back to his home state of Texas sooner, but opportunity smiled upon him and Lootchee never could say no to a pretty face, and he never let a pretty face say no to him.

He made money hand over fist in South America, shipping drugs and laundering money for his associates in the States, and he found a new hustle in the jungle: the untampered, high-profit, and low-risk business of the phone cards.

But he couldn't live off of money alone. He needed something more that the jungle couldn't provide; there was unfinished business in the States that was keeping him awake at night. He had to teach his ex-girlfriend a lesson. He didn't get to where he was in life by allowing anyone to steal from him and live to tell, write, or laugh about it. But in order to get away with it, he knew he had to calculate and bide his time. Lootchee always got what he wanted: money, revenge, power, respect, women. Always. And by any means necessary.

• • •

Lootchee was having breakfast with two of his bodyguards in one of his favorite diners when his cell phone rang. He had been waiting for this call since last night, so he answered quickly. "Hello."

"I just landed," Isis said. "Where are you?"

"Be there in fifteen minutes. I'll meet you at baggage claim."

"Okay. Thanks," she said.

Exactly fifteen minutes later Lootchee called Isis back to tell her that he had been caught in traffic but he was only ten minutes away and to meet him at the departures gate instead of the baggage claim. Isis stood on the curb beside the cart with her luggage in it looking divalicious. She was wearing a velour, all-white Juicy Couture sweatsuit with white Juicy sunglasses when

Lootchee pulled up in a black 1995 Impala. Two large men hopped out. One put her bags in the trunk while the other watched.

After Lootchee felt like everything was good, he got out of the car and gave Isis a hug. "Let's bounce, Sweets," he said. "We got a lot of things to do."

Isis wasn't expecting Lootchee to be traveling with two 300-pound bodyguards, which made her a little nervous. "Did you set up the meeting with a lawyer for me?" she asked. She planned to get out of dodge as soon as she got Phoebe out of jail.

Lootchee pulled out his cell phone and made a call. "What is your sister's name?"

"Phoebe Cross. It's spelled P-H-O-E-B-E."

Lootchee told the person on the other end of the line Phoebe's name and then said, "By all means, get her out of there. I want to be having dinner with her at six o'clock, so you got until five to have her out." He hung up and then told Isis, "It's done."

Isis wasn't impressed. She wasn't going to be satisfied until her sister was standing right in front of her, free and in the flesh!

The first stop that they made was at a car wash, the kind where everything was done by hand. Every fly car in the city must have been dirty that day because it looked like a car show was in progress. There was everything from old-school pimped-out 6-4's to fresh-off-the-showroom-floor Mercedes Benz's. But the automobile that stood out, hands down, was a triple white Phantom. Lootchee drove the Impala to the side of the building and got out with the car still running. "Stay in the car," he instructed her.

Isis sighed. She was starting to dislike this dude more and more, and she didn't really like him that much in the first place. She just needed a contact in Texas. And now this fool was playing around at the car wash.

When Lootchee got out the car people crowded around him like he was a rock star. Everybody wanted to talk to him, shake his hand, or embrace him in some way. When he looked back to see if Isis was okay, she was admiring the Phantom that was parked in the corner.

Man, I could really use one of those in my life. I gotta get my hustle turned up to the tenth notch so I can make it happen, Isis thought.

Taking a better look at what was going down—it was more than just a car convention—these brothers were straight up balling. And there were a few sisters in attendance as well, not just on groupie status, but doing the damn thang, too.

A few of the fellas made eye contact with Isis. There were plenty of Black Widow potential customers that had already given her the eye, but Isis ignored them. She didn't want to seem disrespectful to Lootchee by acknowledging them. Regardless of how macho a man acted on the outside, Isis knew that deep down most of them were as insecure as a hooker in a room full of nuns. And right now, for her sister's sake, she needed this man's help.

No more than five minutes had passed, when one of the two goons that were riding with Lootchee popped the trunk and removed her bags. Lootchee walked back over to the car and opened the door to the Impala for her, held his elbow out to her and said, "Right this way, Sweets." He then escorted her, arm in arm, to the Phantom.

"Where to, Lootchee?" the driver called out.

"The Ritz," Isis answered for him.

"The Boat Showplace," Lootchee corrected.

"What? Why are we going to a boat place?" Isis asked. Lootchee seemed cool and all, but she wasn't feeling all the stops, nor did he at any time ask her what she wanted, which was to get her sister out of jail and get the fuck out of Texas.

"I got you, Sweets, but I need to go make sure everything is straight with this boat that I just bought."

"That wasn't the deal," Isis reminded him. "I know I sprung everything on you last minute, and the last thing I want to do is inconvenience you, so all you have to do is drop me at my hotel and give me the name and number of the lawyer and I can take it from there."

"Listen, Sweets, ain't no need for all that. I got the best lawyer in the state on my payroll, and he's in the process of taking care of the business as we speak." Lootchee's words poured out like syrup. "Just relax. Your sister will be out by five p.m., and afterward, I'm treating the both of you to the best damn celebration steak Texas has to offer."

Isis had to give it to him, the man didn't lack confidence. "Can I ask you a question?"

"Anything, Sweets."

"Why do they call you Lootchee?"

"Well, the plain and simple version is," he started, "back in the '80's Lootchee used to be slang for money, and that's what I am—pure dee money. So the name stuck."

Isis thought that they were balling at the carwash, but the Boat Showplace was off the meter.

Lootchee had bought a beautiful thirty-footer with all the amenities. The fact that he never piloted a boat before didn't slow him down. In his eyes this was $50,000 of well-spent money. You only lived once.

Lootchee, the owner of the store, and Isis were all on their way to check out the boat when she spotted a stunning sixty-foot yacht. Isis pointed. "I hope that's the one you bought," she smiled. "It's beautiful." Isis walked around the boat, admiring it.

Rick, the owner of the store, smirked when he heard Lootchee say, "That's why I came back today, because I wanted to see if this one had come in." When they went aboard to take a closer look, Lootchee lagged behind with Rick and asked, "How much for this one?"

Rick smiled. "Three hundred and fifteen thousand. Your wife has wonderful taste."

Not bothering to correct Rick's wrong assumption that Isis was his wife, Lootchee did the math on the difference in the prices of the two boats quickly in his head. "Yes, she does. So it's mine for another hundred and sixty-five thou' then?"

"I'm sorry, Mr. Fonzworth, but the other yacht that you purchased was custom-ordered. I can't take it back," Rick explained.

"There's no such thing as a man that can't do something, now is it?" Lootchee wasn't really asking a question. He was making a statement.

"I'll tell you what I *can* do," Rick said. "If you don't want the other one, I can buy it back from you for seventy-five thousand."

"Man, you know I am a businessman. You gotta do better than that."

"Well, you could leave the boat here and resell it for a ten to fifteen percent commission?" he said, not wanting to rub Lootchee the wrong way. Lord knows he wanted the sale of the boat.

Lootchee thought for a minute, looking from one boat to the next. Finally he said, "Deal." The two men shook on it. "Sweets!" Lootchee called out to Isis. "We gotta go. I need to make a run."

Great, Isis thought, throwing her hands up. "Where to now?"

"I gotta go to the bank to get another cashier check for $315,000 to buy this here vessel. We in Texas for gud-dam'it— if it ain't big, it ain't right," Lootchee boasted as he winked at Isis.

Isis smiled and shook her head as she made her way toward the exit of the boat. This dude really did feel as though he was a king and deserved only the best.

Lootchee was determined to impress her. The boat was just another thing, but the beauty that Isis possessed was priceless.

"Rick," Lootchee said before the two of them exited the boat, "being you like my wife's taste so much, you probably would like to do some business with her. Especially since she's the reason you just got such a big sale."

"What type of work does she do?" Rick inquired.

"She's the best damn jewelry designer on the east coast, North and South Peninsula, and I'm sure she could make something real nice for your wife that won't run you much more than thirty-five thou'. Your wife does like jewelry, doesn't she? I mean, what woman doesn't?"

Isis turned and faced the men after hearing the word jewelry.

"I was just telling Rick here that you design jewelry," Lootchee said to Isis.

"Oh, yeah," Isis said, "that's what I do. Designed this one myself." She held up her hand.

Rick couldn't miss the rock that Isis was wearing on her ring finger even if he was blind—and he wasn't—so he saw exactly where Lootchee was going with this. "I would be honored to purchase something for my wife," he said. *Fair exchange ain't no robbery,* he thought. "Do you have a business card?"

"I sure do." Isis opened her rhinestone card case and passed him one.

"Black Widow Jewels, huh?" Rick scratched his head. "I think I might have read something about you."

"The one and only." She smiled.

"May I have a few of the cards? I may have a few folks I can refer to you."

Isis obliged, handing the man a few more.

"Make sure you use them." Lootchee pointed to the cards as they headed to the bank. As soon as they got in the car, Lootchee's cell phone rang. "Hello," he said, taking the call.

After Lootchee had been trying to woo Isis all afternoon, he finally made some headway when he got off the phone and said, "That was the lawyer. Your sister is out of jail."

Isis had never been so relieved in her life. She exhaled. "Could you please take me to get her?"

"We're on our way now."

On the way to the jail to pick up Phoebe, Lootchee finally engaged in a conversation that didn't involve him. "What made you decide to be a jeweler? And why did you name your company Black Widow Jewels?"

"Jewelry has always been a passion of mine," she confided. "My mother and father always gave me a piece of jewelry for my birthday up until I was thirteen, and my mother had the most beautiful and interesting jewelry when I was young. It's always intrigued me."

"But why Black Widow?"

"Let's just say I wanted to take something negative and make it positive."

Loochee was quiet for a minute. Then he spoke. "You sound like a scorned woman."

"Well, I have been."

"Then we have more in common than you know," he said.

She looked at him. "Don't tell me you're a scorned woman?" Isis joked.

"No, not exactly," he said. "I had an ex-girlfriend that I loved dearly. In return for my love, she cut me pretty deeply with a knife called betrayal. So you tell me, what does that make me?"

Isis could see the anger in his eyes when he spoke of his ex-girlfriend and didn't like what she saw. "So you going to let me make a nice medallion or something for you?" She changed the subject to lessen the tension that had filled the car.

"No, you can't sell me a ring or something," he said. "I want an entire set; maybe two."

"Well, tell me what you want and what your budget is and I'll get it done."

"It ain't no budget, Sweets. Knock yourself out. The Lootchee is endless."

I opened the door wide open for that one, she thought.

"That's what I'm talking about, playa playa! Do the damn thing!" She stroked his ego even more. And Lootchee liked how it felt.

After arriving at the jail, both Lootchee and Isis were surprised when the guard informed them that Phoebe wasn't there and had been released a half hour ago.

"Then where is she?" Isis asked.

"Little lady," the guard said, "I don't keep up wit 'em after we release 'em. Got enough to babysit as it is."

"She probably caught a cab to the airport or something, or is on foot somewhere. Since she hadn't talked to you, she probably had no idea you were in town and on your way to get her," Lootchee added.

Isis immediately tried to call her sister's cell phone. She hoped the battery was still charged. The phone rang about six times and then she heard, "What up, sis?"

"Hey, sister, you okay?" Isis said, relieved.

"Yes, I am." She sounded just as relieved. "Thanks for getting me out."

"You know that's what we do for each other. Where are you?"

"I just left from down there so I am up here taking care of a few things," she said.

"Up where?" Isis asked again.

"I'm just trying to handle my business, that's all." Phoebe continued to be evasive, but the chiming of the grandfather clock in the background didn't lie.

"Tell me you're not at that monster's house. Matter of fact, don't even lie to me. I'm on my way to get you."

"You in Texas?" Phoebe thought since the lawyer said that he was sent to get her out that Isis was still in Florida somewhere.

"Of course I'm in Texas. You called me to come get you, didn't you? So, I'm coming to get your ass." Isis turned to Lootchee. "Put this address into your navigational system." She reached for her little mini notebook and handed it over to Lootchee. "We have to go get my sister."

Lootchee followed orders. "No problem, Sweets."

Phoebe asked, "Who are you with?"

"A friend of mine and we'll be there in a few."

"Good. I got time to get my stuff together; that's what I came here for anyway."

"Didn't I tell you to leave that shit? That I would get you some new stuff?"

"Yeah, but I got some nice shit. I can't leave with nothing."

Isis couldn't believe her ears. "Listen, you are leaving with your life and your freedom. It could be so much worse, but I am not trying to lecture you. I know how that shit feels. But anyway, I will be there in a few minutes." She hung up the phone and breathed hard. "I can't believe she done went back over to that nigga's house."

When Isis pulled up to Randy Vanz's house, police were all over the property. As they got closer, Isis saw her sister being escorted to a police cruiser in handcuffs.

"You are having me locked up because I don't want your steroid-taking, little dick behind anymore?" Phoebe screamed at

Randy. "This is what you do to me because I won't let you whip my ass?"

Isis got out of the car and ran over to the police car. "Please let me speak to my sister. I promise, I will only be a second."

Seeing the desperation in Isis's eyes, the officer agreed. "You got one minute, ma'am," he told her.

"Thank you, officer," Isis said anxiously, making her way to Phoebe. "What happened, Phoebe?"

"I only wanted to get my things and leave." Phoebe had tears in her eyes. "And this motherfucker told me that I had to abide by his rules and be taught a lesson. I just said fuck the shit; left everything and went to the gate to wait on you. Next thing I know the police are arresting me for trespassing and some more shit he made up."

"Time is up, ma'am," the officer interrupted.

"Sister, don't worry I will figure something out," Isis assured her.

Isis wanted to talk with that no-good ass Randy, but with so much commotion, he managed to stay clear. She did get his number from Phoebe and she would try to call him later and convince him to put an end to this madness.

Once back in the car, Isis shared with Lootchee what Phoebe had told her.

"We gotta come up with something to stop his crazy ass," Isis said.

Lootchee was already two steps ahead of her. "Sweets, I called the lawyer as soon as I saw your sister in the cuffs. He said it would be at least a day or two before he could do anything under the circumstances. He said it may prove to be to our advantage if I could talk to Mr. Vanz man-to-man about dropping the charges and letting bygones be bygones.

"That would be wonderful if you could make that happen."

"I'll do all I can do, and that's a lot. But there isn't much more we can do right now. So I suggest that we go to dinner; get a clear head and a full stomach to boot."

"Thank you, Larry, that'll be cool, but first I'm going to need to be dropped off at the hotel so I can change my clothes."

"I don't live too far from here," Lootchee said. "I have an extra room. Actually, I have a guest house," he bragged. "You could change there since we've got a reservation, and we're pressed for time and your bags are still in the trunk."

She hesitated, not wanting to give Lootchee the wrong impression nor put herself in a vulnerable situation. "I would much rather stay alone."

Lootchee shrugged his shoulders, taking no offense. "Either way is cool with me. It's just that I have more than enough room," he said. "I tell you what. Being that we are so close to my house, you can go ahead and just change there, then after we eat, we can get you a room if that's still what you want. How does that sound?"

Isis agreed to his terms and they were parked in his driveway within ten minutes. "You live *here* alone?" she asked after seeing the size of his home. Lootchee's house resembled something off of MTV's *Cribs*.

"Well, my security guard, Max, stays here, but he really doesn't count. My sister was house-sitting for me while I lived in South America. She's supposed to be finding a place of her own, but she keeps telling me that it's hard to live here and then turn around and go live in some apartment."

"I know that's right," Isis agreed, still looking over the place, which looked like a palace fit for a king.

Lootchee offered to take Isis on the grand tour before getting changed, and she accepted. They were walking room to room when he said, "I must admit, I'd probably have a hard time staying in an apartment after living in this place too, but I told my sister, there isn't anything like having your own. She's cool though. She stays out of my way, and one of the good things is, that she keeps things going for me; it doesn't matter if I'm here or away. I don't know what I would do if anything ever happened to her. That's why even though I'm back and she seems to be procrastinating about finding her own place, I don't pressure her to move out.

"So, shall we head toward where you'll be changing?" Once again Lootchee held his elbow up for Isis to latch onto as he led her toward the guest house.

He called the suite that she would be using to wash up and get dressed the master guest quarters. There was a sitting area toward the back of the bedroom that was set up like an entertainment room. The third adjoining room, which was much smaller than the other two, had a full-size refrigerator stocked with beer, juice, and sodas and a little cabinet with chips and snacks.

Lootchee left Isis to handle her business as he went to do the same. The only thing about the suite that wasn't to her liking was the ceiling fan, which was set on high speed. It had been annoying her ever since she had gotten out of the shower. She had to get dressed in the sitting area to keep from getting goose bumps. For the life of her she couldn't figure out how to cut it off.

It was almost like Lootchee could read her mind the way he appeared at the door, but like most men, he was late when he said, "Is it too cold in here? I can turn down the air."

"No. But I wish you would've come and turned that ceiling fan off before I got wet. I hate those things blowing on me," she said. "My husband and I used to debate all the time about whether to turn it on or leave it off. My husband loves it."

"So do I," Lootchee said, not really interested in hearing about her husband. Then he asked, "Do you mind if I share something with you?"

"No, I don't mind at all."

Lootchee cleared his throat and interlocked his fingers forming a steeple, then said, "You remind me a lot of my ex-girlfriend."

"How so?" she asked, remembering the look in his eyes earlier when he was talking about her betrayal.

"She was from Virginia too. But not only that, she was so radiant, filled with energy and confidence just like you are."

"Well, thank you. I guess I can take it as a compliment then," she said with an unsure smile on her face. "But if she was so great, then why is she your ex?"

"It's kinda complicated. I made a wrong assumption. I thought since I was down for her that she would be down for me, but she wasn't. Instead, like I told you before, she took me for a lot of money, lied and betrayed me in the worst way."

Isis's heart went out to him. She knew exactly what it felt like to be betrayed and lied to. "I am so sorry that happened to you."

"Don't be. It only made a better man out of me for real. As a result, I traveled across South America, made some major contacts, and put together one of the best business situations I could ever be in."

"You know what? I felt like that when I was with one of my ex's. He did some pretty mean things to me, things that I don't even care to elaborate on, but at the end of the day, I prevailed."

"I feel you," Lootchee said, "probably more than you will ever know."

"For a long time," she continued, "I thought that I had some kind of black cloud over my head when it came to men, but things have a way of working themselves out. There's a reason for everything."

"You are so right," Lootchee said with a smile, thinking Isis was the match that he'd been waiting for. "I see so much of me in you. I think we should get to know each other better."

"Lootchee, I speak for many women when I say that I think that you are a really great guy. You are a really good catch. You have class, style, and swagger that won't quit. Plus, you're business minded and seem to really be financially stable. You're definitely a catch."

"I'm not trying to be a catch for any ol' woman. I want you. And make no mistake about it: I always gets *whatever* I wants." He smiled, meaning every word.

"Lootchee, I am married, and I love my husband with all my heart."

"But does he love you? If he does, how come he hasn't called you all day?" Lootchee boldly asked. "If he was really concerned, he would've checked on you by now. Or even came with you, for that matter."

Isis reluctantly told him her situation. "He's locked up now."

"And you still call him your husband?" Lootchee chuckled. "How much longer will he be gone?"

"I don't know," Isis said honestly, with some sadness in her voice. "And yes, I do still call him my husband. Prison can't change that for me, only death can."

Lootchee was willing to be number two for a moment, but only a moment. In his mind there was no way a man in prison could be any real competition to him. "Well, while he's locked up, what if I'm just your friend on the side?"

Now it was Isis's turn to change the subject. "Where did you book those reservations? I'm starving."

Dinner was at a five-star restaurant, and Lootchee had everyone from the owner to the cook jumping through hoops for him. Isis knew that he was trying to impress her, much like he had been attempting to do all afternoon. And to be honest about it, the man was damn good at it. It cost a lot of money to be the king of Texas and Lootchee didn't cut any corners.

Chapter 26

Nobody Likes the Rat

After wining and dining her, and extending an indefinite rain check on going out dancing, Lootchee took Isis to her hotel as promised. She decided to follow her first instincts and not give Lootchee the wrong idea by staying at his place. Because it was after midnight by the time they arrived at the hotel, he walked her in to be sure she was safe. At the check-in counter, the woman on duty informed Isis of a problem with her reservations.

"I'm sorry, Mrs. Wiseman, but if you don't check in or call the hotel by six PM, the reservations are considered void and will be charged to the credit card on which the room was reserved," the clerk said.

"No problem," Isis told the clerk as she whipped out her wallet. "I'll just book another one now."

"I'm sorry, Mrs. Wiseman, but there are no more rooms available. There is a NASCAR race this weekend and a church convention, and we are renovating our north tower. I'm so sorry, Mrs. Wiseman. Your room was booked at 6:05 PM. Demand for rooms was just that great. Again, my sincere apologies that you weren't informed about our policy."

Although Isis was fit to be tied like a hog in Texas, this was the best news Lootchee had heard all day. "Excuse us," he said to the clerk, then ushered Isis a few feet from the desk so that their conversation couldn't be overheard. "Of course you know that my offer is still open."

"That's really sweet, and you have a wonderful home, but I wouldn't feel comfortable there."

"Why?" he asked. "Because you're afraid that the more time we spend together the more time that gives us to bond and develop feelings for one another? If you are scared of falling for me, then say that you are scared."

Isis decided that now was not the right time to set Lootchee straight, so she gave him a polite chuckle. "Since this is your town, *your kingdom,* it shouldn't be hard for you to find me a hotel room. Can you do that for me?"

Lootchee tried to call in a few favors but came up empty. It seemed as if every single room in the city was booked. They even rode around to a few of the less-reputable motels because Isis was so insistent on not staying with him. It was beginning to look like an impossible mission when finally they spotted a sign that read: VACANCIES: WE HAVE ROOMS W/ JACUZZI.

"Stop the car," Isis said. "Let me try in there."

"Are you serious?" Lootchee asked. "Is staying at my place so bad that you would rather stay here?"

"No. Not at all," she assured him. "But my husband wouldn't want me to stay in the house of a man I just met in a strange city, regardless of how nice you are and how innocent your intentions may or may not be."

Lootchee reluctantly submitted. "I'll do as you wish," he said, not liking the idea at all.

When they got inside the hole in the wall of a hotel, a man with a turban greeted Isis. "May I help you?" he said with a heavy accent.

"Do you have any rooms available?" she asked.

"Ha long?" the man inquired. "Ha many hours?"

An insulted look crossed her face. That should have been her cue to walk out right then, but she didn't. Instead she said, "I would like to have the room for a night."

"Check out time ahhh-leven o'clock."

"Okay, how much for the room?" she asked.

"Give me sixty dollars."

Isis said that she would take the room, despite Lootchee's protest. She sent him on his way, but before he left, she made him promise to be there first thing in the morning so that they could check on Phoebe's case. He agreed and walked out of the hotel, sulking like a child who couldn't have his way.

Room 403 wasn't as bad as she expected it to be. As soon as she walked in, she could smell the lemon disinfectant that had been used to clean the room. The bed even had a couple of pieces of chocolate waiting for her on the pillow. The flowery carpet was a little worn down and the matching wallpaper was peeling a little bit from the bottom of the wall, but it would do for the night. It wasn't as if she was trying to vacation there.

When she walked into the bathroom, she was pleasantly surprised, because the sign outside hadn't lied. In the corner, there was a big round Jacuzzi that could fit four. Then she noticed that there weren't any washcloths or towels hanging on the rack or on the shelf.

No problem, she thought. She went back into the main room and picked up the telephone to call the front desk.

"Yah," the same man who'd checked her in answered. "Front desk."

"Yes, I'm sorry to bother you, but I need towels and wash-cloths."

"No problem. Me get chu whateva chu need."

She thanked the clerk and hung up. The towels and wash-cloths were delivered within five minutes. Not bad service for what appeared to be a one-star hotel. She went into the bath-room to wash up before lying down and getting some rest. Al-though the outside of the hotel looked kind of shabby, the rest of it seemed surprisingly clean. She couldn't imagine Logic wanting his princess to have to lay her head in a place like this, but she couldn't imagine him wanting her head to be lying on another man's pillow either.

Isis peeled off her black spandex dress, which was embroi-dered with clear rhinestones, and her undergarments, and then slid in the shower. It was steaming hot just like she liked it, and the water sprayed from the head in firm pellets—just what she needed to relax. Soaping up three or four times, she enjoyed the exhilarating, refreshing blasts of the water for at least thirty min-utes. Actually she had lost track of time. When her mind did come back to the present, she got out of the shower before her skin started shriveling up. The towel she patted herself down with was fluffy and had a nice scent, as if straight out of the dryer with a fabric-softener sheet. She used another towel to wipe the steam off the mirror and then removed her shower cap to exam-ine her hair: Her free-flowing loose curls were all in place. She determined that they would hold for a couple more days before she would have to get her hair done again. All she wanted now was some rest and to wake up in the morning and hopefully scoop up her sister.

When she walked out of the bathroom, what she saw next caused a loud scream to escape from her lips. "Aaaaaaahh! What the hell?"

A supersized rat was staring at her, as if she was intruding on him. The good-for-nothing rodent was on its hind legs, sitting on her pillow. It was the biggest rat she had ever laid eyes on and was the size of that dog from those Taco Bell commercials. Isis was afraid of hamsters, so the rat had her freaked out big time. She jumped up in a chair that sat by an old dresser that had seen better days. Shaking and scared half to death, she was unsure of what to do. She knew one thing for sure, though: She was done with this fleabag hotel . . . and there went her damn chocolates!

At this point, Isis knew that she had no other choice but to take Lootchee up on his offer. Hopefully, she hadn't offended him too badly by not accepting it in the first place. Still petrified and standing on the chair, Isis scanned the room for her cell phone. *Damn*, she thought after spotting it on the opposite end of the dresser. No way was she getting down from the chair. Thinking fast, she climbed up on the beat-up dresser and crawled the two feet she needed to go to get to her phone. Beside her phone was a drinking glass. She grabbed the glass and hurled it at the dog-rat. It scampered off the pillow and went under the bed.

Isis shuddered and climbed back over to the chair and stood on it to dial Lootchee. "My room is infested with rats!" she screamed into the phone as soon as he answered. "I hate fucking rats! I need you to come back and pick me up if the offer is still open."

A grin spread across Lootchee's lips, as if he had put the rat up to the act himself. "The offer is always open. I'll be right there." Isis could hear the smile in his voice.

"Lootchee," Isis called out before he could hang up.

"What is it?" The smile turned into concern. "Are you okay?"

"Sure. I just wanted to say thank you."

"Don't mention it," Lootchee said, but he thought, *You can thank me later.*

Chapter 27

Tricks of the Trade

It was 5 AM and Isis was up watching an early morning news program with the volume turned down low. There were too many things running around her head for her to get any rest in Lootchee's guest room. Just being in his house twice in one day had her feeling guilty. Although she didn't have sex with Lootchee and had no intentions of doing so, she still felt that she was betraying her husband's trust. And that wasn't all that had her restless. She was worried about her sister, big time. It wasn't easy for a person who didn't live in the state they got arrested in to get *one* bond, much less two. And this was Texas, which was infamous for its harsh criminal laws.

The words *Breaking Story* came up across the national news channel. The newscaster was saying something about a triple homicide in South Beach and sent the viewers live to the scene. Isis grabbed the remote to turn the volume up a bit.

The reporter was standing in front of a house in a neighborhood that was familiar to her. "This is Michael Rosen, reporting live. Julia, we are in front of the house of famed film producer Tre Wilson, where police were called to the scene by a neighbor. What police discovered in Wilson's house were three dismembered male bodies," the reporter announced. "Police would not confirm the identities of any of the deceased and would not say whether one of them is that of Tre Wilson. Someone close to the scene said that it appeared that two of the corpses were Caucasian men dressed as women. As of right now, there are no suspects or motives to this horrific crime. We are not sure if it was a hate crime, a double murder-suicide, or a random act of violence. Police are still at the scene investigating and details are still coming in. Just as soon as we have more information, we will pass it on to you. Reporting live from South Beach, Florida, this is Michael Rosen."

"Thank you, Michael," the anchorwoman said, before moving to the next story.

Isis was stunned. The first and the last time she had seen Tre was at the club when Logic took his car from him to hold for collateral. Now that she thought about it, there had been something odd about those giraffe-tall white girls he had left the club with, but she hadn't quite been able to put her finger on it at the time.

Isis remembered that Logic had said that Tre was one of the people testifying against him, so maybe his death was good news. Her man just might come home sooner than she thought, and if so, maybe she finally would have a shot at happily ever after. She tried to call Sly to find out if she knew anything but wasn't able to get a signal on her cell phone in Lootchee's house. She drifted off to sleep thinking about all the things she and Logic would do together, only to be awakened a few hours later by a knock at the door, followed by a familiar voice.

"Sweets," Lootchee called from the other side. "Sweets, are you up yet?"

"Yes," she said, and yawned.

"You want to come have breakfast with me in twenty minutes?"

"Sure, that'll be nice."

"I tried calling your phone to ask you so that I wouldn't disturb you if you were asleep, but you didn't answer."

"Yeah, I can't get a signal here. Let me get up and pull it together."

At breakfast Lootchee explained that he had some running around to do and that he'd be back at 12:30 to pick her up so that they could meet with Phoebe's attorney. He also informed her that she could use his house phone if she needed to make any calls but to be ready when he returned, because they had a lot to do.

. . .

Agent Stephen Newman was at home eating an English muffin with cream cheese and drinking a cup of instant coffee. He had been eating the same breakfast every morning for ten years. He was about to take a sip of the instant caffeine jolt when his phone rang. "Damn," the FBI agent mumbled. "Sorry, Charlie, StarKist is for tuna with good taste." Newman answered the phone with the same line he had been using on his partner since the first day they had started working together more than three years earlier.

"Did you catch the news this morning?" Jefferson asked.

"You know I never watch that stuff before breakfast," Newman reminded his partner. There had to be some balance in his life, a moment that didn't involve work. And he knew that watching the news channel was like getting an itinerary for the day's work. Newly reported crimes meant new cases to work. "What did I miss?"

"Only that the lead witness in our case against Wiseman was found slumped in his house along with two high-maintenance transvestites. The word I got, all of them had their wieners chopped off."

Newman used the thumb and index finger of his left hand to massage his temple in a circular motion. "Tell me that this is a not-funny-at-all joke," he said.

"Like that sorry tuna bit you won't let go of?" Jefferson asked. "I'm afraid not. But you haven't heard the funny part yet. The word is that they found Mr. Tre Wilson's wiener in his mouth with the balls still attached. Besides a lot of blood—all belonging to the victims—the place was as clean as the ashtray in the pope's car."

"Okay," Newman said, "we need to make sure that our other witness against Mr. Wiseman is protected around the clock. I need you to call—"

Jefferson cut him off. "I'm already ahead of you, partner. Our boy has already skipped. He's in Tahiti. He left a message for us with his sister."

"This is getting better by the second," Newman said. "What was the message?"

"You're going to love this. According to his sister, he never saw or heard about Logic Wiseman doing anything illegal. He said he made it all up because he was mad at Wiseman and other people offered him money to incriminate him. And if we went to get him, he would spend whatever time he was forced to stay in prison before he continued to lie about an innocent man."

"This is un-fucking-believable," Agent Newman said. "Do you know what this does to our case?"

"What case?"

Chapter 28

Really Unique

The clock read noon. Isis was dressed and almost ready. She had tried Sly again on Lootchee's phone and left a message telling Sly she would call her from her phone when she got a signal. As Isis painted on lip gloss, Lootchee's house phone started ringing and ringing and ringing. At first she ignored it, but it wouldn't stop. She didn't want to answer his phone, but whoever it was sure was determined to speak to someone. She wondered if it was Lootchee calling and decided that maybe she ought to answer it after all.

She reluctantly picked up. "Hello?"

"Hello. Who is this?" a friendly female voice asked.

"Who would you like to speak to?"

"Let me speak to Lootchee?"

"He's not in; can I take a message?"

"Is his sister, Tee, there?"

"No, I'm sorry, she's not in either." Isis was getting tired of playing secretary.

"May I ask who I'm talking to?"

"I'm a friend," Isis replied, and then added, "Don't worry, I'm harmless."

"Harmless?" the caller asked. "There's no such thing. Even a beautiful rose has thorns." Isis chuckled at the comment. "Well, hopefully you are taking great care of him and keeping him out of trouble," the woman on the other end of the phone said. "He needs someone who can keep him focused and bring out his good side. I pray that person is you."

"Well, I haven't known him a long time and I'm just a friend."

"An innocent friend wouldn't be in his house, trust me. He must *really* think a lot of you."

"Who is this again?" Isis asked because the caller was giving off a crazy vibe that she couldn't really read. Was this a setup? Had Lootchee had someone call her just to feel her out or feed her some lines on his behalf?

"I'm not anyone. A fly on the wall that's all. One of his slaves you might say," she added.

"You're saying the man has slaves?"

"Yes, and don't ask. Anyway, it was really nice talking to you. I hope you have a wonderful day, and by the way, let him know that *Unique* called. Tell him that I have some important information for him."

"No problem, Unique."

"Be careful, Miss I'm-Just-a-Friend," Unique said before she hung up.

Be careful? She's a slave? What the hell does she mean by all that? What does she do for him?

Isis's thoughts were interupted when she heard the alarm talking. "System disarmed." Lootchee had arrived. He greeted her with a large bouquet of flowers and tickets to a play on Friday. She had to give it to the man, he was definitely persistent.

"You ready?" he asked. "The driver is waiting in the car."

"All set," Isis replied, grabbing her purse and then following Lootchee out to the car.

They were riding in the Phantom on the way to the attorney's office when Isis mentioned the strange phone call to Lootchee. "Just ten or fifteen minutes ago, your phone was ringing off the hook, nonstop, and I thought it might be you, so I answered it. The caller said her name was Unique."

Isis watched as the expression on Lootchee's face changed from happy-go-lucky to majorly on edge. "What did she say? Was she rude?"

"No. Actually, she was very nice. She just said that she worked for you and had some important information for you."

"I'll call her." Isis left it at that and didn't inquire anymore about the caller, but Lootchee added, "Yeah, Unique is someone who owes me her life. I got her out of a real bad situation."

"That was nice of you," she said. "Do you always get women out of bad situations?"

"When I can, yes. She does work for me out east."

"Oh, okay." Isis changed the subject. "So what do you think the lawyer will say about Phoebe?"

"I don't know, but we're almost there, so we'll know for sure in a few minutes. So Unique didn't tell you what the info was about?" Lootchee asked.

"No, she only wanted to speak to you or your sister; that was it. Is she one of your girlfriends?"

"Not at all," he answered quickly. "She's not my type—you are."

Isis kept a straight face but could feel a blush dying to get out.

They pulled into the parking lot of the lawyer's office, which was on the twenty-third floor. Isis, Lootchee, and Mr. Lumpkin, the lawyer, sat in his office at a table. Lumpkin got right to the point. "I spoke with the prosecutor who will be handling the case, and he's a real hard-ass," Lumpkin said. "He's going to ask for jail time. I know your sister has no prior criminal history with exception of the earlier arrest, and he knows it too. The only difference is that he doesn't give a fuck." The lawyer looked to Isis and blushed. "Excuse my French, little lady."

"You mean that my sister is going to have to do hard time?" Isis interjected.

"Slow down, Ms. . . . ah . . ."

"Tatum," Lootchee said.

"It's Mrs. Wiseman, actually," Isis said, correcting him. It seemed to her that Lootchee was trying to disregard her marriage.

"Hear me out, Mrs. Wiseman. I'm saying we need to let her stay in for ten days or so. That way when I go to trial, I can try to persuade the judge to release her on time served if we can't win the case outright. If not, that damn prosecutor is going to ask for at least a year in jail."

"A year in jail? And he was whipping her ass. Now, that's some bullshit."

"Yes, we all know that, but she didn't document it anywhere. If we'd had some police reports of her getting abused by him, then she could walk. It didn't help either that as soon as she got out of jail, she went straight back home."

Lumpkin spoke with such authority that Lootchee agreed with him too. Isis didn't want her sister in jail for one minute longer than necessary, but everything the lawyer said made good sense. Lumpkin said he would tell Phoebe what they discussed about the 10-day jail sentence.

Isis and Lootchee went out for a nice lunch after leaving the attorney, but she didn't have much of an appetite. She just picked at her food as she thought about the mangy jailhouse food her sister was probably eating.

"Are you going to talk to Randy?" she asked.

"I did, and he agreed to drop the charges, but that prosecutor won't."

"So what now?"

"Chris Lumpkin is the best, and he will make sure that he will get the best results," Lootchee assured her.

After lunch, Lootchee dropped Isis back off at the house with a promise that he would be back soon.

Isis called Sly again.

"What's up, girl?"

"Hey, Isis, you don't know the half."

"I saw the news report on TV about that guy, the witness."

"I know—ain't that crazy? He got caught with two men, and all of their dicks were in their mouths. And that changes the game for our team in a fantastic way," Sly said.

"Tell me everything," Isis said with a smile.

"I don't really know anything, but I do know you need to keep checking in with me on the regular until you get phone service."

"You know I will," Isis said.

"Wait a minute; someone is on the other line. Let me see who this is."

Isis held on and waited a long time for Sly to come back to the line. Several times she was tempted to hang up and call back, but she didn't. Then Sly finally did switch back over to her line, and she was so excited that she damn near screamed through the phone. "Ice, you need to come home. Girl, they are going to let Logic out! That was Michael McGetty, the lawyer, looking for you. He said the feds don't have a case. Logic will be home as soon as the paperwork is done."

Chapter 29

Fit for a Princess

After several years of ups and downs, Isis had made quite a splash in her career and had been profiled by the media many times. People were intrigued by the beautiful young woman who called herself the Black Widow. Her story of heartbreak and betrayal was as fascinating as her designs. Celebrities on the red carpet often stated that they wore Black Widow originals. The highlight of her career was that she was being commissioned to design engagement rings for a lot of stars.

It had been three months since Logic's release. Isis and Logic purchased an extravagant home in Bal Harbour. And Phoebe was even going to be coming home soon. The lawyer Lootchee had hired made a plea bargain with the prosecutor. In exchange for the several years the prosecutor was initially seeking, Phoebe was given only six months, and with good behavior she'd be out in a matter of days.

Life was beautiful. Isis felt as if the curse had finally been broken.

• • •

Isis was running late for a meeting. She was rushing around trying to get herself together when Logic stopped her in her tracks just as she was about to dart from the bedroom.

"Slow down, Princess," he told her, smiling.

"I can't, baby. I got a meeting that could land me a deal worth hundreds of thousands of dollars," Isis told him as she tried to push her way past him.

"Would that meeting be with a Mr. Ural Mine, by any chance?" Logic asked, with that same knowing look on his face.

"Yes, it is, and I'm running la . . ." Isis's words trailed off after she thought for a minute. "How did you know who my meeting was with? It was set up at the last minute yesterday. I didn't even think I'd told you about it." Isis observed the devious grin on Logic's face. "What? What's going on?"

"Mr. Ural Mine . . . Ur-al mine. You're All Mine." Logic smiled, waiting for Isis to catch on.

"Logic, you . . ." Isis play-punched her husband before he took her into his arms.

"Sorry, Princess. I had to trick you. This was the only way I could get you to take time to settle down for a minute. So today, you're all mine."

Isis wasn't the least bit angry. She embraced her husband and planted a tender kiss on his lips.

"Now let's go. You've got an appointment with me."

"Logic, where are we going?" Isis asked. "Do I need to change?"

Logic faced his wife with a serious look on his face. "Princess, don't you ever change."

Logic had planned a day that she'd never forget. In his preparations, he had been bound and determined for the two of them to have the most romantic time that any couple could have in twenty-four hours.

He booked a private jet to fly them to the Bahamas, where they enjoyed a couple's massage and had staff members waiting on them hand and foot. As Isis sat on the huge patio by their private pool, she smiled as she thought about how secure Logic was with their relationship as two half naked-men he'd hired, with Olympic-quality athletic bodies, were fanning her to cool her off from the hot rays of the Bahamian sun.

He had a woman massaging her feet and another woman feeding her grapes when he brought her his cell phone. "This is the only call that I'd let you take. After that, you're all mine . . . remember?" Logic winked and extended the phone to her.

"Who is it? I mean, you confiscated my phone, so who could this be calling for me on your phone?"

He smiled and just pushed the phone toward her as she took it from his hand.

"Hello?"

"Hi, sister," Phoebe said. "They just let me out. I'm in Miami. My brother-in-law got me all set up. Sly just picked me up from the airport, and now I'm getting settled in the condo. He said that I could stay there as long as I want."

"Of course you know that."

"And I really like Sly."

"Don't you? She really grew on me."

"Yes, so once you return, I will need your help, big sister, to help me figure out what I will do with my life. I can't live off of you and your man, you know."

"We will work it all out. Don't worry. I feel like Miami is a good start for you. It's the place where anything goes."

"I know, but I gotta figure out something. It just seems like every time I dream of something, it falls through. I'm damn near afraid to even dream anymore."

"Girl, I was in the same boat. Don't worry, we will figure out something together, sis." Isis paused, and then a thought popped into her head. "Your dreams are never shattered unless you stop dreaming."

"What are you saying?"

"Look—so what you didn't make the squad. So what? So what you didn't get the man of your dreams. So what? So the fuck what? We, me and you, have always made dreams happen for us." Isis sat up and shooed everyone away so she could have a private conversation with her sister. "Listen, remember when we were thirteen and finally found out about each other? Your mother wasn't letting you see me, or talk to me, and Samantha told me that I would have to wait to see you when we were adults?"

"Yes."

"What did we do?"

"We cried to each other."

"After that, what did we do?"

"We planned to go to Skateland on Williamsburg Road, and we met. And we met there every Sunday—from two to six every Sunday—for two years until Samantha found out and gave in and helped us see each other."

"Okay, then, and you helped me with Dave's funeral and for the wedding when you came in a matter of six hours."

"Yes, but what does that have to do with anything else?"

"Look, we make our dreams happen! We wait on no one."

"But I'm getting too old for the squad and can't go back to Texas."

"Well, how about this? You can start a cheerleading camp for little girls or teenagers. Make it like a sisterhood, and you can even make it for kids whose families have money, if you want, and you can give some scholarships away to underprivileged kids. Teach tumbling, stunts, and all that, since you know it all."

Phoebe was quiet, but Isis knew she had her sister's motor going.

"You could even have a store to sell cheerleading stuff— clothing, equipment. Shit, I don't know—just an idea."

"Sister, I love the idea, but how do I get started?" Phoebe's excitement was coming through the phone.

"Well, we will figure it out like we always do. I can give you some money for startup, and I am sure your brother-in-law will help."

"No, he's done enough already."

"I'll be the judge of that," Isis said, smiling. She paused. There was no time like the present. "Well, now since I have you back in your right state of mind, what the hell were you thinking with all that Randy shit?"

"Well, sister, I had my hopes up so high, and when I didn't make the squad, I felt like a failure. Then I had been bragging about this fantastic guy who turned out to be a monster, and I just . . ." Phoebe sighed. "I just felt like I was a loser, and I didn't want to face it. And then I turn around and you're marrying the perfect man." Phoebe paused for a minute. "And then with the abuse, I just felt like I couldn't tell anyone I was getting my ass beat on a regular basis. I was the spunky sister, remember?"

"Well, if you ever feel like you can't talk to me about anything . . . that's the real problem! I'm your sister and I love you. I love you through the bad and the good; never forget that."

"I won't, sis," Phoebe said in an apologetic tone.

"Good. Now if you'll excuse me, I'm being waited on hand and foot."

Phoebe chuckled. "All right, sis. See you guys when you get back."

"Ta-Ta," Isis said as she ended the call and summoned the staff members back.

• • •

Logic had arranged for them to go on a picnic later that afternoon. Once they finished eating, he grabbed her hand and said, "Princess, you are truly my princess, and every day you learn more than you knew the day before. And though I never regret anything at all, I do know that there's something that I need to make right."

"What?" Isis looked at Logic, not knowing what to think.

"I feel like every girl dreams of a wedding that is fit for a princess. And I didn't allow that before because I wanted what I wanted right then and there, but now, I want us to get married all over again. We can have a media frenzy, a mini Donald Trump and Melania wedding."

Logic went into the picnic basket and pulled out a white box. "Isis, will you marry me for the second time?"

Isis felt tears of happiness in her eyes, tears she'd never expected to experience. After allowing a moment for everything to sink in, she shouted as loud as she could, "Yes! Yes!"

"This is a Mr. Black Widow design," Logic said with a smile. "I went to your jewel boy in New York and had him re-create that ring that you loved so much, the one you made for that prince's wife. I did a couple of things different so that you can stick to the Black Widow oath that everything is one of a kind."

"Oh, I love it! And the truth of the matter is that I would marry you again with a ring that's made out of aluminum foil."

He laughed, loving the gesture, but knew better.

Chapter 30

That Motherfucker

Three months later, the media and paparazzi worked overtime to cover the story that was on everyone's lips: The Black Widow weds!

Lootchee watched from the comfort of his home as *Inside Edition* gave all the inside dish about the wedding. Isis and Logic's wedding rivaled that of a prince and princess. He had to give it to Logic because of the extravagance of everything. Lootchee wouldn't have done it any differently. But Lootchee wanted to cry that the woman of his dreams, the woman that he felt deep down inside could possibly be his better half, was indeed with another man, and there was nothing he could do about it.

Instead of crying, he fell into laughter, knowing that it was true indeed that Lootchee always gets what he wants, and if he wanted Isis, then guess what?—he'd have her.

Chapter 31

The Curse

Thirteen days after Isis and Logic arrived back from their honeymoon, Isis was back to work. A contractor had called the house and informed Logic that workers would be by the house to install all the new ceiling fans and light fixtures that Isis wanted in place of the conservative ones that the previous owners had left. Isis was at a meeting, so Logic stayed home to wait for the workers.

The workers arrived within the two-hour time window that the contractor had told him that they would. Once all the fixtures were in, Logic decided to enjoy what his long money had paid for. After getting a cold glass of lemonade out of the refrigerator, he was ready to kick back and watch one of the games until Isis came home. Before dozing off, he cut on the ceiling fan.

. . .

Isis returned home that afternoon to discover that an electrical fire had burned down their house. The house was destroyed, as was everything in it—including Logic.

The man of her dreams was dead.

Isis

But for now, there's
no room for tears . . .
only revenge.

The Veil

I was a mess at first after Logic died, but the doctors finally calmed me down and told me that I was pregnant. Little Logic is due in a few months, and my mother hopes to be home by the time my child is two years old. Aunt Samantha and Phoebe are staying with me, making sure that I don't overdo it.

They ruled Logic's death a freak accident, but I later found out that it was murder—and Lootchee was the one behind it. Lootchee somehow managed to get the contractors to wire the fans incorrectly. The man really will stop at nothing to get *whatever* he wants. I knew the man was persistent, but I didn't know that he was crazy. The day I told Lootchee that *death* was the only thing that could stop Logic from being my husband was the day I sealed Logic's fate. Although I didn't wire anything, loving Logic as I did and rejecting Lootchee was just like signing Logic's death warrant.

I won't have a problem taking care of our child, because my business is booming. Everyone wanted a piece from the Black Widow after Logic's death, but because I had cut back on working, the pieces that were out there only increased in value. Logic had a $3 million insurance policy naming me as the beneficiary, and the policy paid double because the death was ruled an accident. Remember that black Riviera that Logic entrusted to me before his arrest? That car had $5 million hidden in a stash box, and the keys Logic gave me that day were to safe-deposit boxes that contained an amount of money that I would rather not disclose at this time. Let's just say I'm one rich beyatch! And my child and I will live life as Logic would have wanted us to.

I made a vow, and I've never gone back on a vow in my life—without good reason anyway—that I'm going to pay Lootchee back for what he took from me! And as calculating as he is, I've got one up on him. I've hired the best private investigator that money can buy, and with the information that I found on Lootchee, I know just the person to call to help me out . . .

Unique.

People say that I should probably be mourning the death of Logic. That I should be balled up somewhere in a corner, shut off from the world, crying like a baby. But I've witnessed my father die in my arms, seen my first love die in front of my very eyes, had my ass whipped and a baby literally beaten out of me, seen two men murdered in cold blood, and witnessed my sister go to jail at the hands of an abuser. And I myself slipped through the fingers of the feds! I came through all of that, so what makes people think things should be any different now?

Since that awful day when Logic was killed, I've worn only white because I won't mourn until I avenge my husband's death. Yes, maybe then I'll mourn, cry, and even kick and scream like one of them women in a TV movie. But for now, there's no room for tears . . . only revenge.

Thank Yous

First, all the praise and glory must go to my father in heaven because it was his grace, favor, and mercy that allowed me to write this book.

To my two children and the love of my life, thank you for being so supportive of me and loving me as you do.

I thank my family for all your support. Aunt Yvonne, thanks for always having my back through the storm, fire, and sunshine. And Bet, you are truly the best!

To all my Nikki Turner Presents authors for entrusting your great works and careers, I appreciate your dedication and patience as we go through all the red tape together to put out the best books. I also want to thank you for understanding that the publishing world moves slowly. I have such special relationships with each of you. Seven, you've become a good friend and I appreciate your belief in my vision when it was only a mere thought. Freeze—nothing I can say could ever reflect my gratitude to you for waiting on NTP to manifest. You've shown me that loyalty is more than a word . . . it's a lifestyle. Dana Dane—wow! Who ever thought that one of my favorite rappers would end up on my line? Thanks for your insight and wisdom, which you give to me so freely.

My friends that keep me encouraged on a daily basis: Joy, Latina Tunstall, and Tammy Saunders (NJ). You are three of the deepest sisters that I have ever met. Tammy, your positive words and overall insight on this game called life are sometimes the only things that can get me through. I thank you for being you and dropping everything to read the very first draft of this book. Latina, thanks for being backup when the walls are tumbling down. Joy, you have grown so much over the years and I am so proud of the person you have grown into spiritually. Time and time again you continue to show me that you have my back— with words of wisdom, a lesson on life, or a laugh. But I thank you the most for knowing what to do when there is nothing else to do but pray.

Tim Dawg, I know at times I have a crazy way of showing you that your insight, input, and opinions are appreciated but they are—you will never know how much. Melvene, thank you for reading the first draft and cheering me and my books on the entire way.

Melody, you are such a great editor but an even better friend. I thank you for all the passion you put into my vision and dream, and insight into my crazy life. I do love you so much. To my dear publicist, Sarina Evan—thank you for your tireless hard work and for putting my book and face in places that I never imagined. I love you, and I couldn't have done it without you. Marc, I thank you for our friendship and for always listening to all my new ideas.

To everyone reading this, including my loyal readers—I could never thank you enough for showing me as much love as you have.

About the Author

Nikki Turner is a gutsy, gifted, courageous new voice taking the urban literary community by storm. Having ascended from the "Princess" of Hip-Hop Lit to "Queen," she is the bestselling author of the novels *A Hustler's Wife*, *Project Chick*, *The Glamorous Life*, *Riding Dirty on I-95*, and is the editor of and a contributing author in *Street Chronicles: Tales from da Hood*. Visit her website at nikkiturner.com, or write her at P.O. Box 28694, Richmond, VA 23228.